StorM ThieF

ALSO BY CHRIS WOODING

Poison
The Haunting of Alaizabel Cray
Crashing
Kerosene
The Broken Sky series

CHRIS WOODING

Storm Thief

SCHOLASTIC PRESS / NEW YORK

Library of Congress Cataloging-in-Publication Data available

ISBN 0-439-86513-1

12 11 10 9 8 7 6 5 4 3 2 1
06 07 08 09 10 11

Printed in the U.S.A.
First Scholastic edition, September 2006

Book design by Steve Scott

PART ONE:

The Seabird

1.1

The seabird slid through the black sky beneath the blanket of cloud, its feathers ruffling fitfully as it was buffeted by the changing winds.

The ocean was the colour of slate. It bulged and warped in angry swells. Above, spectral light flickered within the thunderheads, and the air boomed. A steady rain fell, slipping off the seabird's oiled feathers in droplets.

It was alone. Somewhere on its solitary journey towards the breeding grounds, it had lost its way. A magnetic storm was stroking the upper atmosphere, confusing its instinctive sense of navigation. The oppressive cloud hadn't dispersed for three days now, so the bird couldn't even use the sun as a guide. It glided over an endless expanse of steely waves, completely without direction.

It was a hardy sort, a species that had evolved for long flights without rest. Their migration took them many days coast to coast, and they never stopped flying in all that time. There were beasts in the water, toothed creatures and quick, nimble, biting fish that attacked in swarms. It was too dangerous to rest on this ocean.

A sudden gust hit the seabird, blowing it aside. It adjusted the tilt of its wings, the wind rippling violently across the short white down of its smooth head and along the feathers of its tail.

It had endured the storm for a long while now, but for how long it couldn't have known. There seemed to be no passage of time in this howling, skirling void. The seabird was aware only of the wind against its body, the constant need to move onward. These were its only concerns.

Until, impossibly, it found land.

At first it was a grey mass nearly indistinguishable from its surroundings. The tired traveller angled towards it. It wasn't troubled by the presence of land where there should be no land. Nor did it care that it couldn't have crossed half the ocean yet, and so it could be nowhere near the breeding grounds. Land meant shelter.

The shadowy mass loomed as the seabird battled through the storm. It widened and rose, emerging from the bitter rain like the blunt prow of some gargantuan ship. Colossal cliffs, pocked with abandoned dwellings, were topped with sheer walls of riveted metal and weathered stone. Dour outposts hunkered atop rocky pillars, linked by narrow bridges and winding stairs. Vents gushed dismal waterfalls, plunging to the sea below to join the foamy churn as the waves battered the feet of the cliffs.

It was a city. A city on the sea, standing atop a great plateau that rose from the ocean.

Behind the enormous wall that surrounded it, skeletal cranes hung against the skyline, creaking in the wind. Thin towers rose above ugly, squat temples, webbed with delicate walkways. And in the darkness, a million tiny lights glimmered, a net of baleful stars in the gloom.

Grim and storm-lashed, the city of Orokos filled the horizon.

The seabird angled downwards, between the raking spires and the walkways and the pulleys and scaffolds, seeking a secure place to rest. Thunder boomed and rolled across the sky. Flashes of lightning high in the clouds illuminated huge, folded shapes that watched the bird pass from nooks and eyries. The people of the city called them jagbats, but the seabird knew only what its instinct told it: They were predators, and it was prey.

4

Wings spread, and something launched itself into the air, soaring towards the seabird.

The bird sensed the danger and reacted, plummeting towards safety. Ahead of it was a five-sided tower of red-and-black stone, scabbed with ancient bedrock up its sides. A large oval window was hanging open near its tip.

The seabird accelerated its dive and arrowed towards the window. The jagbat chased it down, but the bird was too quick, and finally the larger creature banked away to prevent itself from colliding with the tower. It flapped sullenly back towards its perch.

The seabird, still travelling at maximum speed, shot through the window into the shadows. It saw the obstruction in its path far too late to do anything about it. It tried to brake, but it was going too fast. It crashed violently into the side of a brass pipe with a cracking of its hollow bones, and fell out of the air.

The dreary glow from outside spilled onto the floor, spreading across the maze of pipes and tanks and gauges and valves that dominated the chamber. The seabird lay paralysed, its small heart thumping wildly in shock, its broken wings limp.

Something moved. An inhuman hand reached down and picked it up.

Half in the shadow and half in the light, the golem looked uncomprehendingly at the dying thing in his palm. His long fingers opened. The jointed rods that ran from the back of his fingers to his forearm sighed with the movement. He watched in puzzlement as the seabird died, felt its heart stop beating through his thick and scarred skin.

For a time he was motionless, gazing at the tiny body in his grip. Then he squatted down and began to try to wake it.

5

1.2 "You ready?" Rail asked, as they lay in the cramped and cold metal duct, looking through the grille to the room below. They had crawled through the darkness for what seemed like hours, and their elbows and knees were scraped and scuffed.

Moa couldn't keep a tremble from her voice. "Ready," she replied. She reached across the distance between them and clutched his wrist, the patterned grille of the duct striping her thin arm in light.

Their gaze met for the briefest of instants. Rail, dark-skinned, dreadlocked, his face obscured beneath his respirator. Moa, pale as milk, eyes smudged black and lips painted dark green. Then he looked away, and she let him go.

He drew a small cylinder from his satchel, unscrewed the top, and tipped it out onto the rusty hinges of the grille. The hinges began to sizzle and melt, giving off a thin smoke that stank of acid. She licked her lips nervously, eyes flickering up and down the duct. He lifted the grille gently and set it aside.

"Let's do it," he said, and he slipped through.

They lowered themselves down onto a beam, one of several that crisscrossed the room up near its ceiling. The beams were wide and made of some kind of material like ebony, which was somewhere between wood and metal but seemed to be neither.

The chamber beneath was heavy with shadow. Once it must have been grand, back in the time before the Fade. Now it smelled musty, and mildew had settled in the corners. Curious shapes were sculpted into the walls — spirals and sprays and seashell patterns.

Some of them glowed with a faint radiance, providing the light in the room.

There was junk everywhere: broken chairs, scraps of material, shattered bowls, and a few gnawed bones. Human bones. Evidence of the new occupants of this place.

Rail hung from the beam and dropped the rest of the way, landing soundlessly on the floor. He reached up and caught Moa by the hips, helping her down. There was a single doorway in the room, leading farther into the building. They took it.

Rail went first, Moa followed. It was always this way, ever since they had met in the ghetto, all that time ago. Ever since he had taught her how to be a thief like him. She had a natural talent for the craft, even though her conscience bothered her sometimes. Unlike Rail, she suffered pangs of guilt at the thought of taking what wasn't hers.

Not this time, though. This time they were stealing from the Mozgas. Those monsters didn't deserve her pity.

They emerged at the top of a stairwell. It had been constructed so that it flowed downwards in a half-circle. Wood and metal and other substances that they couldn't identify had been moulded together like water. Parts of it were chipped now, and graffiti in some bizarre language had been painted across one wall. A globe of light hung unsupported in the air above the stairs. A marvel of ancient technology, now faded out of memory like the hands that had built this place.

So sad, Moa thought, distracted for a moment. *So sad that there was once a time when the world was full of wonders like that. So sad that we've forgotten how to make them.*

Rail hadn't given it a second glance. He was creeping down the stairs, listening.

There were voices below. Muttered phrases suddenly accelerated into high-pitched, squeaky chatter and then returned to a drone, as if someone had recorded a voice and was randomly speeding it up and slowing it down, rearranging the syllables in different orders, playing them in reverse. The warped speech of the Mozgas.

Rail proceeded a little more slowly. He could hear them moving around below. Their footsteps went from sluggish, heavy thuds to quick scampers and back again. He looked up the stairs at Moa and put his finger to where his lips would have been, if he hadn't been wearing his respirator. It was a muzzle of smooth black metal that fit over his mouth, covering his face from the bridge of his nose to his cheekbones and chin. Two cables ran over his shoulders to the small power pack that sat between his shoulder blades. Moa had rarely ever seen the features beneath, but that was only natural. Without his respirator, Rail couldn't breathe.

The footsteps and voices faded away as the Mozgas moved elsewhere. Rail calculated his route, recalling the floorplan they had been given by the thief-mistress Anya-Jacana. The building was massive. That would work to their advantage. There were only a few dozen of those creatures living here, and if they were careful then they could avoid them entirely.

He crept to the bottom of the stairs and looked up and down the corridor. It was lit dimly by overhead tracklights, its walls made of patterned metal that reflected the dull glow strangely. Nothing moved.

Moa was behind him, at his shoulder. She practically radiated fear. She was pretending that this was all a game, an adventure like the ones she lived in her dreams, but she couldn't fool her body. Her heart was pounding against her ribs, sweat prickling her scalp.

Rail believed it could be done. That was what she held on to. Rail thought they could do it, and she trusted him. She took some of his calmness for her own. She thought of how he had reacted when she had expressed her doubts yesterday. *I'll look after you*, he had said. *I always look after you.* And that had been enough for her.

But Moa knew the kind of things these creatures were capable of. This particular gang had been snatching people from the streets in this area for some time now. Those people got eaten. They only killed you first if you were lucky.

She put it from her mind. It was too late now. They had taken the job, and Anya-Jacana didn't like it when her thieves failed her. She got *very* angry. Moa never wanted to be on the receiving end of that. She was more afraid of Anya-Jacana than of the monsters in this lair.

Rail passed silently from the stairwell along the corridor, and Moa kept close to him. A distant jabber of speech startled them, but it quickly faded away. She brushed the straggling black fronds of hair from her face and looked around, searching for movement. This wasn't the same as dealing with slow-witted guards in some rich factory owner's house. She and Rail might not even see the Mozgas coming. These creatures could appear in the blink of an eye.

Rail peeped around the edge of a doorway, then ushered her through.

It was a small room, scattered with bits of debris and clearly unused. Something that looked like an operating table, contoured to the shape of a person's body, stood in the centre.

9

Recessed tracklights ran around the room in the corners where the ceiling met the wall. On the other side of the room was a metal door.

"Through there," Rail whispered, motioning with his head.

Moa picked her way through a pile of old boxes, bent spokes, and bits of slate to get to the door. She pushed it gently, but it didn't give. A quick glance at the locking mechanism told her all she needed to know. Meshing tumbler system. Easy.

From her pocket she drew out a pair of thin, serrated blades, and with them she began to probe around in the triangular keyhole. Rail kept watch on the corridor from the doorway.

Moa worked at the lock as quickly as she could, fiddling at the catches to release them one by one. Rail always left her to do the locks. She was better at it than he was — better, in fact, than almost every thief in the ghetto. There wasn't a lock she couldn't get through, except those old-style Functional Age locks that nobody understood and that didn't use keys or bolts.

This was a stubborn one. It hadn't been used for a long time, and it had rusted. She was only halfway through when Rail hissed quietly at her.

Something was coming along the corridor.

She squeezed her eyes shut, took a breath, and carried on. She could hear it now — a dull thudding of footsteps, slow and ponderous. As if whatever made them weighed a ton. They were already speeding up, becoming higher in pitch, turning into a mouse's patter, coming closer.

The footsteps stopped. Not far away. Rail had retreated, and was by her shoulder now.

"I don't mean to hurry you . . ." he said.

"I know," she murmured. Her arms were shaking, but she

forced her hands to keep still. She was on the last tumbler, and the frecking thing wouldn't drop. If she could only . . .

There was a click as a catch came free, but as it did another tumbler locked in place. An extra little bit of security. Moa breathed a curse.

They could hear a scuffing noise out in the corridor.

"Moa . . ." Rail whispered.

"You're not helping," she singsonged quietly.

She chewed on her bottom lip as she scraped at the tumbler with the tip of one of her blades, trying to work it loose. Visions of what was outside flashed through her head. She had never seen one of the Mozgas, but she had heard the stories. She willed the lock to open. It seemed determined to be awkward.

The footsteps began again. Heavy and deliberate. Coming along the corridor. Any moment, any moment now the thing that was making those noises would step into the open doorway. It would see them and it would all be over, everything would be over. . . .

The lock clicked. She pulled the door open and shuddered as it squealed on its hinges. Rail was through in an instant, and she went after him.

She pulled the door closed behind her as they ran into a tiny storage room piled with crates, some of which had split and were oozing nutrient gruel. Rail was already looking for the hatch, the one that they had seen in the floorplans. He knew as well as she did that the Mozga would have heard the sound of the door opening. It would be coming to investigate. It was only a matter of time. But with these creatures, time was the biggest uncertainty. They might move faster than an eye could see, or so slowly that they appeared not to be moving at all. Moa could only hope, desperately, that fortune was on her side.

She and Rail ducked behind a pile of crates, and there it was: a metal trapdoor, half-hidden beneath a box that was leaking some sort of fibrous stuffing. Rail shoved it out of the way and pulled the trapdoor, expecting resistance; mercifully it wasn't locked. Moa slipped through into the crawlspace beneath, and he followed. He closed it just as he heard the door to the storage room open and the Mozga come in.

"Go!" he hissed through his respirator, and Moa went, squeezing through the tight gap between the floors of the building. There were pipes here, and ancient mechanisms with a purpose she and Rail could only guess at, but there was light and enough room to wriggle.

They only relaxed when they came around the corner, and the crawlspace opened out into a tiny chamber full of dials and cables, all cold and inactive. They sat together on the hard metal mesh floor, letting their breathing slow. They didn't think they had been seen, and the Mozga was too big to get in after them anyway. There were some advantages to being small, with bodies lean from a lifetime of hunger. Nobody really counted weeks or months or years in Orokos, but both Rail and Moa were somewhere between children and adults, in that hazy area where adolescence occurred. In the ghetto, there was little time for childhood. They seemed older than their true ages.

After a time, Moa grinned at Rail. "Close one," she said.

Rail was grinning back; she could tell by the creasing around his eyes.

"Never worried for a second," he lied.

1.3　They made their way down through the levels, using crawlways whenever they could, sneaking along corridors when they had to. The floorplans they had memorised were sometimes wrong — parts of the building had changed since the drawings had been made. But Rail and Moa were adaptable, and they dealt with such problems as they arose. Between them, they managed to get down to the lowest level of the building, some distance underground, without being noticed at all. Sometimes they heard the inhabitants chattering and groaning in their dreadful tongue. Then they backtracked and skirted around the danger zone. Though there were many dead ends and a few close shaves with the Mozgas, they eventually found the room they were looking for.

They came to it from above, slipping through a door onto the balcony that ran around the top of the chamber. The balcony, like the chamber itself, was a work of art — a blend of metals and woods and strange plastics that swirled and swooped as if it had grown naturally, not crafted by hand. The walls of the chamber had once been breathtaking, panelled with translucent coloured glass, arcs of black wood, and sprays of gemstones. But the beauty had been ruined by time and vandals. Many of the gems were missing, and the wood was scratched. Obscenities had been splattered across the walls. Waste and dirt and rubble had gathered in the corners.

Worst of all was the cairn in the middle. The Mozgas had built a tower of bones, the height of a man, carefully constructed from the remains of their victims, held together with some kind of gluey mortar. Bits of dried flesh still clung to the yellowing femurs and clavicles.

Long after anyone had stopped believing in any gods at all, these creatures kept to their worship of some dark deity. This was their altar to him. In front of it was a small brass casket.

"There it is," Rail murmured. For the first time, he began to really believe that they were going to do this.

He looked back at Moa, letting none of the relief show on his face. It was easy to disguise his feelings with the respirator hiding his features. Sometimes he was almost glad for it. What if Moa had sensed that he was a lot less sure of himself than he pretended? What if she had known that his insides had turned to water when he'd thought they were about to be caught? She looked to him for strength, and if he let her down she would crumble. So he kept up his façade of brash confidence, because she needed him to.

He had met her, all that time ago, because he had been thinking about robbing her. She was wandering around the ghetto, gazing wide-eyed at everything. She couldn't have looked more lost and helpless if she had been wearing a sign. It was blind luck that Rail saw her before anyone more ruthless did. He had introduced himself and she had asked for directions to someplace — he forgot exactly where. He offered to take her. He wanted to determine whether she had anything worth stealing, or whether she was just another homeless waif. At least, that was what he told himself.

By the time they had reached the spot, Rail knew two things about her for certain: first, that she was poorer than he was and had nothing worth taking; second, that she would last approximately half a day in the ghetto before her throat got cut. Violence wasn't Rail's style, but there were many who would kill her first and steal from her later.

She was devastated that the man she had come to see — her uncle, he later learned — was long gone, and the shack he had lived in was burned and deserted. Against his better judgement, he offered to let her stay in his den for a night until she could make a new plan. She was wary of him, but she agreed.

After that, she never left, and he never asked her to. He introduced her to Anya-Jacana, the thief-mistress, and they became partners. That partnership had made them among the most successful thieves in the ghetto.

It was a living.

They found stairs leading down from the balcony, and took them. Rail scanned the room, searching for signs of traps: spiderweb tripwires, clockwork dart-guns, springblades, and the like. His own specialty was disarming and avoiding those kinds of mechanisms. The Mozgas weren't smart, but it paid to be careful.

He saw nothing, but he told Moa to wait on the stairs in case. He walked towards the gruesome cairn of bones, treading lightly, alert for pressure plates in the floor. If he was being thorough, he would have been crawling on his hands and knees, testing as he went. But he didn't believe the Mozgas were sophisticated enough to use those kinds of tricks, and he didn't have time anyway. He wanted to be away from here as fast as possible.

He reached the brass casket without incident. Once there, he checked it over, looking for secret catches. Nothing.

This is too easy, he thought. *It's not even locked.*

He opened the chest and looked inside.

The majority of the haul was power cells, tiny cylinders that glowed yellow-green from within. Some of them were a little dim, but they would still fetch a good price. Power cells were always in demand. There were a few bundles of platinum chits and three velvet bags of assorted coins, mostly triangular and made from polished stones of various colours. Plus other odds and ends, bits of machinery that Rail couldn't identify, and something else.

It caught his eye immediately. The rest was standard; the kind of currency used every day in Orokos. But this was different. He could tell at a glance that it was Functional Age technology, but beyond that it was a mystery. There were two small loops of bronze-coloured metal side-by-side, and at right angles to them was set an amber disc, about an inch in diameter. It was exquisitely made, and though Rail was no expert, he could imagine it was valuable. Very valuable.

"Everything alright?" Moa stage-whispered across the room. She had seen the hesitation in his eyes.

He nodded and began filling his satchel with the contents of the chest. But his mind wasn't on what he was doing. Possibilities were racing through his head.

This is Fade-Science. Real, genuine Fade-Science. This must be worth a fortune.

Never before had he come across anything like this. He doubted that the Mozgas even knew what they had. But the real question was this: Did *Anya-Jacana* know they had it?

The thief-mistress had offered them this job. She would take her pick of the treasure, as she always did, and leave a percentage to Rail and Moa. That was the way it worked. If she saw this, she would take it from them.

But who was to say she even knew it was here? She didn't know the contents of every safe and every chest in Orokos.

Chances were that she had only heard rumours of where the Mozgas kept their money, the loot that they took from the people they kidnapped and ate. Nothing more than that. That was why she sent her thieves.

He had emptied the casket now. All but the Fade-Science thing, which lay alone. He stared at it for a moment.

Is it worth the risk? he asked himself.

He snatched it up and slipped it into his pocket, then stepped away from the casket.

He felt the pressure plate click under his heel an instant before the alarm began.

It was a basic system, mostly clockwork, but the din of bells it made was loud enough to wake the dead. Moa shrieked in alarm at the sudden noise.

Rail's gaze met Moa's across the room.

"Time to go," he said, and they ran.

1.4

The tunnel echoed with the drip and splatter of rusty rainwater, spilling from the ceiling into a shallow, dirty stream. Rubble and bits of old girders had fallen here, along with spidery mechanisms that had once been parts of things from the Functional Age. The tunnel itself was a relic of that time — its walls were made of some smooth, dark metal that couldn't be scratched, and great ribs ran along its length. But uncountable days and nights had done their work, and it had buckled and slumped at last. Nothing lasted forever. Particularly not in Orokos.

Silence at first, except for the sound of the water. Then the sharp tap of running feet. Getting louder.

A grille high up on one side of the tunnel screeched open, and first Rail and then Moa slipped through. The grille shrieked closed behind her as they splashed into the tunnel. Rail grabbed her gloved hand, tugging her into motion, and they were running again.

They dodged their way around the heaps of broken stone and metal, ducking past joists that jabbed down from the ceiling. After a short way, they reached a point where the tunnel branched into two. Rail slowed to a halt, looking from one to the other.

"You know where you're going?" Moa panted. She was out of breath and her head was light. They might have gotten out of the Mozgas' lair — through a carefully planned escape route — but their pursuers didn't give up easily.

"It's this way," he replied, his voice humming slightly as it passed through his respirator.

"What if it's changed?"

"It hasn't changed. I checked it."

"When?"

"Ten days ago."

"Ten *days*?" she hissed. She pulled free from him and wiggled her fingers. "Rail, ten days ago I was right-handed."

"It hasn't changed," he said.

There was an explosive burst of noise from behind them, the stuttering nonsense-language of their pursuers. Then came the sound of the grille squealing slowly on its ancient hinges. Moa looked back, but there was too much rubble to see anything.

Rail glanced at Moa with his liquid brown eyes. "Quietly," he said, and they took the tunnel branch that he had decided was the right one. He really had no idea, though. There hadn't *been* a junction here the last time he had passed this way.

They ran as stealthily as they could, keeping close to the tunnel walls and staying out of the water, but their shoes squelched and the buckles on the satchel that Rail carried kept tapping together. The tunnel bent slowly as they hurried along it. The voices of the Mozgas echoed from the ribbed walls.

Moa's muscles burned, and she knew she would not last much longer. She hated herself for being a burden, but she was physically weak and always had been. She didn't have the endurance for a sustained run.

They came to another junction, a crossroads in the tunnel. Overhead, a vast metal fan with a single blade turned behind a discoloured grille, beating the stale air. Lean-tos and little junk shacks crowded the edges of the junction, where the water didn't reach. They were all deserted.

Rail gave Moa a triumphant look. "See?" he said, sounding more confident than he felt. He was relieved that he recognised the place, but he was still not sure that the route he remembered was right. Tunnels and streets had a habit of moving about in Orokos.

Moa didn't give him a response. There wasn't enough breath in her anyway. She was gasping for air. Rail's expression flickered with concern, but he snatched up her hand again and tugged her onward. A jabbering shriek reverberated after them.

They went right, taking a tunnel that was set higher than the one which crossed it, above the level of the stream. They made it a little way farther before Moa began to drag on Rail's hand and she stumbled.

"Rail, wait . . ." she managed.

"We *can't* wait."

"I can't . . . run . . . anymore."

Rail cursed, searching for a solution. There was nothing here but more debris, carried down from other places when these tunnels had flooded in the past.

"We're nearly there," he said, his voice becoming soothing. "You can make it."

He knew that she couldn't. If Moa pushed herself further, she would collapse. She was so sickly and frail. Despite the terror of the things that chased them, he couldn't feel angry at her. Like himself, she had grown up malnourished, and she tired easily. He saw the disappointment on her face, her shame at being the one to hold them back. Even amid everything, it made him want to comfort her.

"Just . . . a few . . ." she said, and didn't finish.

Rail put his arm round her shoulder and steered her behind a pile of mouldering stone and bits of wire mesh. From there, they could see back to the junction. He sat her down and she curled up, arms wrapped around her knees, face screwed tight as she shuddered lungfuls of air in and out.

Rail peered over the edge of the rubble, watching the junction. The cries of the creatures that stalked them seemed to come from far away now, but he knew he couldn't trust the acoustics in this place.

He put his hand on the satchel that he carried, reassuring himself that what he had stolen was still inside. Right now, the only thing he feared more than being caught by the Mozgas was going back to Anya-Jacana empty-handed. Then he felt in his pocket, where the strange Fade-Science artifact lay, separate from the rest of the loot.

Are you really going to do this? he thought. *Are you really going to rip off Anya-Jacana? She'll kill you dead.*

This was all happening too fast, too much at once. It wasn't only a matter of stealing — he was a thief, for freck's sake, stealing was in his blood. And it wasn't only the money that such a thing would fetch. It was the *possibilities* it represented. It was a chance. A chance to make things different.

Did he dare to keep it? And could he live with himself if he gave it away?

Something moved in the distance. Two of them. They seemed to literally *appear* in the centre of the junction. But Rail knew better. They had simply moved too fast to see. And yet they were sluggish now, as if they were dragging themselves through treacle. They were looking about, turning their hairless heads, deciding which way their prey might have gone. They flickered again, suddenly switching positions with no apparent movement in between. A third one joined them, running into view, then decelerating into slow-motion. One of its companions had become a gibbering blur, its head shaking from side to side.

The Mozgas wore trenchcoats of black, hung with buckles and long straps and chains, and they carried slender daggers that gleamed like icicles. Their skin was dead white and cold, limbs and bodies thin inside their coats. Their faces were elongated towards the nose, like a shark or a weasel, with a lower jaw set farther back than the upper jaw, full of narrow, crooked teeth that were translucent like frosted glass. Bulbous white eyes rolled in deep sockets.

Nobody knew exactly how these creatures had come to exist, nor how they had come to be the way they were. It was just one more mystery in a city of mysteries. In Orokos, anything was possible. Anything at all. Even something like the Mozgas, beings that were detached from time itself, never quite managing to stay in sync with the world they lived in. One moment travelling faster than thought, the next as slow as if their limbs were made of lead.

Rail swallowed against the dryness in his mouth and wished he had never taken this job.

"Moa . . ." he said quietly, but she didn't reply. She had gone dizzy and light-headed, and had hung her head between her knees.

The three creatures split up, as Rail had guessed they would. Two of them flitted away and the other, still caught in the slow-motion downswing of its time-cycle, crept into the mouth of the tunnel where Moa and Rail hid.

Sweat broke out on Rail's brow. If they ran now, the Mozga would hear them. And with Moa as she was, they wouldn't get far.

Leave her behind, just leave her behind, whispered a voice in his head, the voice that had helped him survive through a hard and dangerous childhood into an even harder adolescence. *Run!*

But he couldn't leave her. He couldn't. In the time they had known each other, she had become the most precious thing that he had, and he would never give that up. He needed her as much as she needed him.

The Mozga was accelerating now, speeding up into normal time, walking steadily down the corridor. Hobnailed boots clanked on metal.

Rail checked on Moa. Her breathing had become less laboured now. Another few moments would do it — but it was a few moments they didn't have. He searched for a weapon, more to distract himself from the voice in his head than because he really thought he had a chance of using it.

His eye fell on a thin steel pole, about the length of his arm, sticking out from the rubble in front of him. He glanced up the tunnel. The Mozga was still some way away, treading carefully, listening. One of the tracklights overhead fizzed and went out, dimming the tunnel. Another one was flickering, making the shadows twitch fitfully. The soft suck and hiss of the respirator pack on Rail's back seemed far too loud.

He closed his hand around the end of the pole. He began to slide it out, and it came without resistance, making only the softest of scrapes.

It slipped free. A few stones from the heap of debris shifted and rattled to the floor. The Mozga appeared, right in front of Rail's face.

Rail yelled and staggered backwards, the pole in his hand. Shock froze him for a moment. The creature was inches from him, its jaws agape and its teeth wet and shining, a dagger raised to plunge into Rail's neck. It had stopped still. Caught in time like a waxwork.

Rail swung the pole as hard as he could into the side of its head. It was like hitting rock. The creature didn't flinch. The weapon jolted out of his hand and sent a jab of pain up his arm to his shoulder. He took a step back, uncertain of what to do next. Then he pulled the startled Moa roughly to her feet and they fled.

They had got a few steps down the tunnel when there was a dull thud behind them. The Mozga had been sent flying sideways, crashing into the wall and slumping to the ground. Time had caught up with it.

They didn't dare to wait and see if it was out of action permanently. The tunnel bent left and they followed it. Moa stumbled more than once, but Rail was there to bear her up. Finally, after what seemed like forever, they found their way out.

The steps, thankfully, were where they were supposed to be. Moa had almost collapsed again by the time she reached them, but Rail would not think of stopping now, not with the cries of pursuit growing once more. He lifted her onto his back and she clung to him. She was light as a ghost, but he wasn't strong. Only the fear of what came after them propelled him up the spiral staircase. His legs ached with the effort, but he made it to the rusted door at the top. There he put Moa down and pounded out the rhythm he had been taught. Three hits, pause, one hit, pause, four, pause, three.

Nothing. Nobody answered.

He tried the pattern again. He was sure he had it right.

Still there was no sign that anyone had heard him. There was no handle on the door on this side. He kicked it, but it didn't give. He swore and kicked it again.

"Rail . . ." said Moa, her voice thick with exhaustion. She sounded like she had already given up. "They're coming."

The steps were made of slatted iron, and through them it was possible to see to the bottom of the stairwell. There were shapes down there — quick, darting movements. The sound of hobnailed boots, now fast in a rattle, now slow again.

"Open this frecking door!" Rail cried, his respirator flattening the desperate edge on his voice. He pounded the rhythm again, and a moment later there was the sound of grinding as the lock was disengaged. Rail dragged Moa up again. An explosive shriek came from below, stuttering into rapid nonsense.

The door came open and they shoved through it. Moa fell out into the cluttered alleyway beyond. Rail was already slamming the door behind him. He caught a glimpse of one of the creatures racing towards him as fast as a spider, and then the door crunched shut. The wheel-shaped locking mechanism clattered out a jerky manoeuvre, and the bolt thumped home.

Rail leaned against the metal for a moment, listening to the thwarted howls of the Mozgas. Then he turned on the boy who had opened the door. He was runty and small, dressed in a waterproof poncho and a battered hat, and he held a small, half-eaten pie in one hand. He backed away a little under Rail's glare. The rain drifted down from the slice of grey sky visible overhead.

"Where were you, Fulmar?" Rail grated. "Why didn't you answer?"

The boy's face was a picture of fright. "You won't tell Anya-Jacana, will you? You won't tell her?"

Rail took a step towards him and snatched the pie out of his hand. At the end of the alleyway he could see the stalls of a street market.

"You can't do one thing right, can you?" he snarled. He crouched down next to Moa, helping her sit up. "Here, eat this," he told her, his voice softer now. Moa took it from him wearily.

"What is it?" she murmured.

"Best not to ask," he said. "Eat."

"I was only gone for a moment," Fulmar whined from behind him. "I got hungry. I'd been waiting for —"

Rail held a hand up to silence him, not bothering even to look. "I'll deal with you later."

"You won't tell her, will you? Please?" Fulmar was almost shaking now.

Rail ignored the question. He was watching Moa take tiny nibbles from the pie. "Okay?" he murmured. "Can you move?"

Moa swallowed and nodded. Gently, he helped her to her feet.

"Come on," he said, as if soothing a child. "Told you I wouldn't let them hurt you. I always look out for you, don't I?"

She nodded again, barely seeming to hear him. The two of them walked slowly down the alleyway towards the market, his arm around her shoulder to support her, the rain soaking into their clothes. Fulmar cast a nervous glance at the metal door, where scratching noises had begun, and then hurried after them.

1.5 Cretch was watching the panopticon in his battered red armchair when Ephemera burst into the room and said, "Granpapa! Come and look at Vago!"

He tutted and waved at her to go away, not turning from the machine. It was a great brass periscope that hung from the ceiling. He was twiddling the knobs on either side anxiously, making frustrated noises as he did so.

"Why do they make the writing so small in these things? Don't they think of old men like me?"

"That's why they have *pictures*," Ephemera said, as if it was obvious. "Come on, come and look. Vago's doing something silly!"

"What is he doing, child?" Cretch sighed.

"You have to come and *look*!" she demanded.

He drew back from the shielded eyepiece of the panopticon. He was tall and lean, too tall for the armchair he sat in, and his hair was white and wispy. A heavy, false-velvet robe was draped around him. He wore a set of goggles, attached by elastic to his head. They were black half-spheres of metal that fit over his eyes, with a small hole in the centre in which glass twinkled like the lens of a kaleidoscope.

"Read this to me first," he said.

Ephemera scowled at him. "You shouldn't be looking at that thing with your goggles on," she chided. "It gives you headaches."

Cretch didn't answer that. No matter how many times he told her he was blind without his goggles, she never understood. She didn't understand anything. She was young, and she thought

27

she would always be well-fed, healthy, and strong. Didn't know enough to be afraid when the probability storms struck the city, rearranging things, moving streets around. The storms might snatch a person away and put them elsewhere, turn children into statues of ice, or make a man speak in a different language.

Ephemera never considered that she might wake up in the middle of a Revenant den, or with six fingers on her hand, or turned into a boy. She had always been lucky, so she believed it couldn't happen to her. And maybe it never would. Nobody could ever be sure.

But Cretch knew very well what the Storm Thief could do, how he could turn a man's life inside out, and he feared the storms deeply.

Anything could happen when the Storm Thief was abroad. He was a wicked entity who delighted in mischief, as likely to snatch a person's purse as he was to shower them with jewels. He might steal a baby's eyes and replace them with buttons, or turn a house into sugar paper.

The tale was old, invented long ago to make sense of the senseless. Parents used it to explain probability storms to their offspring. But though it was only a legend, they never quite managed to stop believing it themselves. When they talked of the damage wreaked to their lives in the aftermath of the storm, they still talked of a visit from the Storm Thief.

There had been a probability storm five days ago. Cretch had spent it in bed, trembling. Ephemera had played in the laboratory with her toys. The storm that had raged last night was a natural one, and Cretch had slept like a baby.

Ephemera blew out an exasperated breath and snatched the

panopticon from her grandfather. She rotated it around and looked into the eyepiece.

The picture, as always, was hard to see. It was brownish and flickered at the edges, and it seemed very far away. She adjusted the size to make it as big as she could and then turned the focus knob until everything became clear. It was still like looking at a scene down a long, rectangular pipe, but it was good enough. She had grown up with the panopticon, so she had none of the sense of wonder of her grandfather, who still found it a magical thing.

It looked like a battle was going on. There was no sound, but Ephemera could see a couple of Protectorate soldiers firing around the corner of a building. She was used to scenes like this. The Protectorate had been fighting the Revenants ever since she was born, and long before.

All children were taught the difference between the two sides at a very early age. The Protectorate, as their name suggested, looked after the people of Orokos. They were led by the Patrician, who was the ruler of the great island city. The Revenants were evil monsters that killed anything they touched. It was a simple enough lesson, even for a child.

The viewpoint of the panopticon moved, and Ephemera saw a wall and a big iron gate, around which lay a lot of dead bodies. The soldiers were shooting bolts of glowing aether energy at swiftly moving shapes in the distance. Captions appeared at the bottom of the screen, in the spiky, complex symbols of the Orokon alphabet. They remained there for a few seconds, then faded away to be replaced by new ones.

"'Protectorate forces won a great victory today,'" she read. "'Recent probability storm allowed Revenants into the Mereg

Food Processing Complex. Troops have driven them back after days of fighting. Workers will return later today.'" Her voice changed from a drone to a cry of appalled delight. "Eww! They just hit one!"

The picture switched to a dirty-looking man in a coat, with sharp features. His mouth moved, but no words came out.

"'Spokesman for nearby Territory Northwest 43 expressed gratitude to troops.'" She adopted a whiny voice as she mimicked the spokesman. "'*Without their help the people of my district would be starving now. We would like to thank the Patrician for protecting us from the terror of the Revenants.* Later he —'" She broke away from the panopticon. "Northwest 43 is a ghetto district. Who cares what stupid ghetto-folk say?"

"Ephemera!"

She made a face. "What? They *are* stupid. Why else would they live in those horrible ghettoes? Don't they want to be clean?"

Cretch put out his arms, inviting Ephemera to sit on his lap. She did so. He stroked her hair softly. It was a mass of bouncy ringlets, one side dyed black and the other side her natural white. She was wearing a dress of purple with silver lace trim, which she picked at as he spoke.

"Sometimes people aren't all as hardworking as your granpapa," he said. "They're in the ghettoes because they don't want to work, or because they're criminals. That's why the Protectorate puts them there: to keep decent people like you and me safe and sound."

"But they're just *lazy*!" she protested. "And they steal stuff all the time, and you always read about them fighting on the panopticon."

"Don't be too hard on them, child," Cretch told her benevolently. "They don't have the advantages we have. No wonder they give up so easily. No wonder they become criminals. They're inferior, and they know it." He touched his granddaughter's hair on the side where it was bright white. "We should have pity on them."

Ephemera wasn't remotely convinced. "We should just let the Revenants get them," she said.

"Well, when you're the Patrician you can decide that, hmm?"

She laughed. "Silly! I'll never be the Patrician. He lives for*ever!*"

Cretch grinned, showing his brown-veined marble teeth. "Now what was it you wanted to show me?"

Ephemera's face was a comical gasp. "I forgot! You have to see what Vago's done!" She bounded off him and led him away and up the stairs.

Vago lived at the top of the tower above Cretch's laboratories. It was a large five-sided chamber, crowded with brass cylinders and tanks that hissed and thumped, and strange valves and dials that moved of their own accord. The floor was iron, and it was hot and gloomy. There wasn't much space to move between the banks of noisy machines. There wasn't even room to put down a bed, but then Vago didn't sleep anyway.

He spent all of his time up here when he wasn't assisting Cretch. Often he wandered about in the aisles between the steaming pipes, or talked to the faded painting that leaned against the wall in the little corner he had taken as his own. Sometimes he stood there and stared out of the large oval window that looked south across the city. Mostly he just thought about things.

He had a lot to think about, considering he was only a hundred and twenty days old.

Ephemera had brought a mirror up to tease him with once. After he had seen himself, he had been able to make sense of the distorted reflections he often caught in the curve of the brass cylinders. The thing looking back at him was a stranger, half of metal and half of flesh. It was hunched and long-limbed, towering in height. Built like a hunting cat, if hunting cats walked on their back legs. Brown, stringy muscle stretched across his gangly frame, studded with dull silver strips of strange machinery. A ridge of knifelike metal fins ran along his back, flanked by two slender power packs that hummed softly. And he had wings: great, leathery wings like a bat, that grew from either side of his spine and were reinforced with dozens of tiny steel ligaments. He had never understood why the wings were there. He was never allowed to leave the tower, and they caught on corners as he moved, making him clumsy. He had suffered more than one beating because his wings had knocked over something in his master's laboratory.

"Granpapa says you're a *golem*!" Ephemera had crowed. "You didn't have a mama or a papa. Someone made you. Aren't you ugly?"

His face was the worst of it. The skin was stretched tight over his skull, wrinkled and withered like a corpse. Most of the left side was masked in metal, and where his left eye should have been there was a black orb instead. His other eye was yellow and mottled, looking out on the world with child-like wonder. There were hardly any lips on his narrow mouth, and when he spoke, steel fangs glinted in the dim light.

"Am I ugly?" he had said. "Is that what ugly is?"

"Oh, yes!" Ephemera had cried, laughing with glee. "Ugly is what you are!"

Last night, during the storm, a seabird had flown into his room. He had been standing by the window in his little corner when it had flown in and knocked itself dead on one of the pipes.

The event had made him sad. The seabird wasn't ugly. At least, he didn't think so. Even dead it was beautiful. Its feathers were sleek and soft, and he liked the feel of it on his skin. He remembered how it had flown, how fast it had gone. He stroked its wings and thought how much more elegant they were than the unwieldy things on his back. He flexed his own wings as much as the space would allow. Was that what these were for? To make him fly? But how could he? He didn't even know how to use them.

But he liked the seabird. So he found himself a piece of rope, and he tied it to the seabird's feet with his nimble fingers, and he hung it around his neck. That was how Cretch found him, when he and his granddaughter came up the stairs.

"Look at him! Look at him!" she cried, hanging on to Cretch's hand, dancing and pointing.

Vago appeared nonplussed. He didn't understand what Ephemera was so excited about.

"Oh, Vago, what have you got there?" Cretch said. He came closer and peered at the golem's bizarre pendant. Vago shrank back a little, though he was a clear foot taller than Cretch was. "Come, come, I won't hurt you," said the old man. "I just want to see."

Vago reluctantly let Cretch lift the bird off his neck. He was never quite sure when Cretch was liable to hit him, though the knobbly walking stick that was Cretch's usual instrument of punishment was nowhere to be seen. The pain of those beatings was bad enough, but what was worse was the strange and terrifying feelings they provoked in him. Dark, hot, angry feelings. He didn't know where they came from, but he feared what they might make him do one day.

"Fascinating," Cretch murmured, turning the bird over in his hand. "Where did you find this?"

"It flew in," Vago replied. His voice was somewhere between a whine and a growl, shockingly deep. Whenever he spoke, it sounded like he was straining the words out.

"Remarkable. I've never seen its like before."

"But he was wearing it round his neck!" Ephemera squealed, disappointed that her attempt at ridiculing Vago hadn't worked. Her grandfather ignored her.

"Well, I'm no expert, but I think you've got something quite unusual here, Vago," he mused. "If I didn't know better I'd think this came from *outside* the city." He laughed.

"Outside the city?"

"Never mind. An old fool's joke."

Vago's puzzlement showed in his one good eye.

"Don't you get it? There *is* nothing outside the city, you stupid *golem*!" Ephemera snapped. "Orokos is all there is!"

1.6

Rail and Moa made it back to the ghetto by midday. The skies overhead were a monotonous grey, but the rain had stopped and left the city shining wet. They had spent the morning picking their way through the complicated districts of Orokos, detouring around areas where Revenants had taken over. They paused often to check with locals that things were the same as they had been before the last probability storm. Streets and buildings in Orokos had a disconcerting tendency to move. Even entire districts had been known to get displaced.

Old folk still recalled the day when the whole of Orokos reversed itself, turning into a mirror-image. Buildings on the north edge found themselves on the south side, east and west flipped over, everything perfectly symmetrical. It wasn't often you got an upheaval like *that*, they said. Generally the changes were smaller, such as when Moa, who had been right-handed all her life, woke up left-handed. Or when Rail's lungs stopped working properly in the middle of a probability storm and he nearly died. He had been forced to wear a respirator ever since. The Storm Thief had stolen his breath.

The ghetto was a dense tangle of streets and alleyways. It had once been partially enclosed by a wall, but like all walls in Orokos it hadn't lasted. Within, rainswept plazas that had once been magnificent were crowded with rotting shanties. Vast, elaborate buildings reared above clutters of miserable shacks and houses. The grim façades of ancient mausoleums glowered at one another over thundering canals, and gaping metal archways led into the city's subterranean depths.

There were gates watched over by Protectorate soldiers, who checked the identity stripes tattooed on every ghetto dweller's forearm. Ghetto-folk were only allowed outside their assigned areas with special passes, and although people like Rail and Moa flouted the rules regularly, it was a dangerous game. If they were caught by the soldiers they would be taken away — and ghetto-folk who were taken away never came back.

Rail and Moa got into the ghetto through one of dozens of back ways. They had lost Fulmar some while ago. Rail had promised that he would *definitely* tell Anya-Jacana about Fulmar's slip-up unless the boy made himself scarce. He didn't seriously intend to do it — Fulmar didn't deserve the kind of punishment the thief-mistress would deal out — but Rail thought he could let the younger boy sweat for a while. Maybe next time he'd think twice before he deserted his post for a pie.

Rail and Moa lived in a den that had once been a bunker of some kind. From the outside, it was little more than a round, rusted hatch on the concrete bank of a canal. It was hidden underneath a bridge and shielded from sight by a small shack that Rail had erected around it. But beneath the hatch was a ladder, and at the bottom of the ladder were three small, solid rooms that Rail and Moa had taken as their own. The hatch was secured by a combination of dials and switches, which Rail had one day found completely unlocked. Whether it was a probability storm that had done it or some other explanation, he never knew. He memorised the settings and had been living there ever since. Later, when he met Moa, he invited her to stay there with him. She was suspicious at first, but she accepted in the end. To find a place so safe in the ghetto was an extraordinary stroke of luck, and they guarded its location jealously.

It was to their den that they went first, before going to see the thief-mistress. Though the walls and floor were bare metal, the two of them had accumulated all kinds of blankets, rugs, carpets and curtains and cushions, which they used for bedding and for covering the floor. The main chamber had a tiny portable oil stove for occasional cooking and for warming the place. It was cluttered with bric-a-brac that they had stolen or salvaged and were assembling into something they could trade or sell. Moa's room was the smallest and was piled waist-deep in soft fabrics. She literally burrowed into it at night and slept in the plush womb that she had created for herself.

Moa slept a lot. She preferred being asleep to being awake, for she always had the most vivid dreams: dreams of flying or of strange and mystical lands, dreams of adventure and romance. Inside her cocoon of blankets and furs, she could be elsewhere, and in her imagination she lived a life of wonders.

They clattered down the ladder into the main chamber, closing the hatch behind them. There they knelt on either side of a rug while Rail gently shook out the contents of his satchel.

Moa sat with her hands pressed between her knees. Rail glanced at her. Her cheek-length black hair was lank and dirty, her skin so pale that he could see the blue traceries of veins at her wrists and neck. She was wearing scuffed green pants, boots, and a long-sleeved black vest that had frayed at the hem. She looked ill.

He hoped he could score her some decent food off this haul. Maybe getting something healthy to eat instead of the tasteless gruel the Protectorate slop-houses dished up might put some colour back in her face.

"Anya-Jacana will be pleased," Moa said neutrally. She wasn't thinking about how pleased the thief mistress would be. She

37

was thinking about how much money there was, and how much they would be left with. It was a good amount. Not a vast amount, but if the thief-mistress was fair they could live off it for a while. That was something, at least.

Rail studied her uncertainly, thinking of the Fade-Science artifact still hidden in his pocket. Thinking whether he should tell her about it or not. Of course he would share it with her; that was never in question. It was just that if he told her about it, she would demand that they take it to Anya-Jacana. She would say that it was too risky; Anya-Jacana would know if they had cheated her. Moa would say that they shouldn't rock the boat, that the consequences could be terrible. And even if she agreed with him, she wasn't a good liar. She would give them away if she knew.

She was a dreamer, and he was a realist. He knew that they couldn't live like this forever, forced to steal just to survive. Sooner or later, they would be caught, and either killed or taken away. That was what happened to those who broke one of the Protectorate's many laws, or who disagreed with their ideas, or who talked about the possibility of a world outside Orokos.

No. As much as he hated to do it, it was for her own good. She'd thank him for it one day. For making this decision.

He left her counting through the haul while he stashed the artifact under the bedroll that he used as a pillow. Then he came back into the main room.

"Let's get going," he said, and began gathering up the bits and pieces to stuff back in his satchel. Not long afterward, they were on their way to the lair of the thief-mistress.

Anya-Jacana's court could be found deep underground, through many doors and down many tunnels. Their route took them across bridges that spanned dark, rushing streams. They passed by the monstrous flanks of machines that hadn't worked for longer than anyone could recall. Gimlet eyes watched them from the shadows — small, scuttling figures that ran across the walls like geckos.

The thief-mistress herself lay in a room with an arched and ribbed ceiling of black glass. Coiled iron shapes, sculptures from the Functional Age, grew from the walls. A carpet of cured animal skin ran from the oval doorway to the dais where she reclined. On either side of her massive brass couch lurked an assortment of attendants and bodyguards.

Rail and Moa walked into the room along the carpet. Other thieves stood in clusters, their faces deep with shadow, waiting for assignments or passing tips among themselves. Rail acknowledged a few of them with tiny nods, and they nodded back.

"Welcome, my children!" boomed Anya-Jacana. They came to a halt in front of her.

She was grotesquely, enormously fat, swaddled in robes of bright and clashing colours, lying on her side on the couch. Her fingers were thick and banded with jewels and rings, and her fleshy arms were hung with bangles and bracelets. Lank and greasy hair, heavy with ornaments, hung over a frog-like face. When she grinned, her mouth split very wide and revealed yellow, round teeth.

"Greetings, Mother," Rail and Moa replied. She insisted that all her thieves call her "Mother."

"I trust you have what I sent you for?"

"Of course," Rail replied. "Did you think we'd fail you? We're the best."

The other thieves murmured at this, but Anya-Jacana roared

with laughter. "Ah, so cocky for one so young. Such brash arrogance! Well, I can't deny you have talent, that's clear enough. An almost *uncanny* ability to infiltrate any location I care to send you." She looked at Moa, her tiny eyes almost disappearing in the folds of her face as she smiled her wide smile. Her gaze switched back to Rail. "Come, then, show me what you have!"

Two of the attendants came to stand before Rail, holding a strip of leather taut between them. He tipped the satchel onto the leather, and a small pile of money and power cells and other odds and ends spilled out. The attendants carried it up the steps of the dais and held it before the thief-mistress.

She began to pick her way through it. After a few moments, she said, "You did do *exactly* as I told you, didn't you?"

Rail didn't like the tone in her voice. "Yes, Mother. We found the small brass casket and we emptied it. It was there just as you said."

Anya-Jacana was studying them closely now. "You took everything from the casket?"

"Everything," Rail said. He was beginning to get worried now. The thief-mistress's grin was fixed in place, but her eyes were becoming colder.

"And everything you took is here?" Anya-Jacana persisted. "Every little thing?"

The room was dead silent now. Rail's heart felt like it was slamming against his ribs. The world seemed to have narrowed, crowding inwards until there was nothing but himself and the thief-mistress. This was what he had most dreaded. Anya-Jacana had been after something specific. Something that she knew was in that brass casket. Something that wasn't here.

She's going to kill you, he thought. He was terrified. But he held himself straight and looked her in the eye.

"Everything," he heard himself say. Because he knew that if the thief-mistress thought for one instant that he had held something back from her, then she would be very angry. And people died when Anya-Jacana got angry.

Her eyes slid slowly to Moa. "Everything?" she said again.

Moa was frightened and confused. She didn't understand the hostility in Anya-Jacana's tone. She turned to Rail for support, but Rail was careful not to meet her gaze. She looked back at Anya-Jacana.

"Everything," she replied.

The silence scratched out like a fingernail along a stone. Anya-Jacana stared at them hard, her grin fading at the edges. They didn't speak or flinch. The moment became excruciating.

"I will be very disappointed if I find you have lied to me, children," said Anya-Jacana slowly. "*Very* disappointed." She turned her head to one of the assistants. "Fifty percent. Even cut between money and machinery. Give the rest back to them."

Rail's legs were beginning to tremble. He tried to keep it under control, but they wouldn't stop. He took what the assistants handed to him without bothering to count it, and then he left as fast as he could without looking like he was guilty. Moa trailed behind him.

When they were gone, the obese mistress of the ghetto's child-thieves motioned to one of the boys who was lurking in the shadows. He was sallow-faced, his skin jaundiced and yellowish, and his eyes were sunken and had dark rings around them that made him look unhealthy. He wore a dirty assortment of black clothes, and wispy blond hair straggled from beneath the cowl that was pulled up over his head.

"Finch," she murmured. "Follow them. I want what I sent them for."

The boy grinned. His gums were black with decay and his browned teeth were filed to sharp points.

"Good as done, Mother."

"What was that about?" Moa asked when they were out in the open again. She was shaken and trembling.

"Putting the scares on us, that's all," he muttered, staring at the wet flagstones of the plaza they were crossing. "She does that from time to time, doesn't she? To keep us in line." His tone was deeply unconvincing.

Moa glanced miserably around the plaza. Juveniles like them were wandering about or hanging around in gangs. There was little to do in the ghetto. No jobs, no money, hardly any food. They couldn't go elsewhere, not with the stripes tattooed on their arm. Only to other ghettoes where life was no better. It seemed that every few days somebody was taken away by the Protectorate, accused of plotting against the Patrician. Sometimes they were people Rail and Moa knew. Nobody could be certain when it would be their turn. It made an already grim existence that much more uncomfortable.

They were trapped here, purposeless, kept just on the right side of dying but not enough to make them feel alive. The only money that moved through this place was through the under-ground: black-market goods and services, theft, protection rackets, murder. If one of the rich folk needed someone taken out, they went to the ghetto. There were people here desperate enough to do anything.

Rail was twiddling the end of one of his dreadlocks as he walked. He was agitated. Moa could tell, even with the smooth metal muzzle that covered his face. It showed in his wide brown eyes. He was truly a beautiful boy, Moa thought, his features fine and delicate and his skin smooth and flawless. Small wonder that he hated the city that had changed him, forced him to wear that disfiguring mask, that pack on his back, the tubes that ran between them.

"You've done something, haven't you?" she asked. "Rail, what did you do?"

Rail shrugged, as if he could make it less important by acting like he didn't care. "I took something."

"You frecking *what*?" Moa cried. Rail glared at her, and she lowered her voice to a hiss. "You took something? From the chest?"

He nodded. "I didn't think she'd miss it. Didn't even think she knew it was there."

"Oh, Rail . . ." she said, but she didn't have the words to express what she felt right then. An abyss had opened up beneath her, and they were both teetering on the brink. And though it was his fault, she couldn't find it in her to blame him. She knew exactly why he had done it.

They walked on for a way, out of the plaza and into the narrow alleys and paths that ran alongside the canal. He told her about the artifact as they went. The ghetto, like the rest of Orokos, was built around the bones of older buildings from the Functional Age. Towering, alien constructions made of strange material loomed over streets of brick and rusty iron. Indestructible walkways of shining obsidian bridged dirty yards full of junk. What order there had once been in the ghetto had been gradually destroyed by the probability storms, jumbling everything up until it was

43

difficult to tell where the past ended and the present began. It was a maze of many levels, and it moved from time to time.

"We run," Rail said eventually. "It's the only way. We run."

"Oh, no," Moa pleaded. "Maybe Anya-Jacana *was* just scaring us. Can't we pretend the artifact just wasn't there? Maybe she'll just think the information she had was wrong. The Mozgas could have moved it before we got there. She didn't tell us what to look for, so how can she blame us for not finding it?"

"She knew," Rail said. "I could see it."

Moa laid a gloved hand on his arm, bringing him to a halt. "I don't want to leave. Can't we get rid of it? Can't we just throw it away?"

Rail gave her a look that was half pity, half condescension. She was frightened of the unknown. But she knew as well as he that it didn't matter whether they had the artifact or not. If Anya-Jacana thought that they had stolen it from her, their throats would be cut before tomorrow night.

Once the decision was made in his mind, Rail felt strangely exhilarated. "This is an opportunity. It's a chance to change things for us. Maybe." He lowered his head, looked deeply into her eyes as if searching for something there. "You want to throw that away?"

"Things will change on their own, Rail. Things always change, if you wait long enough."

He tapped the side of his respirator muzzle. "I'll make my own luck," he said bitterly. And with that, he stalked away. Moa followed after him.

At a distance, Finch followed them also, with a small gang sent by the thief-mistress to get back what was hers.

1.7

Rail shut the hatch of their den behind him and didn't let go until he heard the heavy clank of the locks slamming into place. Moa had already slid down the ladder and was burrowing around in her room, picking up the scattered keepsakes that she had left among the blankets and furs. Once satisfied that they were safe, Rail went to his room and retrieved the artifact from beneath his bedroll, then put it in his satchel. When he returned to the main room, Moa was sitting cross-legged on a rug, stuffing assorted knick-knacks into a tattered backpack.

"Where are we going to go?" she said.

"I don't know," he replied. "Yet."

"We can't leave if we have nowhere to go!" Moa cried.

"Yes, we frecking can," Rail shot back. "Unless you want to argue the toss with Anya-Jacana?"

Moa was silent for a moment. Then: "I know where we can go," she said quietly.

Rail knew, too. He just didn't want to admit it.

"I know where we can go," she said again, "where we'll be safe, where there will be people who can help us."

She waited for him to say it. Rail liked to be the one to make these decisions, and she liked him to make them. It gave them both a feeling of stability. He needed to be in control, she needed someone else to be in control. That was the way it worked with them.

"Alright," he said at last. "We go to Kilatas."

Moa sprang up, threw her arms round him, and kissed him

on the cheek, behind the cold edge of the respirator that fit over his mouth and nose.

"I'm going home!" she cried.

He pulled away from her suddenly. She had forgotten: He didn't like people touching his face. Embarrassed, she mumbled an apology.

"S'okay," he said, looking away.

It made her sad to see him like that. He was ashamed of himself, ashamed of his condition. He wouldn't accept what had been done to him by the probability storm. Why couldn't he understand that change just *happened*, that there was nothing anyone could do to prevent it? Why did he struggle so hard? You could spend your whole life fighting to make something of yourself, to get out of this awful ghetto, and then one day you find yourself struck down with some disease, or turned into a cat, or dumped on the other side of the city with no way to get back. That was the way the world worked. So why make your life miserable by swimming against the current? It made far more sense to lie back and wait for things to turn your way.

But Rail wouldn't do that. He was angry at being burdened with a respirator. He didn't even think how *lucky* he was that Anya-Jacana had possessed one to give to him. She had saved his life in return for his service, but that wasn't enough for him. He wanted to go to some rich doctor, to have the doctor fix him and make it right. Even though it would cost more than they would ever have, even though no doctor would ever work on anyone with the stripes of the ghetto-folk tattooed on his arm. He wanted to make his fortune so he could change back what the city had done to him.

It was his dream. Moa knew that. And she knew that was

46

what he had been thinking of when he had decided to steal from the thief-mistress.

"Here it is," he said, digging in his satchel and retrieving the artifact. He put it carefully in her hand.

She stared at it in wonder. Suddenly, she could see why he had been so reckless. It was mesmerising. The working of the brass was incredible. The amber disc was made of something like polished stone, or glass, or a gem. But it was none of these. It turned the light in a curious way, so that from some angles it looked like it was *deep*. Instead of a flat disc it seemed like the mouth of a great, amber-lined hole, even though the disc itself wasn't much thicker than a wafer. It was a tiny miracle, an echo of a past long forgotten that Moa believed in desperately. A time when things were different.

"Oh . . ." she breathed. "It's wonderful."

"You keep hold of it," he told her.

"But it's yours," she said, though her protest was halfhearted. She was already entranced. "You found it. It could be worth a fortune."

"You keep that safe. I'll keep *you* safe. How's that?"

She looked up at him and gave him a heartbreaking smile of pure and innocent happiness. She never understood why Rail did these little things for her, these little gestures of companionship, but she loved him for it. Not in the way a girl was *supposed* to love a boy — at least, she didn't think so — but because it made her feel wanted. Neither Rail nor Moa had anybody to care about them but each other.

"That's fine," she said, putting her hand on his arm. He moved his hand onto hers for a moment. Then he turned away and went into his room. It was as if she had never touched him.

For a time, she studied the Fade-Science artifact in the strange light of the den. Rail and Moa had never worked out the source of the illumination in their bunker hideaway. Night or day, it was always light, yet there seemed to be no lanterns or glowsticks or anything of that sort. It just seemed to come from the walls and floor and ceiling.

They hadn't wasted much time thinking about it. There was nobody in Orokos who hadn't come across some wonder from the Functional Age and been baffled. People took the unknown in their stride, because they were surrounded by it. For many generations, scientists and inventors had been struggling to understand the legacy of the time before the Fade. What headway they made was frustratingly slow. For people like Rail and Moa, there was no hope of making sense of the ancient technologies. They were uneducated, without prospects, and denied both because they were raised in the ghettoes. They simply took it as good fortune that they didn't need to light their home and left it at that.

But the artifact . . . that was different. Moa turned it over and over while Rail packed up his meagre possessions in the other room. There were two loops at one end of the amber disc, set at right angles to it, almost like two rings joined together. Experimentally, she slid her middle two fingers through the loops, so that the amber disc lay in the middle of her palm. It was a very tight fit, but it felt right. She turned her hand this way and that.

"Rail! I think I've worked out how you're supposed to wear this thing."

"*Wear* it?" he called back through the doorway. Moa yelped

suddenly. He popped back into sight, alarmed. "Moa, what are you —"

He never finished. Moa was standing transfixed, her hand held out before her and the artifact upon it. Her forearm was sheathed in soft light, swirling veils of purple and green and blue that clung to her like fog. She moved it left and right, and the veils drifted with her.

"Take it off!" Rail cried. He moved towards her and then stopped, not sure what to do.

"No, it's alright," she said. "It doesn't hurt." A faint smile appeared on her face, now that it didn't appear to be harmful. "Look at it."

Rail *was* looking at it. He couldn't take his eyes from it. "You know what that looks like, Moa?" he said. "That looks like what happens when there's a probability storm."

Moa was about to make a reply when they heard a thumping at the hatch to their den, and her blood went cold.

"Come out, come out," cooed a muffled voice from above. "We want to have a word with you."

Rail made a motion to be silent, but he hardly needed to. Moa had no intention of answering. She knew that voice. It was Finch, Anya-Jacana's favourite. He was a superb thief, but he was an even better murderer.

"I know you're down there," Finch called. "Followed you back. You going to let us in?"

Rail looked about desperately, as if there was some kind of escape to be had. But he knew every inch of this den. There was no way out except through the hatch. They were trapped.

"What now?" Moa said quietly.

Rail tried to think, but the answers weren't coming. There had always been one downside to this place: no back door. There wasn't even any way he could get rid of the artifact. They were going to be caught red-handed, and there would be no mercy shown to them. He felt panic rising within him, and if he had been on his own he might well have given in to it. But there was Moa to think of. Always Moa. She needed him to be strong for her.

"Take that thing off," he told her again, meaning the artifact. It was still producing beautiful colours.

She tried to do so. It didn't move. "I can't!" she said, tugging at it. "It won't come off!"

"It has to!" he hissed, but still he didn't dare to touch it. He was afraid of those colours.

There was an ascending whine coming from above now, getting higher and higher in pitch.

"If you won't come out, little rats," Finch called, "then we'll come in."

The whine reached the peak of hearing, and then there was a massive impact on the hatch, like a giant's fist pounding from outside. Dust shook loose from the ceiling.

"What is that?" Moa cried.

"They've got a frecking magnetic ram out there," Rail hissed. The whine began again.

"I can hear you!" Finch yelled over the din. "Mother wants to see you, lovebirds!"

Moa shrieked as the magnetic ram thumped once more and the hatch in the ceiling bent inwards. Though rusty on the outside, that hatch was several inches thick. The ram had been placed over it, pointing down. It stood on four stout legs that affixed themselves to the concrete around the hatch. The legs supported a cannon that fired pulses of magnetic energy. Anya-Jacana had all kinds of devices like this in her secret storehouses. The respirator that Rail wore was from the same place.

Rail and Moa ran through to Rail's room, to get away from the hatch before it caved in. Moa was still trying to get the artifact off, but it was stuck fast. Rail slapped his hands flat against the blank metal wall in frustration. The whine of the magnetic ram began again. It would only take a couple more hits and they would be through.

It was hopeless. He knew it was hopeless. But still he searched for a way out.

The ram fired, this time so hard that the bunker shook. Moa, obsessed with trying to remove the Fade-Science device, stumbled and tripped against the wall. She threw out her hands instinctively to protect herself —

— and fell *through* the wall.

Rail couldn't believe what he had seen. Suddenly, he was alone. Moa was gone. He had seen her pass through solid metal as if she was a ghost. He pressed his hands against the place where she had disappeared, and it was hard and unyielding.

The ram began to power up again. The hatch was buckled now, and its hinges were about to give way. Rail knew that the next blow would break it open, and in would come Finch and his cronies.

But she got away, he thought, though he couldn't imagine how. It seemed like a miracle, but the people of Orokos were used to miracles. *At least she got away. And she took that thing with her.*

He gave in at last, and stopped struggling. Maybe, when she didn't find the device on him, the thief-mistress would be merciful. Maybe she wouldn't kill him. He didn't care too much.

51

Wherever she was, Moa was out of Anya-Jacana's reach. That was all he was concerned about.

The ram pounded again, and there was a crash in the other room as the entrance gave way. He turned around to face the boys who would come clambering through.

Come and get me, Rail thought.

And then a hand grabbed him from behind, and he was pulled roughly backwards. There was a split second when he expected to collide with the metal wall, but he went through it as if it wasn't there. Beyond was a dank metal tunnel, dimly lit by fizzing tracklights, brown with decay. And Moa, holding on to him with her right hand. The other one — the one with the artifact attached — was held against the side of the tunnel.

He looked back in amazement. The metal where Moa was touching it had become transparent, a hole filled with swirling, gentle colours. Through it, he could see the first of the thieves coming through the hatch.

Moa pulled away, and the colours sucked back to surround her hand again. The wall was solid once more.

"It opens *doors*, Rail," she breathed. "It opens doors anywhere."

He wanted to hug her, but he didn't dare. Not while she was wearing that thing. Instead, he looked both ways up the corridor and picked a direction. They had none of the things they had packed, except the satchel full of loot that he had been given by Anya-Jacana. It didn't matter.

"Let's go," he said. And they ran, leaving the thieves in their den to puzzle over how their targets could have vanished into thin air.

1.8

In the small hours of the night, Vago would talk to the painting that leaned against the wall in his room. It was quieter then: Cretch wasn't in his laboratory, and so the pipes and valves that fed it no longer boomed and clicked. The moonlight would paint everything in peaceful shadow. Vago would stand by the window, his scrawny, elongated body of metal and muscle and wing half-hidden by the dark, and spill his thoughts to the picture. The picture never spoke back. But it did pay attention.

It was a small painting in a brass frame. When he had found it, it was covered over with a drape, dusty with neglect. There were no other paintings in the tower. Vago wondered how this one had come to be here, and why his master had left such an interesting picture in this chamber he so rarely visited.

The scene was of one of Orokos's canalside areas. In the foreground ran the water, swiftly flowing from left to right. It was heading for one of the enormous vents that would spew it from the edge of the rocky island to the sea far below. Walkways and bridges cluttered the far side of the canal, and there were doorways and dreary shopfronts set on many levels. In the background rose tall spires and a huge, dark temple. Vago thought he recognised the scene, but he couldn't think why.

The girl was standing on the canalside on the right of the picture, leaning on the railing and looking down into the water. Her white hair spilled down one side of her face. Her dress looked expensive — the sign of a wealthy upbringing. She wasn't a ghetto girl, that much was for sure.

Last time Vago had checked, she had been staring out of the window of a shop, her expression bored. The time before, she had been waving at him from one of the bridges, smiling happily. A few times he couldn't find her at all, and he panicked. He thought of her as a companion, and she was the only one he had. But she would always be back sooner or later. She listened to him, even if she never answered. He could tell.

"Do *you* know where my maker is?" he would ask her.

Vago's memories of the time after he was made were very fuzzy and muddled. He had fleeting impressions of a cell of some kind, a room of black iron with bars on the door. Men in black coats studied him, and he was scared of them. But there were only two things he could recollect with any clarity. One was a face, looking in at him through the curved window of some kind of tank. It was a thin, severe face, more familiar to Vago than his own. The other thing was a name: Tukor Kep. There was nobody else it could be but his maker. The one who gave him life.

Where had he gone? Or, more accurately, where had *Vago* gone?

He didn't know how long it had been since he had found himself in this room. His memory had still not settled by then, and he was like a newborn, unable to understand what was around him. Cretch discovered him there on the morning after a particularly violent probability storm. It wasn't hard to guess what had occurred. The Storm Thief had plucked him from the place he was made and put him elsewhere. Vago imagined his maker's distress at discovering the golem was gone, and it made him sad. But he didn't know how to get back.

He ran his long fingers over the dead bird that hung around his neck. Cretch, in a moment of unusual kindness, had treated it with preserving fluid to stop it from rotting and had given it back to Vago. Its wings were folded now, close to its body so that they didn't get in his way too much. Ephemera had given up laughing at it; she just sneered instead. But Vago liked the seabird, and he thought the girl in the picture did, too. The first time he showed it to her, she was openmouthed in wonder.

When Cretch was working he sent Ephemera up to summon Vago, and the golem dutifully attended. He was a useful assistant around the laboratory. When he straightened up he was very tall, and could reach the highest shelves. His fingers were extraordinarily nimble and strong, good for delicate work. He could crush a stone between his thumb and forefinger, but he could also thread a needle first time, every time.

The laboratory was dark and hot, but islands of bright light were thrown by hooded lamps that hung like vultures over Cretch's workspace. There was a kiln for baking ceramics, a rotating saw and a whining lathe, a blowtorch, and a little dynamo that produced tiny forks of lightning. And everywhere there were devices: mannequins, porcelain figures, miniature animals, and delicate temples. There were clockwork faces that copied the expression of whoever gurned at them. There were wheeled cats that chased wheeled mice around the room, homing in on their darting targets, drawn by some mystical force that Vago didn't understand. There were jagbat automatons that folded and unfolded their wings restlessly. Vago made sure to keep his own wings carefully tucked away.

Whenever Vago returned there was something new to marvel

at. Even half-built, they were masterpieces. Cretch was a toy-maker, and his toys were the wonder of Orokos.

"But whoever made you, *they* could teach me a thing or two," Cretch had said to Vago more than once. "I'd love to take you apart and see what makes you tick."

Vago didn't like the sound of that, and he kept quiet about Tukor Kep. He had asked Cretch once if he knew who his maker was, but Cretch only said, "I have my suspicions," and didn't explain further. Vago didn't dare to press him.

Cretch was in a foul mood this morning, having not slept well the night before. Vago glanced nervously at the walking stick that lay against Cretch's work desk. His master was bent over some tiny jewelled thing, squinting through his goggles while he tapped at it delicately with a pin. Vago lurked in the shadows and tried to be silent. He had learned to fear Cretch when he was like this. He was liable to catch a beating if he put a foot wrong today. He stroked his bird-pendant and watched his master warily.

"Oh, my eyes . . ." Cretch groaned, pinching his brow. He had been complaining about his failing vision for some time now, and it was beginning to hamper his work. "Vago, come here."

The golem came closer, looming over the old man.

"Hold this," Cretch said, motioning at the jewelled thing. It turned out to be a beetle, formed of glittering strands as delicate as spun sugar. "Carefully!"

Vago did as he was told, pinching it with one hand to hold it still. It was tougher than it looked, but even so, it was terrifying to have to squeeze it, no matter how gently. He was afraid he would break it. He might have known Cretch would give him some task like this. It was as if the old man wanted an excuse to beat him.

"Good, good," Cretch said. He peered closer and began to scratch at the beetle again with his needle. "Now turn it a little. The other way, I mean. Good."

Cretch worked nimbly around the beetle with the point of his pin, clearing away minute specks of grit and flaked metal that hid at the edges of the gemstones. Vago began to relax a little. Cretch just wanted him to hold it because it was too delicate for any of his instruments. As long as he didn't squeeze any harder than this, then everything would be fine.

"What do you suppose you were made for, Vago?" Cretch asked absently while he worked.

Vago didn't have an answer. Cretch took his silence as meaning he didn't understand.

"It's not easy, you know. Creating life. *I* can't do it. I can create the best *copies* of life in the city, but none of them are like you."

"Am I alive?" Vago asked, in his strained whine-growl voice.

"Of course you are."

"But I was made. Ephemera says I can't be alive."

Cretch blew his lips derisively. "What does she know? It doesn't matter that you were made. We're all *made*. Made in women's bellies. Just because you're made of different stuff doesn't make you any less alive."

Vago considered this.

"But what were you made *for*?" Cretch mused. "That's what I'm wondering. For someone to make something like you, they must have had a reason."

"Maybe I'm a toy," Vago suggested.

Cretch barked a laugh. "No. I know toys. You wouldn't be much fun. Perhaps —"

He got no further, for at that moment his pin slipped, and jabbed deeply into the dry flesh of Vago's finger. Reflexively, the golem's hand clenched, and the jewelled beetle was crushed to a ball of fibres in an instant.

Cretch howled in anguish as Vago retreated to the back of the room, dread flooding him. He knew, with a child's terror, that he had done something wrong. It didn't matter that it didn't seem to be his fault, that it was Cretch who had stabbed him with the needle. Vago would be punished anyway, the way children always got punished for adults' mistakes.

Cretch was rising from his stool, picking up the knobbed walking stick, turning wrathfully on the golem that cringed in the shadows.

"Do you know what you've done?" he said, his voice low. Then, quick as a snake, he brought up the walking stick and brought it crashing down on Vago's wing. "Do you know what you've *done*?"

Vago flinched under the impact. Pain, awful pain. Something ugly blazed in his mind, a sudden, violent anger. But he was ashamed of that feeling, afraid of it. Each time he was beaten, the anger seemed to be stronger, threatening to overwhelm him. He tried to suppress it, but it would not be kept down. It was something within, something primal. Something that he couldn't control.

"That took me *days*!" Cretch cried. "Days!" He brought the stick down hard across Vago's back, chipping it on the metal fins that ran down the golem's spine.

58

Vago crumpled under the blow and tried to scramble away, but his attempt at escape was halfhearted. He knew that running away would only make things worse. The stick cracked across his metal skull and his vision went white and sparkled. Something was clawing up from within him, terrible feelings of hatred and fury clouding his mind. Cretch was ranting in the background, venting his frustration, and the stick was raised and swung again.

But Vago wasn't there. All he knew was that someone was hurting him, and he reacted. He darted out of the way like liquid, grabbing the stick in one hand as he did so. With a twist of his wrist he broke it in half, and before the pieces had fallen the golem had Cretch's throat in one hand, lifting his master off the floor, his wings outspread. Cretch gasped like a fish, eyes bulging behind black goggles, legs kicking feebly. The golem glared at his master with his one good eye, metal fangs bared, a soft clicking noise coming from his chest.

Slowly, those terribly strong fingers began to tighten.

It was Ephemera's scream that stopped him. She had been attracted by the ruckus, excited by the prospect of seeing her grandfather dish out another beating to the poor freak that she was used to ridiculing. Now she found her grandfather dangling like an eel on a hook, and the golem was suddenly not so comical anymore.

That shrill noise shook Vago back to his senses. The thing hanging in his grip was Cretch again, his master Cretch. The man who had taken him in and cared for him, even though sometimes he did beat him like a dog. Vago opened his hand, and Cretch fell to the floor in a heap, choking. Ephemera watched from the doorway of the laboratory, stunned.

"I hate you!" she shrieked, bursting out of her stupor. "I hate you!"

But Vago wasn't listening. There was only one thing to do now. He dared not stay, dared not face Cretch's retribution for what he had done. He pushed Ephemera clumsily aside and fled down the stairs of the tower, out into the city.

1.9

Vago had never been outside, as far as he could recall. It didn't take him long to realise why.

He emerged from the gate at the base of Cretch's tower and into the daylight. The gate was a massive mechanical thing set within the thick bedrock that covered the lower third of the tower. It led out onto a street set into the side of a steep hill. The hill was utterly covered in buildings, a clutter of rooftops and alleyways and stairs.

He stumbled out onto the road. It was a grey morning, the sky thick with sea mist. Carts and steam engines rolled along noisily. Between them darted riders on high-stepping gyik-tyuks, agile things that looked like a cross between lizard and bird. The gyik-tyuks squawked and hissed at each other, displaying the grey neck feathers to warn off any other gyik-tyuks that came near. Men and women shopped at stores all along the street, buying strange foodstuffs from the hydroponics farms up in the Agricultural Zone. They wore robes in drab colours, and they had curious ornaments around their necks and hanging from their ears.

Vago gazed at the scene in wonder. The clammy air tasted faintly salty and the breeze tingled on his wrinkled and puckered skin. For a long moment, he was paralysed by the sheer busyness of the street, overwhelmed by sight and sound, by the outrageous variety all around him.

Then the first of the screams came. A child's shriek, reminding him of Ephemera. He turned towards its source, and there was a little girl staring at him. Her mother had gathered her close and was gaping at Vago. Heads turned at the sound and eyes fixed on him. There were more screams, and murmurs and exclamations from the menfolk.

He stood before the gate of the tower, feeling suddenly hunted. He wanted to duck back inside. But he couldn't return to that place, not after what he had done.

People all around had come to a standstill, gawking at the golem. He was a mockery of human form, a repulsive hybrid of dry flesh and dull metal. A horror. Probability storms threw up all kinds of weirdness, and occasionally a person might be seen with three arms, or two heads, or a coat of scales, or a forked tail. It could happen to anyone, at any time. That was why people feared them: because it reminded them how fragile their happiness was, how easily their world could be turned inside out. That was why people reacted with disgust and hate.

Vago saw the first stone coming, instinctively tracking the movement. A targeter in his mechanical eye calculated the trajectory faster than thought. He knew exactly where it was going to hit him. But he was still too surprised to get out of the way.

There was a sharp pain as it struck his shoulder. He whirled and stanced in a crouch, his natural eye fixed on the man who had thrown it, his metal fangs bared, his wings half-open. Like a predator, ready to spring. The man went white, and the crowd hesitated, some with stones ready in their hands. There was something in the golem's reaction, something that told them this wasn't some unfortunate thing that could be tormented and driven away, that he was dangerous.

But there were dozens of them and only one of him. The stones started flying.

Vago was pounded under a hail of rocks. They thumped into his flesh and clanked off the mechanical parts of him. He howled and tried to dodge, but the assault was relentless. The crowd was shouting obscenities at him, catcalls and hollers. He didn't understand, didn't know what he had done to merit this kind of abuse. He had harmed no one, done nothing except to share the same street as them.

Oh, yes! he heard Ephemera crowing in his mind. *Ugly is what you are!*

Fury blazed up inside him. He glared hatefully at the men and women and children who were stoning him, and he wanted to murder every last one of them, to pounce upon them and break their bones with his strong hands and bite their necks with his sharp jaws until they —

He caught himself, shocked at the primal viciousness of his thoughts. He had to get away, away from here, from all of this. And so he ran, springing away suddenly, darting through a gap in the crowd. He moved with a fluid grace entirely at odds with his appearance. The mob was too surprised to stop him, nor would any of them have dared. They had seen the killer in his eyes, and they were not willing to tackle him except in a pack.

He fled on all fours. He had never had to run before, but he naturally fell into a bounding lope that propelled him at great speed down the street. Screams and exclamations followed him as he lunged through the crowds, slipping between the slow, wheezing vehicles, cringing from the sight of the people who surrounded him. Everywhere he looked he saw faces twisted in distaste or fear, people pointing or scrambling out of his way. He wanted to hide from their eyes, but they were everywhere.

Into the alleys. That was the answer. Into the alleys, off the street.

A clamour had arisen somewhere nearby. A shrill, pulsing

whistle, joined by another and yet another. He had heard that sound from high up in his tower before. It was the alarm call of the Protectorate soldiers.

He leaped over a cowering boy and plummeted down a set of steps, his wings tucked in close. He landed lightly on his finger-tips and toes when he struck the walkway below. Stone buildings, shops of some kind, reared up on either side of him. Between them was a narrow throughway. He took it.

The buildings closed him in, screening him from the crowd on the street. He felt a desperate relief at being away from them. His skin crawled with reflected loathing. The throughway was empty. As he reached the end of it he slowed and looked back, like a kicked dog that wasn't sure whether to return to its master.

"It's here!" someone cried in the distance. Vago tensed. If he ran, where would he run to? He was afraid of the city, and it was all around him.

Two figures appeared at the end of the alley. They were armoured in pale green, their eyes hidden behind wraparound visors that glowed faintly with the same colour. Both were shaved bald, and they carried with them some kind of devices affixed to their right forearms. Sleek metal shapes, with stubby muzzles that projected past their wrists.

"There it is!"

A sudden memory. Vago recognised these people. Protectorate soldiers. And the things on their arms, that they were now point-ing at him . . .

Aether cannons.

He moved an instant before they fired. The cannons spat squealing globs of burning green energy, a moist slither of pure aether that fizzed and spat as it cut through the air. They struck the wall where Vago had stood a split second before, spraying across it before disappearing with an angry hiss, leaving the stone unmarked. Aether cannons didn't damage inorganic matter like stone. Nor did they affect organic material like flesh. Nobody knew how they worked, but everyone knew what they did. One hit from an aether cannon would blow your soul apart.

Vago was around the corner and into another alleyway before the soldiers had even realised they had missed. He heard the whistle of their alarms as they gave chase. They were answered by others. The soldiers were closing in fast.

This alleyway was cobbled, and a thin stream of dirty water ran down a gutter at its side. It was dense with rickety shopfronts selling strings of animal hooves and spices, cheap ornaments and medicinal concoctions. There was a heavy scent of cooking patties, aromatic smoke, and sweat. Shaggy buta — dim beasts of burden with dirty white pelts that hung over their eyes — chewed handfuls of weeds. Their curling horns were brightly painted and tinkled with little gold charms. They watched Vago pass without interest.

He bounded between the sellers and the buyers, scaring them as he passed. People cursed and fell out of the way, only realising afterward that it wasn't an animal but something else that had blurred by. He could hear the whistle of the soldiers, knew that they were ahead of him as well as behind. But he had to run. There was nothing else he could do.

Then the buildings on either side peeled back and let the sky in, and there before him was a long, curving bridge that arched over a massive canal. The canal was the West Artery, one of the main waterways of the city. It ran from the great pump atop a mountain near the centre of Orokos. There, seawater was sucked up and purified before being released from a colossal reservoir to flow back towards the ocean, travelling north, south, and west along the Arteries. It had flowed east, too, until some time ago when the canal had disappeared during a probability storm. Most of eastern Orokos was flooded. Since then, those areas had become slums, and were plagued with Revenants.

Vago sprang out of the alleyway and onto the bridge. It went from one side of the Artery to the other with no visible means of support. He was terrified by the amount of space around him, by the misty sky and the sensation of great height. He could see the rushing water far below. There was nothing to stop him from falling off except a low parapet.

Down the canal, he could see all the way to the edge of Orokos, many miles away. In the other direction, towards the centre, he could see the spires and rooftops of the city. There were cranes and derricks, and the rotted tooth of an occasional mountain shrouded in white haze. Among them were the magnificent and obscure shapes of constructions left over from the Functional Age.

People were screaming again, and whistles pulsed. The men and women on the bridge scattered. Running towards Vago were three more Protectorate soldiers. He stumbled to a halt and looked back desperately, but he could see two more soldiers pushing through the alleyway he had just come from. There was no escape there. He was trapped.

The soldiers levelled their aether cannons. The people cried out and cowered against the parapets. Vago took one step and sprang over the side of the bridge.

He had been hoping, perhaps, that instinct would take over, that he would spread his leathery wings and fly. He was mistaken.

As soon as his wings unfolded, the wind caught them and the impact sent him spinning, flailing uselessly.

Hopelessly tangled, he plunged like a rock towards the water below. Calculations were flickering through his head, judgements of distance and velocity. The massive canal raced up to meet him, unstoppably fast. After falling this far, the surface would be like concrete.

He hit the water at bone-shattering speed, and after that there was darkness.

1.10

The streets of Orokos went deep.

The city sat atop a plateau of rock in the midst of the ocean, and there was nothing beyond it. Over time, it had grown to cover every square inch of the island's surface, except for the sides of the blunt, lonely mountains that thrust up into the sky here and there. They were too steep to build on.

When there was no more space on the surface, the people in forgotten days had built upwards. They constructed spires and towers and great obelisks of shiny black metal with thousands of chambers inside. But they also dug down, into the rock. They tunnelled out labyrinths of underground waterways, service ducts, and strange chambers whose purpose had long been lost to history. And there were streets down here, long corridors full of apartments, dozens upon dozens of levels. An old superstructure left from a departed time that nobody knew how to maintain.

But whether the city above was basking in the sun or pale under the light of the moon, the Dark Markets were always open.

The market that Rail and Moa found themselves at, some time after they had fled their home, had sprung up in a cavernous Functional Age chamber with a barrel-shaped ceiling. Great branching pillars supported the roof, made of some black substance that was the texture of glistening wood but harder than metal. In between these pillars were dozens of yurts, tents of stiffened fabric that resembled beetles. They were pitched anywhere, in no apparent order. One end was always propped open, to display the wares within. In the Dark Markets, everything was for sale.

Rail and Moa trod carefully through the chamber. It was busy at the moment. Gyik-tyuks and rickshaws made their way among the foot traffic, and the noise of conversation echoed dizzyingly all around. Burning globes of sharp white energy fizzed in the air above. They hung unsupported in space, casting their light on the people below.

All walks of life met and mingled here, where the Protectorate soldiers didn't come. There were rich folk, dressed in heavy, dull-coloured robes, for it was considered vulgar in society to wear bright colours or revealing clothes. With them went mercenary bodyguards with thumper guns. There were hooded Ghost Path devotees, who worshipped and studied the hated Revenants. They murmured among themselves, shunned by the crowd. There were victims of the cruel randomness of the probability storms, men and women with odd-coloured eyes or bizarre deformities. There were boys from the ghettoes, their hair and skin dyed in tribal fashions, representing the gangs that they belonged to. And there was more, and more after that, endlessly.

Rail viewed them all with equal suspicion. He kept his hand on his satchel, watching for thieves, and made sure Moa had the precious artifact tucked away inside an inner pocket of her pants.

She had finally managed to get it off her hand with the aid of some engine oil they had found leaking from an old machine on their way through the tunnels. It hadn't fixed itself to her as they had feared, it was just too tight. Once it had come free, the radiance had faded and it had become inactive. But now they treated it with awe, and she kept checking to make sure it was there in her pocket, as if it might disappear at any moment.

At the sides of the chamber were rows of bars and shops. Short, round-mouthed tunnels were cluttered with advertisements and samples of what lay within. Rail took Moa into one that had steaming vats of ribbonfish outside. A balding man in a smock was frying grain-cakes on a griddle nearby. He glanced at them and then returned his attention to the food.

Inside was a low, circular room, hot and heavy with the scent of aromatic smoke. In the centre was a square bar where cooks took orders from the clientele. Rail ordered each of them a heaping plate of shark cutlets and pumpkin mash. The food arrived with complimentary mugs of cold tuzel, a spicy drink that Moa loved when she could get it.

They took their plates to a small booth and sat opposite each other. Moa attacked the food with an indecent appetite. Rail was forced to eat much more slowly, lifting his respirator between bites. He hated eating in pubic, but they both needed a rest and a good meal. It had been an exhausting journey.

"We can't afford this," said Moa, barely even pausing to speak before putting another forkful of shark in her mouth.

"Bit late now," Rail said, with a grin that only showed around his eyes. "We're loaded at the moment anyway."

"At the *moment* we are," Moa replied, looking up from her plate. "That's got to last."

"You need to eat. Let me worry about the money."

She let it lie at that. She was simply enjoying the taste of real food, and lots of it. Rail watched her indulgently. The times were too rare when he could afford to treat her like this. He knew what she thought of his dreams of becoming rich, of changing the hand that fate had dealt him. What he had never told her was that *she* figured in those plans as well. The rest of the world could take care of itself, but he would take care of Moa. Before anything, before even getting his lungs fixed so that he wouldn't

70

need a respirator anymore, he would see to her. He would ensure that they had a place to live, that they ate a good meal every day, that they didn't have to scratch and scrabble just to survive anymore. That was his secret dream. To make them a life where comfort and safety were not luxuries.

He looked around the chamber while she polished off her food, careful not to catch anyone's eye. It was the usual weird assortment you might find in a Dark Market restaurant. They smoked elaborate pipes, drank their drinks, and watched the other patrons.

"She'll follow us," he said absently.

Moa paused, the fork just leaving her lips. "What are you muttering about?" she said, accidentally spraying a mist of chewed-up shark across the table. She burst out laughing and nearly choked on the food she still had in her mouth. Heads turned to look at them, but she managed to swallow and give Rail a sheep-ish grin, her eyes still watering.

"You okay?" he asked.

"Just about," she said, pounding herself on the chest with the heel of her hand. "Sorry, go on."

Rail looked at her a few moments, concern in his eyes.

"Rail, I'm alright!" she said. "Shouldn't have tried to breathe my breakfast, that's all." She sobered a little. "You mean Anya-Jacana."

"She won't let us go," Rail said, brushing stray dreadlocks over his shoulder. "She must know what it is that we've got. She won't rest until she has it back."

"Then we should get rid of it," Moa said, eating again, a little more carefully this time. "Sell it quickly. Take the money and run."

71

He knew she was going to say that, and had his defense prepared. "We can't. Don't you see what that thing is? We're thieves, Moa. And that device . . . Well, if it does what it seems to, then it can get us into anyplace on Orokos. Can you imagine what we could *do* with that?"

"We're not thieves anymore," she protested.

"We are until we can afford to stop," he said. "If we tried to sell it now that Anya-Jacana is on the lookout, she'd hear about it." He trailed off, sudden realisation dawning on him. Of course. *That* was how she knew. The Mozgas, not knowing what it was, had been trying to sell it on the Dark Markets. The thief-mistress had heard that they were hawking Fade-Science, and realised how valuable it could be. She had found out where they kept it and she sent Rail and Moa to go and get it. Rail felt stupid for having not worked it out before, but he couldn't bring himself to regret it. Not really. After all, they had the artifact now.

"Listen," he went on. "That thing is so valuable that half the people in the city would kill us for it. If we tried to take it to the kind of folk who would have the money to pay for it, they'd cut our throats and take it from us. And don't even think about suggesting that we throw it away —"

Moa shut her mouth. She had been about to do just that.

"We *use* it," he said. "That's what we do. We'd be unstoppable with that thing. We could walk into any vault in Orokos. We could make ourselves rich."

Moa didn't like the idea. It troubled her conscience. "Rail, I . . . it's still stealing. I mean, stealing to survive is one thing, but —"

"It's stealing from the *Protectorate*," he interrupted angrily.

"Them, and the people who support them, the good citizens of Orokos. You remember them? The people who make us live in ghettoes, who hate and despise us? The people who take our families and friends away to a place that they never come back from? The people who blame all their problems on us and punish us for it? The ones who spit at us for being lazy and useless but who make absolutely sure by putting tattoos on our arms that we can't work ourselves out of poverty?"

Moa subsided, staring at her food.

"They deserve it," he said.

Moa nodded slightly. "Yeah," she said.

Rail sat back and watched her for a moment. He hated to play that card. Her own mother had been taken away by the Protectorate.

"What do you think it was for?" she asked. "I mean, in the first place?"

"The artifact? Who knows? Maybe the Faded used it for mining or something, like tunnelling through rock. Maybe it was for spies to sneak in and out of places. Maybe they had a Secret Police like we do and they had all kinds of tricks like that to root out dissenters."

Moa scoffed. "Why would they need Secret Police? They didn't have any crime."

Rail made a noise that indicated he didn't really care either way. "So the legends say. You believe everything you hear? Anyway, it doesn't matter what it was for — what matters is what it can *do*. Now, first things first. We need a place to stay, a place that's safe. We go to Kilatas. Even Anya-Jacana won't find us there. Your friend Kittiwake can help us, right?"

"If you think we'll be followed, then we shouldn't be going

to see Kittiwake at all!" Moa said, alarmed. "We'll lead them right to her!"

"I know, I know. We won't do that. First we have to be sure that nobody can follow our trail."

Moa gazed around the room, suddenly paranoid.

"Relax," he said, reaching across the table and laying a hand on her thin, pale wrist. "They won't catch us. Eat."

Moa was nervous now, but she ate the rest of her food, and half of Rail's as well, after he insisted that he wasn't hungry.

They found a Coder and traded a few power cells for coins and platinum chits, then left the Dark Markets, heading away into the winding tunnels. There were whole towns down here in the dark, subterranean communities beneath the city. People who lived their entire lives beneath the glow of the tracklights. They never once questioned where the energy that illuminated the tunnels came from, nor did they consider what might happen if it suddenly all went black. The false light in this dim world was as eternal as the sun to them.

Rail and Moa kept away from the settlements, not wanting to be seen or remembered. Rail knew most of the places they passed, shanties or tent clusters that sprawled across old, empty chambers, but most of them would not welcome strangers. Sewer dogs roamed about, and hobos shuffled on never-ending journeys, passing from community to community, leaning on their sticks. Down here lived other creatures like Mozgas, subhuman monsters birthed of the probability storms. Most kept to themselves, hiding from the Protectorate, which would hunt them down if they found them.

Rail checked his compass often to make certain that they were still heading in the right direction. He knew where he was going, for Moa had told him long ago where Kilatas lay and how to find it. She never could keep a secret, not from him. But it paid to be sure, in case the route had changed since she had walked it last. Compasses always pointed to the centre of Orokos, to the Fulcrum, the ancient heart of the city. Within the Fulcrum, it was said, lay the Chaos Engine, the source of the probability storms. The source of the Revenants.

Eventually, they came up to the surface, to the streets, and found that night was falling.

They emerged on a service walkway that ran alongside the West Artery. The sky overhead was clear and cool and spattered with stars. A dozen feet below them, water rushed by, glittering with the lights of the buildings on the canalside.

"Look at that," said Moa, leaning against the railing of the walkway. She was heady with the joy of being outside again. "Isn't it amazing?"

"Not really," said Rail, who was more concerned than he showed about being followed, and was eager to get on.

She looked back at him, a frond of black hair hanging over her face and across her nose. "Don't you ever wonder who made all this?" She gestured up the canal, towards the centre of the city. "*Why* they made it?"

Rail, seeing that she was in a speculative mood, gave up and joined her. "The Faded made it. Everyone knows that. And then they left us or died out or something, and then there was the Fade, and we've spent the rest of the time trying to remember the things we've forgotten."

But this answer clearly didn't satisfy Moa. "But why, though? Where did they come from? I mean . . . how did they *get* here, if there's nothing else but Orokos?"

Rail shrugged. "Fact is, it doesn't matter. People like you and me, we just have to worry about surviving."

She was disappointed by this, and it showed on her face. "You really think that Orokos is all there is? That there's nothing out there? What about the legends? How is it that you don't believe in a past when everything was peaceful and in harmony? You only have to look at what the Faded left behind to imagine how beautiful it must have been."

"They left us the Chaos Engine as well," Rail replied. "Now if they *did* live in this perfect world as the legends say, why the freck did they build that thing? Why make something that creates probability storms? And why did they disappear and leave us to deal with it?"

"You know I don't have an answer to that. Nobody does. We don't know enough. It's just about what you believe."

"You and Kittiwake, you're two of a kind. Dreamers. What evidence have you ever had that there's anything out there?"

"I told you about the lights in the sky, Rail. They —"

"Exactly. That's all they were. Lights in the sky. Could have been anything. And listen, even if — and I say *if* — there was anything out there, how would you ever find out? Nothing is allowed to leave Orokos. Nothing. The city itself won't allow it. You know that better than most."

She did know that. It was how she had lost her father. He had tried to escape Orokos, to sail out into the ocean in search of that promised land. He hadn't gotten far.

"But that's the point!" she snapped, a little angry at Rail for

76

bringing up her father. He never could understand why she still believed in the cause that her father had died for. Maybe it was only that she didn't want his death to be in vain, that she wanted to prove him right. Or maybe it was just because she needed *something* to believe. "Why won't it let anyone leave? Why does it keep us imprisoned here?"

"So we don't all sail off in search of another land when there *isn't* one?" Rail suggested, exasperated. It was an old, old argument. "I don't know, Moa. Maybe it's for our own good. Maybe there's no reason at all. It's just the way it is."

Moa gave up. It was clear that Rail wouldn't be persuaded. He dared to try and change his own life, but refused to accept the possibility of a different life away from Orokos. Moa thought that trying to struggle against the world they were born into was foolish, but she clung to the idea that there was some other place out there. A place where there was no oppression, no Protectorate, no probability storms, no Revenants. A place where they would not be forced to live in ghettoes.

She looked down into the water again. "Sometimes I just want to throw myself in," she murmured. "To let it carry me out of the vents, into the sea, and over the horizon. Maybe I'd wash up on another shore."

"You'd wash up dead," Rail said impatiently. "Come on."

They followed the Artery for some distance before the walkway ended and they were forced to go underground again, through a subway tunnel that ran beneath the canal. It was deserted and in a bad state of repair, filled with the echoing roar of the water overhead. Nobody used this way, which was why Rail had taken it. They clambered over bits of rubble, avoiding the steady drips from cracks in the concrete.

77

Moa almost stepped on Vago before she saw him. He was curled up in the shadow of a small heap of broken stone. Moa let out a little shriek and jumped back. Rail was at her side in an instant.

The golem cowered at the noise, flinching back against the wall of the tunnel. In the fitful glow of the malfunctioning track-light overhead, he was partially hidden. But what they could see was bad enough. Rail muttered a curse under his breath at the sight.

"Scared the freck out of me," Moa said, her heart fluttering, then let out a little laugh.

Rail tugged her arm. "Leave him. Let's go."

"Wait a minute," she said. She looked closer at Vago, who cringed like a cur under her gaze. "What happened to you?" she asked him.

"It's not our problem, Moa," Rail said. He knew how dangerous it was to get involved in other people's troubles. The city was a nasty place, and no good could come of it.

"Just *wait*," she said, firmer this time. Rail's heart sank. Moa was digging her heels in. She was in one of her stubborn moods. Usually she went along with anything he said, but her tempers were so changeable. He knew that trying to persuade her would just make her angry.

She crouched down in front of Vago. "You're a mess, aren't you?" she said. "Probability storm did this to you, right? Can you speak?"

There were a few moments of silence. Then: "Not a storm. Someone built me."

"*Built* you?"

"I don't know what for," he added, as if she had asked him.

Moa thought about that for a moment. "What's your name?"

"My master called me Vago," he replied slowly.

"Okay, Vago. I'm Moa and this is Rail."

"We're *supposed* to be keeping a low profile!" Rail cried. "You just gave him our names! You *want* to get caught?"

"He's in trouble!" Moa snapped. "Can't you see that?"

"The whole damn world is in trouble, Moa! *We're* in trouble! We don't have time for this."

"Well, make time," she replied.

Rail scowled and kicked a stone in annoyance. Moa's soft side was going to get them killed one of these days. In the real world, strangers didn't thank you for helping them. In fact, more often they were liable to mug you and rob you. By the time they got to the stage when they needed help they were usually too far gone to want it. But Moa didn't think that way. She believed in some sunny, shiny dream where good deeds actually *meant* something.

"Where's your master now?" Moa was asking Vago, using a soothing tone, as if she was gentling an animal.

"I can't go back to him," Vago replied.

"He threw you out?"

Vago didn't answer her, merely looked away. Moa took that as a yes, though it really wasn't.

"What's that you've got around your neck?" she asked. It was hard to see in the shadow. Vago reflexively clutched his pendant.

"I don't want to take it from you, Vago," Moa said. "I was just asking what it was."

Vago eyed her suspiciously for an instant, then unfolded himself up and into the light. It had been hard to tell his size when he was curled up, but now he towered over them. Moa

79

took a step back, suddenly wishing she had listened to Rail. The sight of the golem in the light was horrifying.

But Vago was showing her the pendant, still attached to his scrawny neck, and she couldn't help but look. A black-and-white bird, smelling faintly of preservatives. Her first reaction was repulsion, and she drew away from it. It was *dead*. He had a dead thing around his neck. Rail was right, she should never have gotten involved.

Then: "Rail," she murmured. "Look at this."

"What?" he said, coming closer. He made a noise of disgust when he saw it. "Great. Really great," he commented.

Vago looked eagerly at Moa, who had shown more enthusiasm for his prize.

"No, *look* at it," Moa urged. "Can I touch it?" she asked Vago, who leaned down so she could reach it more easily.

Rail came closer. Moa turned it over in her hand, studying it in wonder.

"I see a bird," he said flatly. He wasn't comfortable being this close to Vago. "It doesn't look in the best of health. What am I supposed to be looking at?"

"My father studied birds," Moa said. "He had books and books of them. I used to look through the pictures all the time when I was young. He made me learn them all." She shook her head. "I've never seen this kind before. Never."

"So it's a rare bird."

"It's not rare," said Moa. "It *doesn't exist*."

Rail raised an eyebrow. "Not anymore, it doesn't."

Moa let the bird go and Vago retreated a little, watching the two of them.

"No, I mean there is no bird even remotely like that on

Orokos. Look at the plumage, look at the bone structure, look at —"

"Where are you going with this?" Rail asked in exasperation.

"It came from *somewhere else*!" Moa said.

Rail pinched his nose between his eyes and sighed. Moa turned to the golem, who wore an expression of puzzlement on the half of his face that was mobile.

"Where did you get it?"

"It flew through my window," Vago said.

Moa was excited. "We have to take it to Kittiwake!" she cried. "It's another one! It's another bird, like the first, like the one that she caught."

Vago pulled away, shielding his pendant protectively. Moa held up a hand in apology. "I meant, we have to take *you* to Kittiwake. If you want to go."

"Moa . . ." Rail said warningly. "It's not like he doesn't attract attention."

"This is important!" Moa insisted. She turned back to Vago. "Well?"

He returned her gaze with his mottled yellow eye. Ever since he had dragged himself out of the Artery, he had been contemplating a miserable existence alone in this subway tunnel. He had been wishing that the fall had killed him, but he was built tougher than that, it seemed. His bones didn't break like a normal person's. He wasn't sure his bones were made out of bone at all.

"I will go with you," the golem said. There seemed no better alternative.

"Moa, he's *baggage*," Rail said.

"Well, now he's *our* baggage," she replied firmly.

Rail threw his hands up in frustration and stalked away. He

knew she would not be dissuaded now. What burned him up about Moa was that she was usually so passive, but she clung so tightly to her dreams that she sometimes lost her grip on reality. It was a *bird*, for freck's sake. Who cared about a bird?

But it was what she wanted, and in the end he could never say no to her. He heard Moa coaxing Vago to follow them. Sometimes he wished he hadn't ever gotten mixed up with this girl. But he never wished it for long.

1.11

"There he is," said Rail.

Moa scanned the city below them. A labyrinth of under- and overpasses coiling around each other, shot through by slender bridges. The streets were blotched with illumination, and darkness lay in between. The moon was hidden by cloud and only the arclights and lanterns held back the night in patches. The pallid gleam of the West Artery could be seen in the distance, peeking between the spikes and towers.

A cool wind plucked at them where they hid, on a stone walkway that ran between two browned chimneys of metal. They were crouched behind the parapet of the walkway, the low wall that ran along the edge to stop people falling off.

"I don't see anyone," she said. It wasn't strictly true. She could see the odd person passing along the lit streets, an occasional cart or a gyik-tyuk rider slipping through the islands of brightness. But not Finch or any of the other thieves who had chased them from their den, who Rail believed were hunting them. Rail had been making cryptic hints about a plan that he had to get rid of the thieves, but first he had to make sure that they were really being followed. To that end, they had doubled back on themselves in the hope of catching a glimpse of their pursuers.

"Down there. In that little square."

Vago hunkered closer, his tendons whirring softly as his fingers closed over the edge of the parapet. They had bought a voluminous hooded cloak for him in a vain attempt to disguise his freakishness. It made him look like something that mothers would terrify their children with. They travelled at night now, and they took deserted ways. As long as nobody came too close, they would not know him for what he was.

"I see them," Vago said. He pointed one long finger.

"Get down!" Rail hissed, and Vago withdrew quickly like a scolded infant. Then, because Vago was cringing again and Moa would snap at him about it afterward, he added more gently, "We don't want them to see us. Okay?"

Vago nodded, his good eye darting uncertainly from Rail to Moa. Moa gave him a reassuring pat on the shoulder with one gloved hand, then looked over the parapet again.

This time she spotted them, far away. They were passing through a tiny plaza that nestled between a thick clot of buildings with slanted metal walls. She could make out little detail in the harsh white glare of the arclights, but she could see enough to recognise the black-clad, cowled shape of Finch, and the five thief-boys who lurked with him. Then Finch moved away, into the shadow at the edge of the plaza, and his companions followed him.

Moa looked at Rail, who was regarding her expectantly. "You were right," she said.

"They've got our trail," Rail murmured. "There are informers everywhere."

Moa slumped against the parapet and wrapped her arms around her knees. Vago hunkered down next to her, his hood shadowing his face.

"So what's the plan?" she asked.

"We're about a mile from Territory West 190. It's also the most direct route to where we're going. I say we take it."

"West 190?" Moa queried. She thought a moment, then

realised where she had heard the name before. "That's one of the districts taken by the Revenants during the last surge."

"Exactly," said Rail. "They'd never follow us through there."

Moa shook her head wearily, her lank black hair swaying with the movement. "It's too dangerous," she said. But her protest was already halfhearted. Rail always determined these kinds of things. He was the one who made the big decisions, he was the one with the answers. She drifted along in his wake, happy to be guided by him. The responsibility of choice was something that she didn't want.

"You said yourself that we can't lead anyone to Kilatas," Rail told her. "And any chance we might have had of giving them the slip ended once you decided to adopt your little friend there. Eventually, they'll catch up with us. We have to take the chance."

Moa seethed inwardly. He had been needling her about Vago ever since the golem had joined them. He had made it quite clear what he thought of having Vago with them. Typical of him — one of the few times she made a decision and stuck to it, he made her feel foolish.

"I don't like it," she said. "It's such a risk."

Rail peered over the parapet again, searching for another glimpse of their pursuers. "Sometimes you have to take a risk, Moa," he threw back at her.

PART TWO:

Revenants

2.1

The crumbling warehouse stood amid the clutter of Territory West 217, a brutal block of mortar and bricks, built ugly. An enormous Functional Age building rose behind it, like a fin of greenish metal in the dim afternoon sun.

How primitive they seemed in comparison to the Faded, thought Lysander Bane as he studied the buildings before him. Like dull apes awed by the magic of gods. How much greater was the glory of those past times, when everything worked as it should, when there was order and discipline. What mockery it seemed that they were left with this random world, where any attempt at bringing peace was rendered impossible by probability storms. For the storms brought the Revenants.

He strode towards the warehouse, across a forecourt scattered with rubble and strewn with the dead. Most of them had fallen without a mark on them. They lay gazing emptily at the cloud-misted sky — men and women and children.

The door to the warehouse was guarded by several Protectorate soldiers. They were shaven bald and clad in ballistic armour, with wraparound glimmer visors over their eyes. Bane was wearing a visor himself. It gave everything a curious, sickly hue. The faces of the soldiers looked strangely unreal through it, like luminous charcoal sketches. But walking around Territory West 217 without a glimmer visor was foolish. Revenants were invisible to human eyes, and without a visor he might never see them sneaking up on him.

The soldiers recognised him by sight, even though none of them knew exactly who he was.

He was a familiar face on the panopticon. Often he was seen standing in the background during the Patrician's speeches. He cut a memorable figure, with his lean, stern face and short-cropped white hair. Always standing to one side of the lectern as their great leader spoke. Always dressed in black jackboots and a long trenchcoat with a high collar buttoned to his chin. He never said a word during the speeches, and nobody ever referred to him. He was simply there.

Legends had sprung up around this mysterious figure. People wondered who he was, why he stood always at the right hand of the Patrician. Some said he was their leader's son. Some that he was the greatest warrior in the Protectorate Army. Some that he was the Patrician's personal assassin. They called him Grimjack, and made up their stories.

Lysander Bane, Chief of the Protectorate Secret Police, let the rumours fly. It was good to have people afraid of him. They had reason to be.

The soldiers saluted him as he neared, snapping their heels together and each raising one clenched fist to his shoulder. Lysander barely gave them a nod in acknowledgement. He looked them over with cold grey eyes.

"What's the situation?"

The soldiers looked uncertainly at one another, trying to determine who should reply. "The district has been cleansed," the bravest of them said. "We have the last of the Revenants cornered in the warehouse. It'll all be over soon."

Bane nodded slowly, letting his steady gaze rest on the soldier long enough to unnerve him. The faint sound of aether cannon discharge came from inside the warehouse. He raised his right arm, where the blunt stub of his own cannon projected from beneath the specially adapted sleeve of his coat.

"Good," he said, and walked past the soldiers without another word. None of them tried to stop him.

The warehouse was gloomy and smelled of mildew and decay. Great drums of nutrient gruel were stacked like walls. Massive aisles of storage crates stretched into the distance, full of all manner of foodstuffs. The gruel had come from the Mereg Food Processing Complex; the rest was from the hydroponics farms in the Agricultural Zone. Mereg was one of dozens of complexes where much of the city's food was produced. The gruel went to the ghettoes. It was mainly to prevent the people there from starving, for starving people were liable to riot, and that meant disorder. To the rest of the citizens went vegetables and meat from livestock herds bred in battery conditions. Much of the diet of the people of Orokos consisted of seafood, but there were measures in place to ensure that only licensed Protectorate fishing vessels caught any, and that the food went to the right people. Everything was taxed, regulated, controlled. That was the way it should be, thought Bane.

But the Revenants . . . well, the Revenants didn't fit into anyone's scheme. They lived by their own bizarre rules, caring nothing for the well-being of the city. They unmade what the Protectorate made; they ruined instead of creating. And Lysander Bane hated them for it.

The Revenants: invisible ghosts of energy that could possess the body of a person, could take them over entirely and live inside their skin. These possessed husks, animated only by the will of the Revenants, were called the Taken. The Revenants were the enemy. And Bane had sworn to stamp them out.

Some would have said it was unwise to even be here, to risk himself in combat against the dreadful spectres. But he believed that the only way to know an enemy was to meet it face-to-face. And besides, he just couldn't resist killing them. Nothing gave him such vicious satisfaction as being personally responsible for eradicating a Revenant.

He followed the sound of aether cannon fire — and the occasional dull *whomp* of a thumper gun — until he found another soldier, who directed him onward.

"They're pinned in the southeast corner," the soldier said. "We're just mopping up the last of them."

Bane stalked through the aisles, staying alert as he neared the firefight. Many of the crates had been broken open, and the Taken had eaten what was within. Stinking slicks of gruel had been left to decay where they spilled. Taken ate like animals, with their hands. Bane kept an eye out in all directions, even looking up to where metal beams hanging with hooks and pulleys crisscrossed the warehouse. The cursed things might drop on a man from above.

A soldier darted into the aisle in front of him, raised his cannon in fright, and then relaxed a little.

"Are there any left, soldier?" Bane asked.

The soldier had clearly recognised him from the panopticon. "We've brought down the last of the holdouts. But we think that there were one or two that slipped through . . ." He hesitated, unsure of how to address the man before him. "Sir," he finished.

"Very well," Bane said. "I'll join your sweep until your commander is satisfied that every last one is gone."

The soldier nodded and headed off again. Bane walked a little way behind him, treading silently through the wide, shadowy aisles, his glimmer visor cutting through the darkness.

It didn't take them long. They turned a corner and there it was, just standing there as if waiting for them.

It was one of the Taken. A boy-child, perhaps ten years old, with long blond hair down to its shoulders and wearing a simple blue smock. Its feet were bare. It gazed innocently at them from a distance of a few dozen feet.

But with the glimmer visors, they could see what was invisible to the naked eye. It burned with an inner fire, and its mouth and eyes and nose and ears glowed furiously. Raw aether seeped from them like smoke.

Bane raised his cannon. "Get out of my city," he told it, and fired.

The Taken dodged the first blast, its expression of fresh-faced youth dissolving into snarling animal hatred as it attacked. It ran at them with teeth bared, fingers held out before it like claws, screeching. The soldier panicked, squeezing off a shot too early. The Taken leaped over the path of the soldier's bolt and landed on him, hands clamped around his bald head. The soldier dropped without a sound. The mere touch of a Taken meant death.

Bane didn't miss a second time.

He caught the Taken full in the chest as it bunched to spring, and it crumpled. But it wasn't the husk that concerned Bane. The Taken were just the shells that the Revenants possessed. As he watched, the body began to steam aether as if it were a kettle. The vapour uncurled and rose up before him. With his glimmer visor, Bane could see an outline of crackling force, with a long tail and great triangular wings like those of a manta ray. Between those wings was the shape of a head and four thick tentacles of light that swirled and writhed slowly. This was the true form of a Revenant.

It rushed at him, but Bane was ready. He fired again, hitting it square. The blob of green aether sent it flailing backwards with a dull explosion, trailing sparkling gobbets of light. Bane hit it again, striking it on one of its wings. It spun away, swimming through the air like a fish, attempting to make its escape. But it was wounded and slow, and Bane quite calmly aimed and hit it dead-on as it fled. It erupted in a shower of light and was gone.

Two soldiers, drawn by the commotion, arrived to find Bane standing over the child, his head hung. The boy was dead, his eyes open but unseeing.

"What a waste," Bane murmured. "What a waste."

The soldiers watched him as he shook his head, turned his back, and walked away.

There was a man waiting for him outside the factory when he emerged. He was small, dressed in a similar manner to Bane, and his face was narrow and hard.

"The Secret Police have news for you, Chief," he said. "There were reports of a disturbance on the Elbow Road in Territory West 174. Soldiers intervened, but the perpetrator escaped." He looked up into his superior's eyes. "It was the golem. The golem is still alive."

Bane digested this news without expression, staring out over the industrial muddle that surrounded him. After some time, he spoke.

"Find him," he said.

2.2

The streets around the gate to Territory West 190 were deserted, and the buildings stood empty. The Protectorate had evacuated all the dwellings along the wall. Not that anybody would have stayed anyway.

The great city of Orokos was divided into hundreds of uneven sections called districts or Territories, and virtually every one was surrounded by a wall. The walls had been built by the Protectorate long ago. The energy ghosts could appear anywhere, and where they appeared they possessed the bodies of men and women, creating armies of the Taken. So it was necessary to devise a method to stop them from infiltrating all of Orokos. If one section of the city was breached by the enemy, it could be sealed to prevent the Taken from flooding out.

The energy ghosts were a different matter. How could the Protectorate contain beings that could fly through solid stone? Guards with aether cannons stood on the walls, but they were really only there to make the citizens feel better. There was little they could do against those Revenants that had no bodies, for the energy ghosts could pass under or over the walls as they liked.

However, for reasons the Protectorate didn't understand, the ghosts were not usually interested in crossing the walls. Though the Revenant ghosts could spread out through all of Orokos if they wanted, they never did. They tended to stay in tight groups, sticking with their Taken hosts, overwhelming one district at a time. There was purpose in their movements — though what purpose, nobody really knew.

Usually, gates were left open and unguarded, but in some cases — such as the ghettoes, or in districts where Revenants were rife — both gates and wall were patrolled by Protectorate soldiers.

So it was with the gate to Territory West 190. It was a great mass of grey iron, two sliding halves interlocked in the middle like clenched teeth. On one side, blistering out of the wall, was a squat rectangular guardhouse. Standing before the gate were eight Protectorate soldiers, their glimmer visors glowing pale green in the night. Arclights along the top of the wall cast a dream-like, hazy illumination, haloed in the soft sea mist that had gathered out of nowhere. The mist had brought with it a chill and the salt tang of the ocean far below. Eerily silent streets surrounded the gate, crowded with rickety buildings of wood and stone and metal and clay.

Rail, Moa, and Vago had scouted the wall for half a mile either way, and found it impenetrable. It was walked by guards and topped with plasma wire that could cut through flesh and bone like it was butter. Eventually they had returned to the gate, and they observed it for a time from the safety of a thickly shadowed street.

"Alright," Rail said, satisfied. "Nobody is getting through here. Nobody except us, anyway."

Moa touched the artifact that was stowed in the inner pocket of her pants, reassuring herself that it was still there. Would it even work a second time? Had the miraculous escape from their den been an accident? Maybe she had done something that had activated it without knowing, and she would not be able to do it again. Fade-Science was a mystery.

"We'll need glimmer visors," she said.

96

"I know," said Rail. "And an aether cannon. We're not going into a Revenant district without a bit of protection."

"I do not need a visor," Vago volunteered.

Moa raised an eyebrow at the golem. "You sure?"

"I can see Revenants without a visor."

"Somebody made you with glimmer technology built in? Why?"

Vago didn't have an answer for her. Though he hadn't had the opportunity to test it yet, he simply *knew*. His mechanical eye — the black, reflective orb — was capable of seeing the energy ghosts that were invisible to others. Just like it could calculate trajectories, target threats with astonishing accuracy, and resolve images so sharply that he could count the legs on a spider two districts away.

Rail shook his head; they didn't have time to puzzle it over now. Finch and the others wouldn't be far behind.

"This is the plan," he told them. "That guardhouse is where they'll keep spare equipment. We go through the wall using Moa's trinket, and we sneak along till we reach the spot where the guardhouse is on the other side. Then we come back, through the wall and into the guardhouse from behind. Nobody will be looking for us. There's only one way into that place that I can see, and that's the door at the front. They'll never expect us to come in from the back — that's ten feet of solid metal."

Moa could hear the excitement in his voice. He was already thinking of the kind of moves they could pull off with the artifact at their command, how they could walk through any barrier like phantoms. They could become the most legendary thieves in the city.

"You take it," she said suddenly. They had drawn back around the corner now, farther into the darkness and out of view of the guards at the gate. Her eyes glittered as she spoke. "You can use it."

She meant the artifact, and Rail knew it. Vago had no idea what was going on, but he didn't feel inclined to question. If they thought they could walk through walls, then that was fine with him.

"I'm not touching that thing!" Rail said with a little laugh. He was still afraid of the colours it made. "Besides, we agreed. You look after it, I'll look after you."

Moa didn't want to be the one to let him down, but she wasn't at all sure that the artifact would work again. She lay back against the wall and sighed. "Is this really a good idea, Rail? Do you think we can make it across a district full of Revenants?" The fact that she was questioning him at all showed how worried she was.

"I've got it covered," he said. "There's a secret way, by the canal. It's not too far in. It's a tunnel that leads beneath the district and out the north side, just near where you told me Kilatas lies. Assuming the route to Kilatas is still the same after all this time."

Moa gave up. He had it all figured out.

"After you," she said.

2.3 Between the mist and the broken arclight a little way from the gate, it was easy to sneak close to the great metal wall surrounding Territory West 190. The guards who patrolled along the top had their attention on the Revenant side, and paid little mind to the uninfected district at their backs, with its deserted buildings that hunkered in close. The two thieves and their strange companion slipped into the patch of shadow left by the broken arclight, and none of the guards saw a thing.

The surface of the wall was freezing and dewed with water from the air. They pressed themselves against it. The guards trod along the walkway many feet above, their footsteps sounding over the gentle hum of the plasma wire. They expected no trouble. The wall was so high that those patrolling overhead would need to lean over to see where the intruders hid in the shadows.

Moa slipped the artifact from her pants and held it in her hand. Vago peered at it with mild curiosity. They waited until the guards had passed, and then Moa slipped it on, so that the rings rested at the base of her fingers and the amber disc lay against her palm. Strangely, it fit her perfectly now, whereas before it had been too tight. She hesitated. Had her fingers gotten thinner? No, that was impossible. Then had the rings expanded?

There was an instant when nothing happened, and she felt her heart sink. Then the colours came, drifting out of the disc and wrapping around her hand and forearm, a glove of soft light.

Vago watched, fascinated now, the purple and blue and green reflecting in the black orb of his mechanical eye.

She gave Rail a look as if to say: *here goes.* Then she put her hand to the wall.

The colours spread eagerly from her hand into the metal, and in moments there was a tunnel there, blurred at the edges and fuzzed with veils of gentle vapour. On the far side they could just see the empty buildings of the Revenant district.

Though the colours that swirled in the gap made him uneasy, Rail knew he couldn't back out now. He had to let Moa believe that he was fearless. So he went in, and through, and it was as simple as that. Vago came next, creeping warily with his wings folded close under his cloak. At any moment he expected the gap to disappear and leave him trapped in an iron tomb like a fly in amber. Moa went last, holding her left hand in the air like a talisman.

She stepped out of the gap, and the colours sucked back into the artifact. She slid it off her hand and the light died away. The wall had closed behind them, and left them on the other side.

"I frecking love that thing," Rail murmured. She could hear the grin in his voice and couldn't help grinning, too.

They made their way along the inside of the wall, towards the gate. There were no guards on this side, but they were still forced to be silent out of fear of those that patrolled steadily above them. Now that they were on the Revenant side, the dark streets and empty buildings took on a new menace. The place could be swarming with ghosts, and neither Rail nor Moa would see them until they were snatched up and their bodies possessed. Rail felt his skin crawl at the thought. He glanced at Vago, and hoped the golem had been telling the truth when he said that he could see the invisible Revenants.

But he only planned to be defenceless for a few minutes, and

Revenants knew better than to come near the walls where they would be shot at.

After a few dozen yards, they halted. Rail estimated that the guardhouse lay on the other side of the wall now. They waited until the soldiers above were heading away from them. Rail could feel the tension beginning to mount in the muscles of his shoulders. Any moment he expected to hear the alarm being raised, to hear the shouts of the soldiers. But their gaze was turned outwards, towards the nearby buildings, and they didn't lean over and look down.

He gave Moa the all-clear, and she put on the artifact and used it again. For a third time it worked perfectly, opening a door through the barrier. Rail's guess had been good. On the other side was a gloomy room, with benches and a small stove and a fire burning in the grate. The guardhouse.

"Stay here," Rail murmured. "Keep this tunnel open. I'll need a way out."

And with that he was gone, leaving Moa to wonder in terror if she even *could* keep the tunnel open. What if the artifact ran out of power? What if it could only make doors for a certain amount of time? What did they really know about it?

Rail hadn't considered any of that. It was a way into the guardhouse, and that was all he cared about.

The room that he entered was evidently where the soldiers came to rest and smoke and eat, but there was no one there now. It was stiflingly warm after the chill of the night, despite the cool air that drifted through a small slitted window. Rail felt a thrill at the realisation that he was back on the other side of the wall. Such an impenetrable barrier, and he had passed through it twice like it was nothing. Plans were forming in his mind. He was thinking of the kinds of places that the Fade-Science artifact could get them access to, the kinds of rewards they would hold.

Later, he thought. *Keep your mind on the job.*

The guardhouse was small, and all the guards were outside. A single doorway led to a tiny box room which served as a junction. He picked another door and opened it, finding a similarly tiny room beyond. Here, mounted on the walls, were gun racks and small equipment lockers. He raided them with expert swiftness, finding two glimmer visors and an aether cannon amid assorted worthless knick-knacks and uniforms. The visors and the cannon he took, and headed back to Moa. He was tempted to stay and steal what he could, but he knew that they were treading a fine line and that their luck would not hold forever.

He hurried back into the room with the stove, and had just appeared at the other end of the tunnel Moa was holding open when he heard a shout from above, and the sound of an aether cannon firing. Moa looked up, her face a picture of horror. Vago scooped her up and pulled her out of the way a moment before a bolt of aether sizzled through the air.

Moa was no longer touching the wall. She wasn't holding the tunnel open anymore. The coloured vapours that swirled in the gap flooded away, returning to the device in Moa's hand. When they were gone, the wall would be solid metal once again.

Rail had only an instant to act, and instinct decided it for him. He ran into the tunnel and dived through the gap. There was a moment of utter and total fear as it seemed as if the air was thickening around him, crushing him. But then he was through, and he hit the ground in a heap, his loot cradled in his arms. The concrete of the street jolted painfully against the power pack between his shoulder blades. Behind him, the tunnel had closed.

He dreaded to think what would have happened if he had been a fraction slower.

Someone overhead was shouting for them to stop, but they weren't that stupid. If they were caught now, they would be taken away like Moa's mother, like all the ghetto-folk who were caught. It would be quicker to just let the soldiers shoot them.

Moa was calling his name. She was halfway across the street towards the buildings on the other side, where the golem had dragged her. She had stopped and was reaching back for him. He scrambled to his feet, gathering up the visors and the weapon, and ran. An aether cannon screeched. Rail felt the air singe as it flew wide of him. Then another soldier fired, this time at Vago. He dodged, tripped on the hem of his cloak, and went down in a thrashing heap.

"Go!" Rail shouted at Moa, his respirator blunting the desperate edge of his voice. Hesitation showed on her face for a moment, and then she fled towards the buildings. Rail ran past Vago, who was struggling with his cloak. He was far more concerned with his own welfare than the golem's.

Another cannon fired and missed, but now Vago stood up and tore his cloak away, his wings outspread. There was a curse of disbelief from one of the soldiers, and the sheer sight of him made them hold their fire. That time was enough for Rail and Moa to disappear into the alleyways between the buildings.

Vago bared his fangs at the soldiers, snarling like an animal, and then ran on all fours after Rail and Moa, into the Revenant district.

2.4

It was several hours later when they came across the first of the Taken.

It had begun to rain by then, a freezing downpour that had gathered in off the sea to wash the city clean. The streets ticked and hissed and spattered, heavy with echoes of emptiness. Moa's nerves had been steadily shredded as she jumped at imagined footsteps and half-seen movements that turned out to be tricks of the weather.

Rail had wanted to take shelter until the sky cleared, for Moa's sake. Her constitution was frail and being out in the rain would likely make her ill. But she would not hear of it. They had to travel under cover of night to have any hope of getting through the district, and the rain would help remove their trail. It couldn't have come at a better time, and they would be fools not to take advantage.

So they had crept along the deserted thoroughfares, slinking from shadow to shadow, only the pale lines of their glimmer visors showing in the darkness. Vago scouted ahead as they went. He found he was surprisingly good at it. He instinctively picked spots where he could spy out their route without being seen himself. He moved without sound and used cover like an expert.

"Look at him. He looks like he's at home here," Moa commented at one point.

Rail scowled. "That's what I'm worried about."

It was Vago who warned them before they walked into a plaza full of Taken, and Vago who led them to a place where they could observe the enemy. They took some stairs to a roofed stone walkway, high up on one side of the square. There they hid, and looked down on what was below.

The Taken were at work in the rain. Moa and Rail watched, fascinated and afraid, as the quiet figures moved unhurriedly to and fro across the plaza. Had Moa and Rail not been wearing visors, they would have seen only men and women and children, completely unremarkable except for their almost supernatural calm. They went about their business without ever saying a word, their eyes glazed. Like sleepwalkers.

But with the visors on, it was possible to see them for what they really were. They seethed aether. Greenish-yellow energy, fine as vapour, wisped from their bodies or trailed behind them as they moved. Their eyes and mouths and nostrils were like tiny torches, blazing with blinding energy. It was as if their bodies were merely shells to contain the spectral glow. When they moved their heads, fizzing particles of aether detached from them and floated away, slowly fading into nothingness.

They were dismantling a building. Though they used no tools but their hands, the structure came apart easily, as if it were made of bread and not bricks and metal. Slowly, and with little apparent effort, they were pulling it down bit by bit.

On the far side of the square was an empty pedestal where a statue had once stood. There was enough left to identify what it had once been. Like all other statues in Orokos, it was a likeness of the Patrician, who ruled the city from the top of the Null Spire. Everyone was familiar with his image. He was broadshouldered and tall, dressed in a long uniform coat that buttoned from neck to ankle. Rail had always thought it looked uncomfortably like a surgeon's smock.

But most unsettling was the face, or rather the lack of it. For the Patrician had no face at all, only a black oval of emptiness. His skull was clad in a tight-fitting black headpiece, like that of a wetsuit, and his face showed only an abyss. It was made of some material that threw back no reflection. Instead, it seemed to swallow the light. It was a face to inspire fear and awe, for the Patrician was as cold and merciless as the void. He would stop at nothing to bring order to the chaos of their world.

Moa had grown up with stories of the past, when there had been a thing called the Democracy, where leaders were elected and laws passed by a council of many. Her parents loved those kinds of stories, and Kittiwake had talked of them endlessly. But they told of a time long before she had been born and they seemed like myths.

Then the Protectorate had arisen. It was one of the many political parties that had existed back then. Its message was simple: The Democracy wasn't strong enough to contain the Revenants. A firm hand was needed to bring safety to the people of Orokos and destroy the ghosts once and for all.

The people were tired of being afraid, tired of the constant war against the Revenants that had been raging ever since anyone could remember, ever since the Fade and maybe long before. And so the Protectorate had taken power. They built walls, many walls to separate the districts and keep the Revenants contained. Everyone felt safer. They put soldiers on the streets, and the panopticon showed everyone how brave they were in cleaning out infested districts and reclaiming areas of the city long abandoned. The citizens cheered.

Then one day the Patrician outlawed all other parties, because they were becoming obstructions to him. They were always complaining about rights and liberties, debating when they should have been *doing* something. By the time the Patrician declared himself sole ruler of Orokos, his support was overwhelming. It didn't matter that they made no real headway at all, that the more soldiers they sent against the Revenants, the more Revenants appeared to fight them. What was important was that the people of the city felt stronger, they felt safer, they felt like they didn't need to hide in fear anymore. And so the reign of the Patrician became absolute, and there was nobody left to challenge him.

"Well, the Taken got one thing right," Rail murmured. "They tore down that dog-son frecker."

Moa made a soft noise of agreement. Like Rail, she hated the Patrician. After all, those walls that separated the districts did more than protect against Revenants; they protected the Protectorate, too. Behind those walls they had set up ghettoes. They herded the poor and the sick and the rabble-rousers and the criminals all in there together. That way, there was more space to grow food for everyone else on Orokos, more space for training grounds for soldiers. Everyone was happier, everyone praised the Patrician for making their lives better. Everyone but the people who had paid for it: the people in the ghettoes; but nobody really cared about them.

"Look," Moa said quietly, watching the Taken below. "The rumours are true."

"It's a Protectorate building," Rail said. "They haven't touched anything else."

Vago made a puzzled noise. Moa elaborated for him.

"We've heard things about the Revenants. Everyone's heard them, but nobody's certain," she said. "They take over a district and they . . . erase things. Protectorate things. They take apart

107

everything that the Protectorate built. They leave everything else alone. Like they've got some grudge against the Protectorate or something."

Rail joined in now. "Where I came from, they used to say the reason Revenants possess the bodies of people is because Revenants can't touch anything. But the Taken can. They can tear down what the Protectorate makes."

"I heard it was because Revenants don't last very long as ghosts, and they need a human body to live in," Moa said, remembering a conversation from long ago. It was just one of several dozen theories about the Revenants, and she hadn't given it much credit back then.

"Yeah, I heard that, too." Rail turned back to Vago. "Anyway, when they've stripped a district of every trace of the Protectorate, they attack a neighbouring district. All at once. They pick one and overwhelm it. That's how they work. They clean one place, and then move on to another. That's why they don't just spread everywhere. They're doing the city piece by piece."

"I never knew that bit," said Moa, her gaze roaming over the rain-lashed plaza below, the silent figures at their industry. "You'd think we'd . . . you'd think more people would know about all this."

"They keep it quiet," Rail said.

"The Protectorate?"

"Of course the Protectorate. Would *you* want everyone to know? People used to say that the Protectorate *causes* the Revenants somehow. That the only reason they appear is to get rid of the Protectorate."

"That's stupid," Moa said. "Revenants were around before the Protectorate was."

Rail shrugged. "That's what they say."

For a time, there was silence between them, and only the loud and constant splatter and trickle of the downpour intruded on their thoughts.

"We should go," Moa said eventually, hugging herself against the cold.

Rail was about to agree when there was a sound in the distance that froze them all. It was a soft, eerie cry, like whalesong, that echoed across the cloudy night.

"Tell me I didn't hear that," Rail said, when it had fallen into silence. But nobody had a chance to reply before the noise sounded again, cutting through the breathy hiss of the rain. The Taken in the plaza ignored it. Rail was thinking as fast as he could, but nothing was coming to him. Nothing except the primal and useless desire to find shelter as fast as he could.

"Let's move," he muttered, and they were off, racing along the stone walkway to the far side of the plaza. Another cry chased across the rooftops. His heart was thumping from fear. As if it wasn't enough that they had Revenants to deal with and pursuers on their trail, *this* had to happen. If he had believed in any gods, he would have cursed them now.

Though he couldn't see it, he pictured the scene in his mind's eye. In the very centre of Orokos stood the Fulcrum, the vast impenetrable fortress of the Functional Age. Next to it, much smaller, was the Null Spire, seat of the Protectorate's power, a thin black spike in the night. Strange colours were flickering in the sky above the Fulcrum, and the Null Spire was bleating an alarm to the people of Orokos, because everybody knew what it meant when the Fulcrum woke up.

A probability storm was coming.

2.5

Some distance south of where Rail and Moa listened to the siren of the Null Spire, Finch had switched from hunter to hunted, and he wasn't happy about it.

He crouched in the rafters of a recently evacuated attic, a place of bare boards with a few pieces of rickety furniture lying about. The rain pattered on the roof, inches above his head. He held in one hand a long, serrated knife. His eyes were fixed on the hatch in the floor nearby, beyond which he could hear the sounds of movement. He was cornered, deserted by the other thieves who had run in different directions. Maybe they had been caught, maybe they had escaped. It didn't matter to him. All that mattered was that he get out of here. But his pursuers had corralled him expertly, driving him up and up until he had nowhere else to go.

He ran his tongue lightly over the tips of his sharp brown teeth. This would never have happened if it had been simple soldiers that they were dealing with. What were the Secret Police doing here?

He had thought it an easy game to catch Rail and Moa. Dragging that third person with them, a being of freakish size, they left a trail an amateur could follow. Whenever he was uncertain as to which direction they had gone, people remembered the stranger and set him on the right track again.

It should have been simple enough to find them. But now this. In following them to the gates of a Revenant district, he had somehow stumbled into a nest of Secret Police. One of his clumsier cronies had been spotted, and the men had given chase. But these were not fools that could be evaded with a few quick turns down the alleyways. The Secret Police were well-trained and dangerous, and, try as he might, he couldn't seem to shake them.

So here he was. Trapped. He knew they would search the attic, but at the moment they were not sure where he was. He guessed that there were only two of them down there. Two he might be able to handle, if he could take them on one at a time.

He listened. Clad in all black and with his straggly, thin blond hair hidden beneath a cowl, he was all but invisible in the shadows of the rafters. The men below didn't speak, but his ears were sharp and he could hear their careful tread as they walked from room to room.

His pulse was barely up. He knew that being caught meant the end for him. Simply running from the Secret Police was enough to get him executed. The Protectorate didn't look kindly on those who chose not to cooperate with them. But even when the stakes were this high, it didn't excite him much. Fear wasn't something that he was particularly familiar with. He simply didn't care enough to be afraid, even when his own life was at stake. He had never been scared of dying.

He waited for the hatch to open, and as he waited he thought of Rail and Moa. With a wry twist of his lips he realised that he had underestimated them. Twice now they had got away from him. After their frankly impossible escape from their den, Finch had to ask himself: Were they much better than he had given them credit for? Or was there more to the artifact they carried?

Anya-Jacana had confided in him about the artifact she had sent Rail and Moa to steal. He had always been her favourite, her pet killer, even if he wasn't as loyal to her as he pretended. He stayed at her side because it was a good deal, but he had none of the fondness for her that she had for him. Perhaps she sensed that. Perhaps that was why she sent Rail and Moa instead of him, her right-hand boy. The Fade-Science artifact represented a fabulous amount of money, and maybe she had thought that letting Finch get his hands on it was a little too dangerous.

But in the end, it was Rail and Moa who had cheated her. He was forced to respect them for that. She had hoped they would not recognise its true value, because the Thieves' Code demanded she would have to give them a cut. Even Anya-Jacana had rules to obey. But she had underestimated them as well.

The thief-mistress hadn't thought what the artifact might actually *do,* only what she could sell it for. As far as she knew, it was just an extremely valuable trinket. But Finch had got to wondering now.

He heard the footsteps halt at the bottom of the hatch. Then the soft creaking of someone ascending the stairs. He flexed his fingers around the grip of his knife.

Only two of them. He could do this.

Lysander Bane stood in the rain, lit on one side by the white arclights shining from the top of the wall, and looked into the darkness. Around him, his men were questioning the soldiers on duty. The soldiers shuffled nervously and answered as best they could. They were meek and cowed. They knew about the Secret Police — or at least, they knew what Bane *allowed* them to know. The siren of the Null Spire was disconcerting them further, and their gazes flicked to the sky in expectation of the coming storm.

The report had come through a short while ago, and Bane had decided to attend to it personally. The soldiers had been forced to tell their superiors how three figures had somehow got into a heavily guarded district and made off with valuable Protectorate equipment, and the report had reached Bane's ears through his spies. He wasn't interested in punishing the soldiers. All he cared about was the description of the winged flesh-and-metal thing that they gave. The golem had been sighted again.

Now that he had talked to the soldiers, he had to admit he was puzzled. First, why were the golem and his companions even going into a Revenant district at all? Second, how did they manage to get over or under the wall? And third, how did they manage to steal from the guardhouse when the only way in was watched over by eight soldiers?

There was more to this than he knew. The golem had fallen in with some very interesting company, it seemed.

But perhaps this one has the answer, he thought as he saw a prisoner being led towards him at gunpoint.

The boy they brought to him was a vile-looking thing. His eyes were sunken and dark. His cowl had been pulled back and revealed a head of blond hair so thin and patchy that he looked like he was suffering from a terminal illness. What little of it hadn't fallen out was plastered to his pale skull by the rain. And his teeth! Rotted fangs. A ghetto boy.

Bane regarded Finch without the slightest hint of emotion. There were still fresh bloodstains on his clothes that the downpour hadn't washed away.

"Gelver's dead, Chief," muttered the man with his gun on the prisoner.

"Your handiwork?" Bane asked the boy.

Finch grinned horribly.

"I'm impressed," Bane said. "You realise, though, that we will have to execute you now?"

"You want me to beg?" Finch said sarcastically.

Now Bane really was impressed. He was extremely good at reading people's reactions, to know when they were lying, or secretly afraid. He had a nose for guilt. It had made him such a success in the Secret Police that he eventually ended up leading them. But this boy was absolutely unconcerned. He had the flat eyes of a killer without a conscience.

Suddenly Bane found himself thinking of a better use for Finch.

"No," he said. "I want to make you a deal."

2.6

The probability storm sank drowsily onto Territory West 190 and upon the three fleeing figures that ran through the empty streets.

Probability storms bore little relation to natural storms. They were not loud and furious, but soft and gentle and insidiously deadly. The alarm of the Null Spire was joined by other cries as the storm gathered. Strange coos and distant wails echoed through the cloud-wracked night. They sounded like the voices of alien things, or ghosts of the dead. Some said they were the calls of the Storm Thief's minions, combing the city in search of targets for their master. Protectorate scientists had another theory — something to do with friction and particles, with atmosphere and pressure. Most people didn't understand it, but they trusted the Protectorate. It was better than believing that the cries were souls taken by the Revenants, or that beings from foreign dimensions were peering hungrily into Orokos through the windows of possibility that the storms provided.

The rain still fell, but the undersides of the cloud were streaked with colours now. The black sky raced with gentle blues and purples, a hint of yellow, a phantom green. Channels of light swayed and switched fitfully, changing direction like a shoal of fish or a flock of birds. It was an aurora borealis that covered the great island city. Where the isolated mountains of Orokos rose, their spired tips almost scraped the underbelly of the storm; where Rail and Moa and Vago hurried through Revenant-infested alleyways, the brick and metal of the district was painted in bruise shades. Even beneath their feet, where tunnels and sewers ran, where whole communities lived without sight of the sky, the storm could be felt. For there was no protection against its influence, no place to hide that was safer than any other. If the storm chose to change you, you were changed.

After a time, the colours began to slip from the clouds, peeling away and drifting down in veils, draping themselves across the city like the tentacles of a poisonous jellyfish. They passed over the streets, sometimes sweeping delicately through the tips of the highest towers, sometimes licking deep into the stony heart of the city, far into the earth. They passed through stone and metal and flesh with equal ease. And whatever they touched might be altered, or might remain as it was. In the heart of the storm, creatures like the Mozgas were born, lives were lost and saved, grief and joy mixed and mingled. The veils fell silently onto entire districts, dragged in tatters across the streets, or hung like underwater fingers of seaweed, waving with some ghostly motion. And as the spectral cries echoed across the rainy night, the Storm Thief went about his work.

Rail was trembling, and not from the chill of his soaked clothes or fear of the Revenants. He and Moa were pressed against a wall as Vago peered around the corner. Beyond was a street where shopfronts stood hollowed out and abandoned, their signs swaying and creaking, battered by the downpour. Moa had noticed that Rail was shaking — of course she had noticed, she knew him to the bone — but she pretended that she hadn't. He didn't want comfort from her; it would make him feel weak. He was supposed to be the one that protected her. He was ashamed to be afraid of the storm.

But all Rail could think about was that terrifying time when he hadn't been able to draw breath, when he lay on the verge of dying because his lungs would not work the way they should. A storm had done that to him. And no matter how Moa tried to persuade him that probability storms brought good things as well as bad, he could never forget what had happened. He could never forget what had made him the way he was: the mask on his face, the power pack embedded between his shoulder blades. He had been a good-looking boy, and the storm had turned him ugly, obscured his features with the black metal muzzle of a respirator. He hated the storms, and he hated being at their mercy. He believed he could change anything he wanted with enough will and effort, but he still couldn't resist the touch of the Storm Thief.

"It's safe," Vago murmured, and they ran. Around the corner, skirting close to the shopfronts, trying to stay in the shadows cast by the glow from the sky. The night was alive with noises of movement. There were Taken nearby; perhaps in the next street, perhaps waiting in the darkness of the empty shops. Rail and Moa were constantly looking about, wary of attack. Rail had the aether cannon affixed to his forearm, taking strength from the weapon. Their glimmer visors shone faintly in the night.

They came to the end of the street and the district fell away before them, opening out. At their feet was a wide set of metal steps that led down into a large square, set lower than they were. The square was surrounded by terraces with tall, shuttered windows and coiled-iron balconies. In the centre was a many-layered fountain, where water flooded over sculpted fish and whales and monstrous, half-mythical creatures of the sea. Ahead of them, they could see great ribbons of colour descending from the livid sky and touching the city, swaying slowly as they tracked across the distant buildings.

Conscious of being exposed, Vago darted into a sunken trench that ran across the front of the nearest building, a kind of ornamental moat. Rail and Moa followed. From their vantage point, they could see across the square. Nothing stirred.

"I think it's clear," Moa murmured as she looked out. Then she felt Rail go rigid next to her, and she followed his eyes upwards.

A thick streamer of gauzy blue slid into view above them, coming from behind, looming over the square. Dragging behind it, gliding through the buildings, was its coloured tail. Moa let out a cry and shut her eyes in terror, for it was too late to get out of the way. The streamer slid from the building behind, a vast swathe of turquoise, and passed through them.

The moment was too fast to really feel it. It was swift as an eyeblink, a dislocation, where everything seemed suddenly *wrong* and they were a fraction out of step with the pulse of the universe. Then, the aftermath: their nerves fizzing, an unpleasantly tinny sensation. They had been scoured through by chaos. The streamer was sweeping away down the steps towards the square.

Moa gasped. She hadn't realised she had been holding her breath. Then she was on Rail, grabbing him to make sure he was still there, searching his face and demanding, "Are you alright? Are you alright?"

But even he couldn't tell. Maybe one of them had just contracted a fatal disease. Maybe a cancer had been born in their stomachs. Maybe they had just gained the power to heal with a kiss. Maybe somebody's kidneys had turned to glass.

He sobbed once and hugged her, biting back the tears of fright. She felt something knot hard in her chest as she clutched him close. The two of them huddled together in the stone trench overlooking the square. One sob was all he gave, but that was enough. He almost never cried. He had been brought up to know that tears did no good. The fact that he was distressed enough to let Moa hold him — Moa, who trusted her whole life to chance and didn't fear the storms as he did — was an indication of how badly shocked and shaken he was.

Moa closed her eyes, felt his heart slow to match hers. She could have stayed like that a long time, if Vago hadn't said:

"Something is happening."

She turned her head to him and caught him gazing intently at her. The golem looked away with a guilty speed, back to the square. She studied him a moment longer. There was something here that she should know, something in the way he reacted. But then she saw what Vago had been referring to, and she forgot everything else.

The streamer that had swept through them had passed on across the square, and was now melting into the buildings on the far side. In its path it had left three patches of brightness, shapes that dazzled without shining, like the afterimage of the sun. It was as if a layer of the world had been scraped away, a worn patch in reality. Within, shapes thickened, becoming more and more defined. Rail pulled himself away from Moa, suddenly embarrassed to look at her. He stared at the shapes as they took form. He knew what they were long before they had fully solidified. He recognised them from pictures, the upside-down triangle of the manta-ray wings, the small head and moth-like body, the slender tentacles.

They were watching Revenants being born.

Moa had barely had time to recover from the touch of the storm. This sight, on top of everything else, was almost too much. She felt tears spring to her eyes behind her visor.

Beautiful, she thought. *Beautiful.*

She had never observed a Revenant in its natural state before, for she had never had a glimmer visor with which to see them. Now that she did, she could understand why the followers of the Ghost Path saw fit to worship them. They were breathtaking. It would be easy to be mesmerised by these beings of sparkling energy as they moved with lazy elegance in the air. She watched as they coiled and looped around one another, flapping their wings, testing themselves like infants. Though they represented a fate worse than death to humans, Moa couldn't help being awed by them.

Even in a city that had been so cruel to her, so dark and cheerless, even here there was beauty to be found. Even their most feared enemies could be wonderful. She glanced at the seabird hanging round Vago's neck, and it awoke all kinds of dreams in her heart. If there was such magic in a hard, cold place like Orokos, what might the world outside hold for her? What if there really was another land out there? A land where everything was different?

Maybe Rail didn't believe, but she did. After all, wasn't Orokos built on possibilities?

Rail hefted the cannon, all trace of his previous weakness forgotten. "I'm thinking we should take another way around."

"Where are we going?" Vago asked.

"North. To the canal. I can find the way from there."

"You're sure?"

"Course I'm sure. Come on."

The three of them slipped away, out of the trench and back the way they had come. Moa followed unquestioningly, Vago with obvious misgivings. He didn't have Moa's blind faith in Rail, but he trusted her. She had been kind to him, defended him against the boy more than once. He didn't like the boy at all. She was a different matter.

Rail was oblivious; he was too busy looking out for signs of movement. He kept one eye on the sweeping veils of the probability storm in case they should threaten him with their dreadful touch again. His skin crawled with shame at the way he had humiliated himself in front of Moa. Even now he wasn't certain that he had escaped unscathed. Perhaps he had been rendered sterile and would not find out for years. The thought of what terrible things might have been done to them lay in his mind like dark threads of poison. He forced himself to think only about the immediate future. About escape.

He was beginning to regret taking them into a Revenant Territory at all. Maybe he had been hasty. Maybe he could have shaken off their pursuers some other way. Too late now. Too frecking late.

But what was worse was this: Now that they were in, he wasn't entirely sure how he was going to get them out. The secret route he knew was hearsay, passed on by another thief a long while ago. He had a good memory for rumour, storing little tidbits of information away until the day when they might be useful. But if the secret route really existed at all — which Rail wasn't certain of — then it might have moved by now.

There was a backup plan, of course. With the artifact Moa carried, they could slip out through the wall again. But the soldiers were on the alert now, and he didn't much rate their chances of making it there unseen. To get to where they were going, they would have to cross the whole district above ground, and that was desperately risky.

He wondered how Moa would feel if she knew how slipshod

his plans were. It was far from the first time he had got them into something with no clear idea of how to get out of it. More than once he had been saved by chance. But the art was to make it all seem intentional, to always appear confident. He valued her trust more than anything, and she needed to believe he knew what he was doing.

And so he led them, never letting the doubt show. Through the rain and the unnatural storm, along narrow passageways, down steep steps.

They had almost made it to the canal when one of the Taken spotted them.

2.7

It was crouching on the lip of a wall on an empty street, where expensive houses stood behind yards and tiny rockeries. Rail saw it far too late. It was a young woman, hair blonde and sodden, glowing aether leaking from its eyes and between its teeth. It was watching the road, surveying its territory, as they came round the corner and froze, discovered.

Its lips peeled back in a slow snarl, and Rail and Moa ran. Vago hesitated a moment, a memory surfacing in his mind —

enemy

— before he sprang away on all fours. The Taken lifted its head up and emitted a shriek that went high above the pitch of human hearing, a cloud of bright vapour pluming from its mouth. Then it dropped from the wall, hit the street with feral ease, and sprinted after them.

Rail and Moa didn't even look back. The fear of the Taken had been drilled into them since birth. The Taken oozed aether, and aether was fatal to humans. One touch from this creature meant death.

They plunged down a narrow alleyway. Open doorways and dark windows blurred past them. The Taken was right behind, bare feet splashing on the wet flagstones. The coo and squall of the probability storm blended with the soft pulse of the Null Spire's alarm, filling the night.

The alley switched suddenly left and Rail took the turning. The rain slashed at him from the narrow slice of sky overhead. He burst out of the alley into another street, this one a sloping, winding road of cobblestones. On either side were rows of dull metal dwellings, faceless and cold.

Two other Taken were here, both men dressed in battered factory workers' overalls. He saw them emerge from a narrow slit of a doorway, alerted by their companion's cry. They spotted Rail immediately and came after him.

Rail didn't break stride, heading down the street with only a swift glance at Moa to check she was still with him. She was sodden and bedraggled, achingly thin. Vago was bringing up the rear, even though Rail suspected he was much faster than either of them. He was putting himself between the Taken and Moa. That suited Rail fine.

Freck, how did I get us into this? he thought desperately.

From where they were on the flank of a hill, he could see a long way across the city. The overlapping veils of the storm were sweeping lazily through the streets of Orokos. At the bottom of the slope the district splintered into dockyards, with tall warehouses and cranes standing grim against the dark. Beyond was the canal, a thin stripe of glittering black.

Too far. They weren't going to make it.

He cursed under his breath. There was no way Moa was going to be able to outrun three Taken. She didn't have the strength for a long sprint. There was only one other thing to do, then. He stopped, swung up the muzzle of the aether cannon that he carried, and fired up the slope.

The cannon bucked against his arm with a metallic shriek as it spewed a glob of sizzling energy through the air. The shot flew wide of its mark by some way. The Taken didn't even pause in their headlong charge downhill. Moa ran past him, her breath rasping in her chest — he could hear that she wouldn't make it much farther — and he fired again, missed again.

The Taken raced towards him, and his blood chilled. He realised with a dreadful certainty that he had made a mistake. He would never stop them in time.

Vago ripped the cannon off his forearm and snapped it onto his own. Rail was too shocked to even resist. He could only stare as the golem swung the weapon up, braced it like an expert, and began to shoot.

His first salvo cut the enemy to pieces. Two shots hit the female Taken in the stomach and chest, and before it had even collapsed Vago had taken down both of the men, one in the leg and one in the shoulder. They tripped over themselves, all strength gone from their muscles, and rolled to a halt, limp.

Rail wasted a few moments on surprise. Through the visor, he could already see the aether seeping from the fallen bodies, re-forming, taking on shape. Ghosts of energy, Revenants in their natural form.

"Go," Vago barked. Rail didn't need a second prompt.

He caught up with Moa easily. She was staggering to a halt, holding her ribs where a stitch was causing her agony. Somewhere nearby, more screams were echoing across the district, so high that he could barely hear them. They made his head ache. The Taken were coming, and they would come in their hundreds. He and Moa were far from safe yet.

He got his arm under Moa and supported her as they half-ran, half-stumbled down the steep road. She was shivering, though whether with cold or fright he couldn't tell. The aether cannon sounded again, and he looked over his shoulder. Vago was walking backwards, stepping delicately on his oddly jointed legs, like a cat standing upright. As he retreated, he fired at the ghosts that rose from the human bodies on the ground. The weapon seemed an entirely natural extension of him. He held it like he had been born with it, moving with military precision.

Look at him, Rail thought suddenly. *This is what he was made for.*

Rail didn't stop to watch Vago shooting down the Revenants. He could already see movement near the top of the slope. Other Taken were appearing. Energy ghosts swam through the air over their rabid human hosts, who were sprinting furiously down the street.

Hopefully they would go for Vago, Rail thought. He dragged Moa to the side of the road, his dreadlocks and respirator dripping. An alleyway beckoned, promising shelter and the hope of concealment. They had almost reached it when a great wave of scarlet lashed down from the sky. He clutched Moa as it swept towards them . . . and then past them, missing them by mere feet. It slipped through the faceless metal houses on the other side of the street, and as Rail watched, several of the houses simply disappeared, fading like a dream upon waking. Their foundations lay open to the rain. Where the Storm Thief had taken them, he would never know.

The sound of Vago's cannon spurred him out of his gawping, and he propelled Moa into the alleyway.

Vago's nearly lipless mouth had peeled back, exposing his metal teeth. It could have been called a grin, if his face had been capable of humour. The targeter in his enhanced eye tracked this way and that, and his muscles moved to match it, aiming and firing with uncanny precision. For the first time since he could remember waking, he felt *right*. The exhilaration of combat, the recoil of the weapon, the sight of his enemies destroyed: It was joy to Vago. They raced at him, crazed with fury. He battered them back with cannon fire, and they dissipated into wisps of energy.

But even through the fierce joy of combat, he knew he couldn't take them all on. Revenants were appearing faster and faster now, from all directions. He had backed up almost to the mouth of the alley where Moa and Rail had disappeared. With a final burst, he turned tail and ran, his wings tucked close to his body. The Revenants followed.

He bounded through the alleys on three of his four limbs; the other one was encumbered by the cannon. These alleys were all rusted iron and grillework, their arclights dead. Power was always cut off to Revenant districts. The glow from the clouds painted the scene in shades of nausea. Vago jumped down a set of steps, took a sharp corner, sprang off the wall, and leaped along another passageway. He had lost sight of Moa and Rail, but he knew which way they were headed. Towards the canal, down the slope where the dockyards were. They couldn't be far ahead, not in the condition Moa was in.

The thought of Moa gave him new speed. The boy didn't have a hope of protecting her if the Revenants caught them. It was *him* that she needed. Her golem.

He could outpace the Taken with ease, but the energy ghosts were a different matter. They swept through walls, cutting corners, diving into and out of solid matter as if it was nothing at all. He darted and pounced through the pouring rain, always half a heartbeat ahead of the glowing things that chased him, their tentacles lashing the air as they dived.

He turned into an alleyway that ended in a balcony. Beyond it there were no more alleys, only a view across the canal to the buildings on the far side. Somehow he had taken a different route from Moa and Rail. Here the slope cut off as sharply as a cliff, and there was no apparent way down.

No way apart from gravity.

Vago raced towards the end of the alleyway, knowing that he couldn't stop with the Revenants behind him. He hoped only that if he jumped, there would be something there for him to jump onto. It was too late to change his mind now. He sailed over the balcony, the ground disappearing beneath him.

He saw his mistake a moment after he had made it. Below, the cliff face fell to an empty road, a fall that even he doubted he would survive. Ahead were a row of warehouses, roofs that he could land on. But his jump hadn't been strong enough. He knew that he was going to fall short, even without the assistance of his mechanical eye plotting his trajectory.

For a few terrible instants he felt the arc of his jump begin to dip . . . and then he spread his wings.

He didn't know how to do anything else with them. He certainly didn't know how to flap them. But he remembered how they had failed him when he had jumped off the bridge into the West Artery, so he held them as stiffly as he could against the pressure of the rushing air. Almost without noticing it, he picked up enough of a lift to glide the last dozen feet to his target.

He hit the flat roof of a warehouse, tucked his wings and rolled, then sprang up aiming in the direction he had come from. The Revenant ghosts were caught out in the open as they boiled out of the alleyway, and he destroyed them with a screeching fan of cannon fire.

The echoes died away, leaving the golem standing on the rooftop, the rain beating at him. The cannon was drained now. He pulled it off his arm and tossed it aside. The wail and sigh of the storm swelled around him as it waved its colourful tendrils of change over Orokos. He looked at the fringe of dark buildings on top of the cliff, at the alleyway he had jumped from. The leap had been far beyond anything a human could have managed. He took a strange pleasure in that.

My wings, he thought, uncurling them distrustfully. He studied them a moment. Had he really flown with them? No, not flown — not like the bird around his neck had flown. But he had glided. Only a little way, but still.

His maker had built him with wings. What did it mean? What did his *life* mean?

He was seized by an overwhelming feeling, a sensation strong as anger or fear. He needed to know who he was. He *needed* to know his place in this world. He had to have the answers. And for that, he had to find his maker. Only his maker could tell him why he had wings. Only his maker could tell him why he had been created at all.

At that moment, he made a decision. As soon as he had a chance, he would search for Tukor Kep. Vago would track him down. And like a father and son, they would be reunited. Perhaps there he would find a place that he belonged.

Somewhere below him, Moa screamed, and he was moving again.

He crawled down the outside of the warehouse wall, scuttling like an insect, his powerful fingers and toes digging into the brick. Halfway to the bottom he launched himself into the air and fell the rest of the way, landing in a crouch. The metal tendons in his legs wheezed as they took the impact. He barely noticed, not even enough to marvel at the wonders of his construction. That scream had focused all his attention on one thing.

He had to get to her. The one person, the only person he could remember who had ever shown him kindness.

He bounded on all fours along the road that ran near the foot of the cliff. Somewhere ahead, he could hear Rail shouting. High-pitched cries were coming from the same direction. Taken. They would be swarming all over the docks now.

He dodged between the warehouses, where there lay a labyrinth of gantries and walkways, of sliding doors and distant cranes. Whether by luck or by instinct, his navigation was good. He skidded to a halt on a thin, rusty bridge of meshed metal. There below him, in an alleyway lined with pipes of black iron, were Rail and Moa.

Rail had the exhausted girl encircled with one arm, dragging her along with him as he ran. Three Taken were sprinting down the alley after him, and with Moa as a deadweight he had no hope of getting away. Rail looked up and spotted Vago crouching on the bridge, but between the glimmer visor and the respirator there was no expression visible on his face.

Vago squatted and reached down to them, his long arm stretched to its limit. "Lift her!" he said.

Rail didn't think twice. He picked up Moa by the hips and boosted her up. Vago caught her and hauled her onto the bridge like she was no heavier than paper.

Rail looked over his shoulder as Vago reached down again.

130

The Taken were shrieking, pelting towards him with renewed fury as they saw their prey escaping. Rail felt his skin prickle with terror. They were too close, too close!

"Jump!" Vago snarled.

Rail jumped as high as he could. It was just high enough. Vago caught him by the wrist and wrenched him upwards as the howling Taken sprang for him, their fingertips missing his feet by a second. Rail was dumped on the bridge next to Moa. His shoulder blazed with pain where it had almost come out of its socket. Below them, the Taken jumped and swiped at the air.

Neither Rail nor Moa said anything. They were shaken and frightened and knew that it wasn't over yet. Rail helped Moa to her feet.

"Give her to me," Vago said to Rail. She could go no farther, and Rail wasn't strong enough to carry her.

But Rail would not do it. "I'll take her," he said, panting behind his respirator.

"We will go quicker," the golem growled in his strained bass. "Give her to me. I'll keep her safe."

He's a killer, said a voice in Rail's head. *You saw how he dealt with those Revenants. He was enjoying it.*

But that wasn't the true reason he hesitated. If he gave her to Vago, he was admitting that the golem could look after her better than he could.

"Let him . . ." Moa gasped. She was shivering, sickly, on the point of collapse. "We have to."

At that, the golem grabbed her from Rail, and he could do little to stop it. Vago picked up the girl in his arms, holding her like a child. Rail felt strangely abandoned and forlorn. He glared at the golem from behind his visor, the rain running down his face and hair. Below them, more Taken had joined the three in the alley, and they were trying to climb on each other's backs.

"Let's get to the canal," he snapped.

There was a metal door at the end of the bridge, leading into a building. It was the only way left to go. They took it.

2.8

It was some kind of factory, cool and dark. It was also full of people. The screaming had begun soon after the lights went out, when the first of the Taken poured in through the doors and the workers realised what had happened to them.

The factories in Orokos never slept. There was never enough production capacity to satisfy the great metropolis, so shifts worked constantly to meet the demand. These people had been in the middle of a shift when the lights died. None of them knew at the time that it was a result of their building being suddenly moved to a district where there was no power. They thought it a malfunction. By the time they understood, it was too late. The Taken were in, through the windows or through the main gates, which had been open.

Rail, Moa, and Vago came out of the dingy service corridors and onto a gantry that ran above the factory floor. The scene beneath them was bedlam. Between the huge machines, all pistons and presses and levers, the Taken chased down their prey. The screams from below were deafening as hundreds of panicked men and women fled towards exits that were swarming with Taken. They trampled the living and the dead underfoot as they ran. The Taken were clambering over the machines to drop down on the workers. At their touch their victims simply sighed and sank to the ground, extinguished.

Those Revenants that didn't yet have bodies swooped and glided over the bloodless carnage. They would dive at one corpse or another, pick it up with their tentacles, and stand it upright. Then they would melt into it, pulling themselves inside the dead body and awakening it again. A fire of aether ignited in their breasts that burned and glowed through their eyes and mouths. The newly born Taken would then race away, seeking out living beings to kill.

Rail felt his knees go weak at the sight. The gantry they stood on was crisscrossed with other gantries, and on this network of walkways there were still some people alive. They were the guards and overseers who used the walkways to get a bird's-eye view of the workers below. They had been trapped up here when the Revenants had invaded. Now the energy ghosts soared up and around the roof of the factory, plunging down to take new victims now and again. They skimmed along the gantries to grab the hapless guards, who fired at them ineffectually with thumper guns. Those that they had already snatched and turned into Taken now prowled along the walkways, hunting.

On the far side of the workspace was a row of open windows. Going down to ground level would be suicide, but the windows promised a way out, and Rail guessed that they faced out onto the docks. With Vago they might just make it down. He glanced at the golem, whose eye was asking him the question. And though he was so afraid that his insides had turned to water, there were no choices left to him. The enemy was behind and all around. The only way was forward.

"Do it," Rail murmured.

Vago set off at a sprint, taking great strides along the gantry, his long body hunched over Moa as he carried her. Rail ran full tilt in his wake, as if the golem could somehow shield him. All they had to rely on was luck, to hope that in all the disorder the Revenants would be too busy to notice them. This was Moa's way: to surrender themselves to chance and hope for the best.

Rail hated being put in that position. Chance hadn't been kind to those factory workers below, after all.

But it seemed that luck was with them. They fled across the walkway, and nothing arose to block their way. There were so many other targets for the Revenants. By the time they were halfway, Rail began to believe they might pass unhindered through the chaos.

He saw it only an instant before it struck, just long enough to give a cry of warning. It was an energy ghost. He saw its sparkling form though the slatted metal of the gantry floor, winging up from below them. He braked himself instinctively, but Vago wasn't fast enough. The Revenant flew through the gantry floor, coming up underneath the golem, passing *through* him . . . and suddenly dissipating in a cloud, as if torn to tatters.

But Rail barely even noticed what had happened to the Revenant. He cared about one thing only:

Vago had been holding Moa.

"Moa!" he cried, the sound of her name plaintive and desperate.

Vago turned slowly, dazed. Aether was sparkling along the bladed fins that ran down his spine between his wings. Moa was limp in his arms, unmoving. The dead seabird that hung around Vago's neck lay across her chest.

"No!" Rail howled through his respirator, reaching for her. But at that moment Vago seemed to come back to himself, and he pulled her away from him.

"Run!" he told Rail, and he was off towards the window. Rail followed, not because of the grave danger he was in, but because the golem had taken Moa.

They reached the window, the screams of the factory workers

thinning behind them. They were right by the bank of the canal. There were no Revenants visible, for they were all inside. The probability storm was quieting now, the colours turning muted and fading in the clouds overhead. The rain had become a fine drizzle that misted down from the sky.

As the docks met the water, the warehouses fell back and turned into a ropy clutter of jetties and gangways. There, berthed and silent, were the small boats that plied the canals of Orokos. They rocked under the barrage from the sky, low and long and sombre. One of them had been turned into a diamond by the probability storm and had sunk. Only its prow was visible, where the mooring line kept it anchored to the dock. Still another appeared to have been turned inside out, its engine parts on the outside of its hull, but by some twist of physics it was still afloat.

They had reached the canal, but they were high above the ground, and the wall of the factory was sheer. There was no way down.

Vago shifted Moa's weight to one arm, carrying her as if she were a sack of grain. With the other, he snatched up Rail, and before he could protest or squirm, Vago jumped.

Rail was too surprised to even yell. The rush of the wind, the awful anticipation of impact, the ground rushing up to meet him . . . and then they hit, and he felt a hefty jolt but nothing more. He blinked. Vago had absorbed the force of the landing through his machine-augmented legs.

The golem put him down. Rail reached for Moa immediately, but Vago held him back.

"Boat," he said, and pointed one long finger.

Even through his grief, Rail saw the sense, but he hated the golem for interfering, hated him for being right. Hated him because he was carrying Moa when the Revenant got him. Hated him for being alive when Moa . . . when Moa was . . .

He bit back tears and ran for the jetties. If there was one thing he could do, it was steal. Taking a boat would be child's play to a thief like him.

2.9

The storm passed by, the rain stopped, and darkness claimed Territory West 190 again.

The canal made its steady way towards the edge of Orokos, where the great plateau ended and dropped into the sea. It took with it a narrow boat, a long, thin vessel shaped like a canoe, painted black as the waters it floated on. It was a crude thing compared to some of the cargo haulers that had once plied these lanes, but it was small enough to slip along unnoticed. The Revenants had quieted after their feeding, and the district was deserted once again.

Rail sat next to Moa, holding her hand. It was cold. Vago hunkered at the prow of the boat, scanning their surroundings. He had his back to them both.

The golem was confused. He wasn't practiced enough at the art of emotion to know what he should be feeling now. On the one hand, what had happened to Moa had made him terribly sad. It was like when the bird had died; that was how he recognised it. On the other hand, he felt better than he had felt since he could remember. A Revenant had touched him. He should be dead. And yet instead he felt more alive than ever. His heart was a muddle, and he tried to make sense of it; but everything was too jumbled up inside him now.

Rail had taken his glimmer visor off and stashed it in his satchel. Moa's he had laid aside in the boat. It seemed wrong to view her through that strange lens. He relied on Vago to spot Revenants, but in truth he wasn't sure whether he cared about them now. Moa was dead. He might as well die, too.

Her eyes were open, and she was staring at the sky. It was only when he had taken off her visor that he saw her eyeshadow had changed colour, from black to red, clashing with her dark green lipstick. So the probability storm had changed something when it touched them, after all. He almost laughed at how trivial an alteration it was, but he knew if he laughed he would start to cry, and he would not let himself do that.

"What is it I am looking for?" Vago murmured ahead of him. The sound of the golem's ruined voice ignited fresh anger in Rail, and he held on to that.

"A tower," he snapped. "A tower with three spires, on the north side."

Vago didn't reply, nor did he turn around. He seemed to be furiously ignoring what had happened to Moa, as if by not acknowledging it he could pretend it hadn't happened. Rail wanted to kill him.

If you hadn't taken her from me, she'd still be alive.

How had the golem survived, when Moa hadn't? It wasn't fair. Nothing about this frecking horrible world was fair.

But he knew in his heart that he was blaming Vago because he couldn't cope with the truth. He was the one who had led them into Territory West 190, who had come up with the idea of braving a district full of Revenants. It was his fault.

He closed Moa's eyes with his fingers. Now she looked like she was only sleeping.

"I see the tower," Vago said.

Rail hardly reacted. When he did, it was to say: "Can you see a hatch near the base of the tower? Facing the water?"

"Yes," he said.

So the secret route that had been rumoured among Anya-Jacana's thieves really did exist. He had been right. How hollow that victory seemed now.

Vago went to the back of the boat, stepping over the two of them without so much as a glance. He turned the rudder to bring them up to the hatch. Rail didn't take his eyes from Moa as the tower — a Functional Age creation of smooth ceramic and indestructible glass — loomed up before them. He let the golem take them in.

As Vago was getting out onto a concrete shelf just above the waterline, Rail said, "We're bringing her with us."

"I know," Vago replied.

The hatch was set in the sloping wall of the canal bank. Vago took hold of the wheel at its center and turned it. It resisted, but not enough to thwart him. The hatch came open. Vago hunched down and peered into the darkness within.

"A tunnel," he said, and went inside.

For a time, Rail didn't move, and Vago didn't come back. The golem knew instinctively that he wasn't welcome now.

Rail just looked at her, lying in the boat. He didn't have the words to say, and he didn't believe in pointless eulogies anyway. Instead, he took a breath and slipped his respirator off.

"It shouldn't have been this way," he said. "I was going to make a life for us."

And he bent his head down to hers. A kiss, their first and last. It seemed the only way to end it.

But their lips never touched, for as he neared, he felt something. The tiniest of movements in the air.

Moa was breathing.

He pulled his head back, gasped in surprise, and then flailed as his lungs didn't respond. A momentary panic took him, until he could get the respirator back over his face.

"Vago!" he cried, and the golem was there in an instant. Rail was so delirious that he didn't even think of the danger of shouting in the silence of the night.

He put his fingers to Moa's lips, and felt it again. Shallow, barely there, but she was *breathing*! It was impossible, it *should* have been impossible, but the touch of the Revenant hadn't killed her. Yet.

Rail lifted her up in his arms, as gently as he could, and stepped out of the boat. His eyes were wet.

"She's alive, Vago. She's frecking *alive*."

They hurried into the tunnel together and closed the hatch behind them. In their haste, neither of them noticed that they had left Moa's glimmer visor where it lay in the boat. It would have been worth a tidy sum on the Dark Markets, enough to feed and clothe both Rail and Moa for a while. But though his life had been spent in its pursuit, the thought of money didn't even occur to Rail at that point. He had other priorities now.

PART THREE:

Kilatas

3.1 The next day found the city shining wet and cleansed. The sun was bright and sharp, providing little warmth but offering a harsh white light that cut stern shadows from the towers and minarets of Orokos. The sea, stretching forever on all sides, glittered blindingly. The air was specked with bomber birds, hovering above the waves, plunging in and emerging with bulging beak-sacs full of squirming fish.

The jagbats were out in force today, great dark-winged shapes that glided between the highest points of the city and out over the ocean. They took down the birds when they could, or squabbled with each other in the air, hissing and yowling. Earlier that morning, one of them had snatched a Protectorate soldier from the deck of a Dreadnought that was patrolling near the foot of the cliffs. The Dreadnought had fired upon it with explosive shells, but it had flown out of range, over the sea. Jagbats were not the smartest creatures, but they had learned that the armoured ships couldn't go beyond a certain distance from Orokos. The city would not allow it. It had defenses that prevented anything from leaving.

At the very centre of Orokos stood the Fulcrum, surrounded by a loose ring of solitary mountains that thrust up from among the cramped and mazy streets. And in its shadow was the Null Spire.

The Fulcrum was one of the most shocking pieces of architecture left over from the years before the Fade. It was a feat of engineering and construction almost unequalled in the whole of Orokos. Some argued that the serpentine Coil in the south or the shifting mirrors of the Light Gardens in the flooded east and lost to the Revenants — were just as spectacular. But the Fulcrum inspired its own special awe and dread. Inside it, so rumour held, was the great machine that controlled Orokos, that generated the probability storms and created the Revenants. They called it the Chaos Engine.

The Fulcrum was built like a spiral, its base smaller than its top, a fragmented masterpiece of metal and sparkling glass. It leaned slightly westward, defying physics by staying upright when it should have toppled. Its exterior was comprised of many hundreds of blade-like sections, like those of a pinecone. The sections were tilted to follow the swirl of the architecture, so that the whole impression was like a tornado of glittering leaves. It was a bewildering mass of edges, sealed away from the outside world, the greatest prize of Orokos. For nobody had ever managed to see what was within.

The Null Spire, in contrast, was plain and bleak, a thick needle of darkness pointing towards the sky, dwarfed by the colossal Fulcrum. At its tip dwelt the Patrician, immortal ruler of the Protectorate. And it was here that Lysander Bane, Chief of the Protectorate Secret Police, had come to report.

The chamber was small and dim, empty of ornamentation. Everything here was a perfect black: the walls, the circular ceiling, the marble floor. A single globe glowed above them, casting overlights on the figures beneath. Bane stood before the Patrician, who sat on a raised platform on a throne of twisted brass. The Patrician himself was as shadowy as his surroundings, dressed in a high-collared black trenchcoat. His face was hidden behind his mask of darkness, which reflected nothing of the room around them and showed nothing of the features beneath.

Bane wasn't intimidated. Like himself, the Patrician used fear and uncertainty to inspire cooperation and respect.

The Patrician wasn't immortal. He was many people, many leaders, united in a single guise. There had been a dozen or more who had worn that mask over the years. The people didn't really believe that he lived forever, and yet they could never be quite sure. After all, between the probability storms and Fade-Science, who knew whether a man might *really* live forever? In Orokos, anything was possible. So they entertained the fantasy. They would rather have a leader that was like a rock, ageless and invulnerable, than a succession of different faces.

Bane had spent the last hour recounting the affairs of the Secret Police, explaining victories and failures and projects in progress. The Secret Police were the enforcers of the real business of the Protectorate. The carefully edited news feeds on the panopticon were merely there to keep the populace happy and secure. The soldiers on the streets were more for show than for their effectiveness. Like all governments, the meat of the matter was dealt with behind the scenes, where people didn't have to see it. Though they would never admit it to themselves, the citizens preferred it that way.

He had almost finished, and was preparing his conclusion, when the Patrician posed him a question.

"What of the golem, Lysander Bane?"

His voice echoed eerily, though whether because of the room or his mask Bane couldn't tell.

"The golem eludes us for now," Bane said.

"I see," the Patrician said. "Then perhaps we can make another, then?"

"It would be impossible. There was only one. The golem is the prototype."

"You made no copies?" the Patrician said. "Careless."

His tone somehow implied a threat, which Bane didn't like, but he was prepared for this.

"Copying the technology that made that golem would be the work of years," he replied. "And until we knew the technology worked, there was no point in expending that amount of effort on it. So we built a prototype for a field test."

The Patrician considered this. Bane found himself trying to catch his reflection in his leader's face. He knew it *should* be there, but the mask turned the light somehow so that it was empty.

"The golem is probably unaware of its own nature," Bane continued. "We hadn't had time to condition it properly before it disappeared."

"Yes. An unfortunate incident."

Bane gritted his teeth behind his lips. The Patrician had a way of making it sound like it was *his* fault. He knew as well as Bane that nobody could account for a probability storm. The best-laid plans in all recorded history were peppered with their influence. They could turn a brilliant victory into defeat or allow a bungled scheme to suddenly come good against all odds. It seemed to him that the city took joy in ruining the perfection of order, that the better the strategy the more likely a probability storm would turn up and throw a spanner into the works. He hated them as much as he hated the Revenants.

"I don't believe the golem poses any danger to us," he said eventually. "The worst that could happen is if it is destroyed before we managed to get it back."

148

"And what will you do when you recapture the golem?" queried the Patrician.

"We will finish conditioning and field-test it if we can."

"And then?"

"Eventually, after we are sure that everything works, we will kill it and remove the technology for study. Then we can begin to copy it and make more of them."

"See that you get it back, Bane. The Protectorate does not appreciate failure."

And so he was dismissed.

As he made his way down through the Null Spire, he found himself turning the problem of the golem over in his mind. Had he been right to make a deal with Finch? Well, no matter — it couldn't have done any harm. Sooner or later, a freak like that golem would be seen. He couldn't go anywhere without inspiring panic and disgust. Word would get back to Bane, and the Secret Police would have him.

The creature couldn't hide forever.

3.2 At that very moment, the object of Bane's earlier thoughts was creeping through the streets of Territory West 190, thinking about the golem also. For Finch, though, matters were considerably more personal.

He made his way along the north edge of the canal, staying behind what cover he could, alert for movement from any direction. He was wearing the glimmer visor that Bane had given him, and in the daylight it lent everything a pallid yellow hue. The Revenants appeared to be occupied elsewhere for now, and he was thankful for that. He had survived the chaos of the night without being seen, weathering the probability storm by hiding in the cellar of an empty house. That was no protection from the storm, of course, but it kept him out of the Revenants' way until things had calmed down.

By the time he had emerged, Rail and Moa's trail was stronger than ever. Near dawn, he had found traces of aether cannon fire on one of the streets. Most important, he had found a trail of Taken dead. Other Taken were clearing up the mess, or new ghosts were inhabiting the vacant bodies.

From there he got to the canal, where he lost the trail. He could only assume that they had taken a boat, and downstream seemed the logical place to go. He hadn't heard the rumour of the secret way into Territory West 190. But nevertheless, he was drawing near to it. The tower on the north bank, a finger of ceramic and glass pointing at the sky, was rising before him.

Unconsciously, he rubbed at the metal band that was clamped around his upper arm, just below his shoulder. As if it would come off that easily.

"I wouldn't try to get it removed," Bane had told him. "It's very sensitive. It's liable to explode."

Bane, he thought with a snarl.

Perhaps he should have been thankful that he hadn't been executed when the Secret Police had caught him back at the gate. But then, he wondered if he wouldn't have preferred that. Simple and straightforward. Instead, Bane had made him an offer. One he couldn't really refuse.

"You want to live?" he had said. "Tell me what you were doing here."

Finch had lied. Of course he had lied. He had worked out by now that the Secret Police must have come in response to something, though he couldn't imagine what Rail and Moa had done. Perhaps to investigate how they had gotten past the wall? It didn't matter. He told Bane some story about how he was hired to kill them by a rich and nameless man. He didn't know why the man wanted them dead. He just took the money. Bane swallowed it; it was what he expected to hear. It happened all the time in the ghettoes.

Finch hadn't mentioned the artifact. He'd kept that to himself.

"Go in there after them," Bane had said. "I'm not interested in the ghetto thieves. I'm interested in the one that's travelling with them. A golem of flesh and metal. Find him."

Finch hadn't believed his luck at first. The moment he was out of Bane's sight he would disappear. But he should have known it wouldn't be that simple.

Bane had motioned to a companion, and they had affixed the device that was now clamped around his arm beneath his sleeve. He had no idea what they were really called, but street slang had christened them "Persuaders." They were thin bands of metal, thickening at one point where explosive charges were packed. A favourite device of the Secret Police to ensure cooperation.

"If you don't show up at the Null Spire within twenty days," Bane had said, "that thing will blow your arm off. If you try and double-cross me before that time" — he'd held up a small brass device, shaped like a yo-yo — "I twist this, it'll blow your arm off. If you try to remove the armband —"

"I get it," Finch had said dryly. He was seething. Being executed was one thing, but being forced to serve the Secret Police was something entirely different. "How do I contact you?"

"With this." Bane had handed him a short, thick brass tube with a press-stud on top. "You know Tick-Tap, don't you? Of course you do." He brandished another tube. "We call these vox-coders. I'll keep this one. Just tap out your message with the press-stud, and I will hear it. I can contact you the same way."

Finch had been surprised. Tick-Tap was the language of rhythmic taps that was originally used by prisoners to communicate between cells. He had learned it on his mother's knee. What he found remarkable was that Bane not only knew about it, but knew how to understand it. The Secret Police had more secrets than he had given them credit for.

"Take this as well," Bane had said, holding up a small black card of plastic, on which were printed several lines in spiky white Orokon lettering.

Finch had snatched it from him. He knew what it was. A pass, so that a ghetto boy like him would be allowed to travel outside the ghettoes without being arrested. He sneered at it, just as he sneered at the Protectorate's laws that were supposed to stop boys like him from leaving their assigned districts; but he put it in his pocket anyway.

"I see you're not too happy with our arrangement," Bane had observed. "Let me add another little incentive, then. If you bring me what I need and we get that golem, you'll get paid. More than your employer would give you. Call it a perk of working for the Secret Police."

He'd named a price. Finch had raised an eyebrow.

So now he was back on Rail and Moa's trail, and hunting their mysterious companion, too. What did the Secret Police want with a golem? He didn't know. But as long as he got his hands on the Fade-Science artifact that Rail and Moa had stolen, he didn't care. Because he suspected that once he had it, he wouldn't need Bane or Anya-Jacana or *anyone* anymore.

The thought cheered him up a little. Several minutes later he came across a boat moored at the foot of a strange tower, and lying inside it he found a glimmer visor. Moa's visor, carelessly forgotten. Finch looked up at the door that Rail and Vago had taken when they carried Moa away.

"Silly children," he said to himself, grinning his horrible grin. "Finch is coming for you."

3.3

Moa breathed.

That was enough for Rail right now. Breath meant life, and with life there was the hope of waking. For a time, he had believed she would not even make it this far. He had feared that the short and hurried journey from Territory West 190 to the hidden sanctuary of Kilatas would snap the last fragile thread tethering her soul to her body. But she lived.

The cave was plain and bare, cut roughly from the rock with a heavy drape across its entrance. Faint daylight bled in from outside, pushing through the drape and around its edges. It spilled across the boy on the chair and the girl on the floor, wrapped in blankets. The blankets were of coarse buta-wool, cut from the shaggy livestock of Orokos. They protected her from the cold edge in the air, the nipping breeze from the sea.

Rail watched her, hoping it was only sleep and not coma that kept her this way. He had to believe she was resting, recovering. But there was no way to tell. A Revenant had touched her. Would she wake possessed? Would she wake at all?

It had been three days now since they had escaped the district that he had led them into. The first day was the worst, when they were carrying Moa. Rail knew nothing about medical procedure — he hadn't even known to check for a pulse when Moa had fallen — but he had heard somewhere that moving a sick or badly injured person was liable to finish them off. And yet there was nowhere closer than Kilatas that Moa could be treated. No hospital in Orokos would take ghetto-folk.

So they had to carry her, through tunnels and down secret pathways, along dark streets. A golem and a ghetto boy with an unconscious girl, trying to avoid attention. It was a miracle they were not stopped by Protectorate soldiers, but with Rail as a guide they managed to pass through two districts without being spotted by anyone in authority. They could only hope that nobody who saw them decided to report it.

And so they had found their way to Kilatas, following the directions Moa had given Rail long ago. Though the route had changed somewhat since she had last passed that way, most of the major landmarks were still there and they had coped well enough.

They went to a bar owned by a man called Whimbrel. At first they were greeted with suspicion, and he pretended to know nothing about any place called Kilatas. But Rail had been told the old passwords, and it was enough to convince Whimbrel to come out and see Moa. He recognised her immediately, and took them the rest of the way himself, through hidden ways and past guarded gates and along mazes of tunnels. Down, down, deeper into the stone island. And finally to their destination.

Moa had held on throughout the journey. The doctors had seen to her, and made their prescriptions, but all they could do was make her comfortable and stable. They were as confused as Rail by what had happened. She had been brushed by a Revenant. She should be dead. There were no exceptions.

Well, no human ones, anyway, Rail thought, remembering Vago.

Apart from a bad case of chill sweats from being out in the rain, which they had treated with old folk remedies, Moa didn't appear to be any the worse for her encounter. Except that she would not wake up.

Rail had barely left her side since they had arrived. Vago

hadn't come to see her once. The thief-boy was bitter about it. Partly, it was because the golem seemed to be entirely unconcerned about Moa's condition after all Moa's kindness to him. But it was also because he wanted to take his frustration and grief out on someone, and Vago was the best target.

The golem stayed away, however. He was somewhere nearby, his movements shadowed by guards. Nobody was sure whether they could trust the monstrosity that Moa had brought them. These people were awaiting the return of their leader, Kittiwake, to make a judgement. She would be back in a few days, they said. Until then, Rail and Moa would not be allowed to leave and Vago would be guarded at all times.

People had come to visit. People who knew Moa from before, or who had known Moa's father. But they could do nothing, just as the doctors could do nothing. Rail was surly with them. He didn't know them, and didn't trust them alone with her.

He brushed her lank hair back from her forehead. Without the heavy make-up she usually wore, she looked different — smaller and more vulnerable. If he had been asked to do anything to make her better, to take on the Null Spire itself, he would have agreed to it then. But there was nothing he could do. He was helpless, as helpless as he was against the probability storms. No matter how much he tried to fool himself, it was always this way. How much could one boy do against a world like this?

Maybe Moa was right. Maybe it was all a matter of seeing what chance brought you.

He could remember the day they met like it was yesterday. The years before that, though he could recall them well enough, seemed somehow dimmer in his memory. He had always had a marvellous ability to carve his life into episodes, to cut the past loose and distance himself from it.

He had done exactly that when he ran away from home as a child. He'd been unhappy, so he'd changed his situation. It had been that simple, even at that age. His mother and father had treated him as well as could have been expected, but it was a savage world they lived in and they were all starving. He had heard the usual myths about how it was better elsewhere, about other districts where ghetto-folk were treated with the same respect as everyone else. When a fast-talking drifter came through his territory, he'd been bewitched by the man's stories of opportunity and adventure. He'd left with the drifter, without saying goodbye to his parents or the few friends he still trusted.

Of course, the stories were just stories. Eventually Rail realised that. The problem wasn't the district he lived in — the problem was Orokos. But the city was all there was. There was no way out of it, and nothing beyond the horizon but the endless ocean. So he had to learn to live with it.

He and the drifter had parted company, and Rail had ended up in another ghetto, little better than the one he had grown up in. He'd thought about going back home, but there had been so many probability storms since he had left that he wasn't sure he could find the way. He didn't care enough to try anyway. The past was the past; no need to revisit it.

One day he had found himself roped in as a lookout for a couple of acquaintances who were robbing a grand old house. When that went well they'd asked him to do it again, and when *that* went well they'd taken him to Anya-Jacana. The obese thief-mistress liked him, and extended her blessing to him. He could be a thief if he wished, under her protection, as long as he made sure she got her cut. And so he'd begun to steal.

Rail never had a problem with theft. A tough upbringing had left him with one rule which he lived by: to think of himself above all others. You had to be selfish to survive. He knew it was wrong to take what wasn't his, but it was somebody else's definition of wrong. He needed the money, and his victims had it. If he was smart enough to take it off them and they were foolish enough to let him, then that was how it would go. In the ghettoes, it was every man, woman, and child for themselves.

Moa never believed in that. Perhaps that was what attracted him to her. He didn't *want* to be so hard-edged, he just felt he had to be. Moa's occasional flurries of good-heartedness were what gave him faith in humanity, that life didn't have to be the way it was, that not everyone was beyond saving. Even him.

Being a thief came easily to him, and he had a talent for it. Without that talent, he might not have survived when he suddenly found it almost impossible to breathe during a probability storm. It struck without warning when he and some associates were on their way to liberate Protectorate technology from a canalside warehouse. Not knowing what else to do, his companions aborted the mission and took him back to the thief-mistress.

She could help him, she had said, but not for free. He was desperate enough to do anything at that point. So she gave him the respirator that he had worn ever since, and she made him pay it back at an extortionate rate of interest. He still hadn't rid himself of that debt, and probably never would. The interest accumulated faster than he could make money. It didn't matter. Anya-Jacana didn't need the money. She wanted his service.

He had been bound to her by fear, and he had thought he

would never be free of that. But now he had run. He could never return to the ghetto. He was adrift. But at least he was adrift with Moa.

Rail had sat faithfully by her bed for several days, but he had to eat and attend to other matters, and that meant he had to leave her alone sometimes while he went to buy food or use the crude toilets in the tiny settlement nearby. And sometimes he simply had to get out of there, to walk around for a while and clear his head.

"Don't go anywhere," he joked weakly at her, as he did each time he got up to leave. Then he pushed aside the drape and stepped out into Kilatas.

The sight of Kilatas in all its shabby glory always made him feel even more tiny and insignificant than he normally did. He held on to the metal railing that ran along the path outside the cave and looked across the secret sanctuary, and marvelled at what had been made here.

Kilatas was built within an immense chamber of rock, at the very base of the black cliffs that supported Orokos. Hundreds of feet above, the city bustled on unaware, while down here at sea level lived a community — one of many, no doubt — that existed beyond the laws of the Protectorate. The cavern roof soared high overhead, packed with stalactites, blackened with bats in patches. The greater part of Kilatas was taken up by a huge saltwater lake, from which dozens of bleak islands rose.

Most remarkable was the western side of the cavern, where there was a great natural wall. This wall was only a dozen feet thick, and beyond it was the endless ocean and the sunlight, which beamed in through several gaps in the rock. The gaps were high up on the wall, massive jagged rents that allowed the day's light in to brighten the cavern. Kilatas was always dim, except in the early evening when the sun blazed directly onto the outside wall. But that was the price they paid for their limited freedoms.

The dwellings of Kilatas had been put wherever they could fit. Some, like the one where Moa lay, were just caves cut out of the rock. There were many of them, high up on the sheer sides of the cavern, linked by precarious paths to other parts of the community. In other places, where the walls of the cavern were only a shallow slant, thick clusters of buildings had grown, dozens of huts and simple shacks of wood and metal. They were constructed with whatever was available, using skills learned in the ghettoes.

But most of the dwellings were on the islands that stood in the lake. They clung to the bare rock like limpets. A dizzying network of rope bridges connected the islands to one another, a rickety web stretched across the water.

Beneath all this chaos, among these shaggy clots of civilization growing doggedly on the cold stone, there was one thing that drew the eye, one focus around which the whole hidden community revolved: the shipyard.

It was to the shipyard that Rail was heading now, and he made his way down the winding path that hugged the cliff. His hand ran along the thin metal barrier that protected him from a terrible drop to the water below. The path took him through a knot of mismatched huts that had been built on a flat shelf in the cavern wall. He was barely acknowledged by the people there, who sat repairing nets with twine or turning spitted fish over small fires. Their clothes were threadbare and their faces were drawn. They hauled themselves about wearily.

Rail didn't look at them. He had long ago learned to shut out the sight of other people's misery. He had grown up in the ghettoes, after all, and this place was no better. It could do him no good to sympathise.

Is it worth it? he thought to himself. *What's the point of pretending to be free if you starve?*

Kilatas might have been beneath the gaze of the Patrician, but it was also beyond his help. Though Rail hated to admit it, the foul nutrient gruel that the Protectorate provided for the ghettoes had stopped him from going hungry more than once. Here, there wasn't even that. He had heard people whispering about Kilatas in the ghettoes like it was some kind of promised land, where their poor, oppressed people could find dignity. But there was no dignity in scratching out an existence like this.

No wonder they wanted to leave. Between the Protectorate stealing away their loved ones and the hopelessness of their situation, he could understand why they would want to believe in another place where things weren't so terrible. He could understand that they would even risk their lives for it. Humankind wasn't meant to be crushed this way. Sooner or later, they would find a way out.

Even if that way out led only to death.

His mind full of dark thoughts, Rail walked on. Eventually the path took him down to where the cavern floor was more of a gentle slope than a cliff, and buildings sprang up everywhere. There was more life in the eyes of the people now. They called to one another and made jokes, and the children played. Nearer to the shipyards, they felt nearer to the heart of Kilatas, closer to its purpose. For Kilatas wasn't a place where these people intended to live out their lives. Kilatas was a place they intended to *escape*.

Rail picked his way down dirty trails until he neared the shipyards. They were visible from everywhere in the cavern. Towers of scaffold surrounded half-constructed hulls, swarming with men and noisy with the tap of hammers. There were three ships being built here, none of them very large. Something the size of a Protectorate Dreadnought was too much for the limited resources that they had at hand. Instead, they were cobbling together crafts, only concerned about one thing: Would they float?

The docks, where the shipyards met the edge of the lake, were crowded with dozens of strange vessels, wheezing things that looked like they might fall apart at the first hint of a storm. Chimney stacks leaned, paint was peeling, and boards were split. Some of the older rustbuckets were daubed in fading graffiti. Some had engines, some paddle wheels, and some sails. But all of them floated.

Rail looked out across the lake, which glimmered with dazzling patches where the sun shone through the gaps in the western wall. Only a few small vessels moved on the water, catching the fish that slid in through underwater tunnels. Most of the crafts in the docks had never left them. They were built for one journey only. The journey out.

But as yet, there was nowhere for them to go. The wall blocked the route to the sea entirely. They were trapped in that underground lake.

This whole place was built on a foolish dream, Rail thought. No wonder Moa had been so keen to bring Vago here. No wonder she was so keen to come home. She lived for dreams.

Shaking his head at the stupidity of it all, he walked through the shipyards and on. He was stuck here, at least for the moment. And until Moa woke, here he would stay.

3.4

It was while Rail was away that Vago came to see Moa.

He had been watching the cave mouth for a long while, from far across the town. His exceptional eyesight allowed him to spy on them from a distance. The two guards that accompanied him sat around looking bored. Eventually he saw Rail leave, and he set off towards it at some pace. The guards followed, jogging to keep up with him.

Rail thought that Vago didn't care about what had happened to Moa, but he was wrong. Vago cared a lot. He just had no idea how to express it. At first he had tried to pretend it wasn't happening, but that was foolish, and he had learned to stop. Now the problem was Rail. Vago got the impression that Rail blamed him for what had happened. Vago wasn't really sure what it was he felt at the moment, and it confused him. But he knew that being around Rail made things worse, and he disliked the thief-boy anyway.

He had thought about leaving, turning his back on them all and heading off in search of his maker. It seemed a good way to avoid the turmoil of his feelings. But though the need for answers tugged at him, he couldn't go yet, even if the guards would let him. Not while Moa lay in that cave.

When he got to his destination, he had to bend down and fold his wings to fit into the cramped space. He pushed the drape aside. The guards waited outside while he went in, letting the drape fall again behind him.

Moa was curled in her cocoon of blankets, lying on the floor. Vago hunkered down next to her, watching her face.

She came awake with a jolt, then lurched away violently at the sight of the golem's monstrous features looking back at her. Vago recoiled in surprise, cringing as if fearing to be beaten.

Moa gazed wildly about, disoriented at finding herself in a strange place. It took her a few moments to establish that she was in no immediate danger, after which she calmed. She sat up, ran a hand through her matted hair, and groaned. Vago had backed against one wall of the cave, unsure if he had done anything wrong.

She noticed the golem's discomfort. "Sorry, Vago. You're just not the face I expected to see."

Ugly is what you are, thought the golem, remembering Ephemera's words.

There was silence for a moment, before Vago said, "You're awake."

She grinned. "Seems so."

"Why aren't you dead?"

Her grin faded at the edges a little. "What?" she said.

Bits and pieces were coming back to her now, memories falling into place. The probability storm, the factory, being carried in Vago's arms. The smell of his dry flesh. Then . . . then what? Then blackness.

"A Revenant," Vago said. "A Revenant got us."

"Both of us?"

Vago nodded.

For a time she said nothing, just sat up, rubbed the sleep from her eyes, and sighed. None of it seemed real to her. It hadn't really hit yet, how close she had come to dying. It had been a turn of the card, a flip of a chit, a roll of the dice. Luck had seen her through this time.

"Why aren't I dead?" she asked dazedly.

"That's what I was asking you," the golem replied.

"Well, I don't know." And she didn't want to think about it now. She looked around. "Where are we? Did we make it?"

"We are in Kilatas."

"We're *here*?" she cried, then made a face as the exertion dizzied her.

"What is this place?" Vago asked, surprised to find that he was interested.

"This is a town for people who believe there's something out there," she said. "Something outside Orokos. Something beyond the horizon. Kittiwake started this so that one day all of us could sail away from Orokos forever. One day we're going to work out a way to get past the Skimmers that stop any ships from leaving, and we'll escape! Orokos is a prison, Vago. Nobody understands that. It's a prison, and we have to get out of it!"

She was exciting herself with the thought. Just being back in Kilatas was enough to spark the old passion in her.

"My father was a fisherman, back before they stopped anyone fishing without Protectorate approval. He was there when Kittiwake found that bird, a bird from outside Orokos, like the one around your neck. He was with Kittiwake when she decided to build this place. We were one of the first to live here. I grew up in Kilatas, until . . ." She trailed off.

The golem regarded her strangely. "Why did you leave?"

"They took my mother away," Moa said. Her voice was matter-of-fact. She had cried all the tears she ever would about it. Now it only left her numb. "She shouldn't have left Kilatas, but she went to visit someone. She was in the wrong place at the wrong time." Moa shrugged. "Just chance. Nothing anyone could do. After that, my father snapped. One day he got in a rowboat and went rowing out to sea. The Skimmers got him. I think he wanted them to."

Vago didn't know what to say. He thought he should feel sympathy, but he couldn't decide what sympathy felt like.

"I couldn't stay here after that," Moa went on, scratching distractedly at the blanket around her knees. "Bad memories. I wandered for a while. I went east to find my uncle, but he had long gone and nobody knew where. Instead I found Rail. Or rather, Rail found me." She sighed and stopped worrying at the blanket. "I'd always intended to come back, but somehow it never happened. Until now."

She was suddenly tired of her tale. She looked at Vago and shook her head slightly. "It's all random. There's no point fighting it. My being here, at this moment, is the product of so many stupendous coincidences and moments of good and bad luck that you can't even imagine it. It's the same with everyone. How can anyone believe there's any sense and order in that?" She gazed down at her knees again. "Being touched by a Revenant didn't kill me. What are the chances?" Then she raised her head and gave the golem a wan smile. "What's your excuse?"

Vago shuffled his feet. "I don't know."

"Oh," was all Moa could think of to say to that. She tried to sit up straighter, but the effort made her light-headed.

Vago felt he should venture something more. "That Revenant . . . it didn't hurt me. It actually . . . it made me feel good. Instead of killing me." He looked uncertain. "The Revenant came through me to get to you. I think I . . . absorbed it. You were brushed by what was left. Maybe that's why you lived."

"Then you saved my life," Moa said.

"But I don't know how I did it. . . ."

"Still . . ." Moa said. "Thank you." It seemed a pitifully inadequate response, but Moa was too tired and drained to offer anything else. The golem gazed at her for a time.

"I think I was made to be a killer," he said.

Moa put her hand on the back of his. It was cold. "I know," she said. "I saw you. It's okay."

Vago was shocked, not only at her reaction, but at the fact that she was voluntarily touching him. "Aren't you scared?" he asked.

"Of you?" she said, and laughed softly. "I'm not scared of you, Vago. We're both outcasts, you and I. We should stick together."

Something melted inside Vago. He adored this girl, worshipped her with the unconditional admiration of a puppy; to hear those words from her lips was something more precious than he could imagine.

At that moment Rail came back, sweeping the drape aside with barely a glance at the guards, and saw the two of them there. Moa cried his name, and he fell to his knees and embraced her.

Vago felt his momentary joy turn to splinters of ice in his breast. Stupid of him, stupid to think that she really cared about him. Rail was who she cared about. Rail. And Vago, freakish and ugly, couldn't compete with that.

Suddenly forgotten and ignored, he stealthily left the cave, his thoughts thicker and darker than blood.

3.5

Two days after Moa had awoken, Kittiwake returned, and the three newcomers were summoned.

Kittiwake's shack wasn't much grander than any other in Kilatas. It was a low building of rough stone and mortar with a metal roof, set on a slope so that it looked out over the shipyards. It was only with a thief's eye that Rail noted how secure it was, its walls built strong and with few blind spots. A pair of guards stood outside, not particularly watchful. They were there as a deterrent to anyone who might think that the house was worth breaking into.

Upon being shown in, Rail decided that it really wasn't. There was very little, at least in the main room, to tempt a burglar. There was a tatty rug and a few chairs, some half-melted and unlit candles, and a table that stood off-centre, grainy and full of knots. A cheap painting of a busy street, with the Null Spire in the background, presided over all.

The din of the shipwrights from overhead faded to a background medley as he stepped inside and shut the door behind him. The room was cool and its roof rang faintly whenever anyone spoke. The light shone through a grimy window, past which workers walked to and fro.

Vago was here, skulking in a corner. He had been avoiding both Rail and Moa since she had awoken. He had a great deal to think about, and the need for answers was burning at him. He had made a promise to himself, to search for his maker and seek out the answer to why he was created. He couldn't put it off any longer. Moa was safe now, and she appeared content enough. He didn't feel he was wanted here. Soon it would be time to do what he had to do.

Moa gave him a quick smile. He glanced at her, then resumed the intense study of the painting he had been making when they arrived.

Kittiwake came through a doorway at the back of the room and embraced Moa. There was little warmth in it, and even Rail could see the distance between them. Moa had known Kittiwake since she was a baby, but only as a friend of her father's, someone to admire. Though Kittiwake would do anything she could for the daughter of her friend, she and Moa had never been close.

"I have to admit I'm surprised," she said. "I didn't think you'd be coming back."

"Me, neither," Moa replied.

If Kittiwake had been expecting any elaboration, she was disappointed. She shrugged. "Well, so much for pleasantries. What are you doing here, Moa? Who is your friend?" She looked over at Vago, flicked a hand at him. "And what the freck is *this* thing?"

"We need your help," Moa said. And she explained about Anya-Jacana and how they had cheated her, how they had been chased out of the ghetto and met Vago. Of the journey, she said little, and she mentioned nothing about the artifact. Rail had been very clear to both her and Vago that they shouldn't say a word about that. Not until they had time to work out what to do with it.

"Just get her to let us stay here," he had said. "We need to hide for a while until the heat dies down."

Kittiwake didn't probe too far. When Moa was done, she asked Vago for his version of events. Vago told her what he knew about himself, which was very little, and which was nothing new to Moa and Rail. There was only one thing he didn't tell: the name of his creator. Tukor Kep. The man whom he had seen looking in on him through the curved window of a tank, the tank in which Vago had floated. Where he had first come to life, perhaps? He wasn't sure. But that memory was his own, and he would not share it.

Kittiwake regarded them all suspiciously. She had a hard face, made to inspire respect rather than admiration. Her hair was white, streaked with black and tied back in a severe ponytail. Her clothes were similarly practical — drab and hardwearing, with high black boots that were scuffed and worn. She wasn't tall — only the same height as Rail — but she projected a presence that made her seem much larger than she was. She had an absolute and unquestionable confidence that other people responded to. This woman had founded Kilatas, made it out of nothing, and kept it going with the strength of her vision. No matter what Rail thought of her plans, he couldn't deny that she had something about her that made him want to please her, to win from her a nod of respect. It wasn't difficult to see how so many people had become swept up in her scheme. Even Moa would have stayed, if not for the loss of her parents.

"May I see your bird, Vago?" Kittiwake said eventually. Vago hesitantly took it from around his neck and passed it to her, his long arms craning over the distance between them. She turned it over in her hands, studying it. It was stiff and cold, and even through the preservatives it was beginning to decay a little.

"It's true. I've never seen anything of its kind before," she said. "You have a good eye, Moa."

"Father made me study all the birds. After the one that you

170

found. I think he was always hoping that another one might come along." She waited while Kittiwake examined it.

"You were right to bring it to me," she said. "It's not from here. It's from another land."

Moa squealed with delight, and even the stern-faced Kittiwake cracked a grin. Vago merely looked bewildered, and Rail's eyes were skeptical. But he knew better than to voice his doubts now.

"I told you!" Moa cried, grabbing Rail's arm. "I told you!" Then she spun away from him and hugged Vago. His body shape — and the fact that he tensed up — made it awkward. "You beautiful thing, see what you've done!"

Vago still had no idea what he had done, so he kept quiet.

"I'd like to have a few people have a look at this, just to be sure," Kittiwake said. "This is hope for the people of Kilatas, Moa. I want to make certain of it before I tell them."

Vago started, making half a movement to grab it back from her before stopping himself. "It is mine," he said.

"He's very attached to the bird," Rail said dryly.

Kittiwake gave Vago a chilly stare. "Listen, golem. Kilatas is a place for ghetto-folk. Nobody knows what you are. If this bird was the reason Moa brought you here, then that's the *only* reason you're here, and it's the only reason you'll be allowed to stay. Do you understand?"

Vago glared at her silently.

"You'll get your bird back," she said. "I won't hurt it."

The golem's fingers clenched slowly, but he didn't say another word. Kittiwake called in one of the guards from outside, gave the bird to him, and instructed him to take it to a man called Ortolan. She cast a look over at Vago, who hadn't taken his eye from the bird, and then added, "Be careful with it. I want it returned in the same condition."

The guard retreated, and the door was closed again. Vago shuffled uneasily. He was a prisoner here, and he wasn't certain how to react. These people were just like everyone else he had met. They viewed him with mistrust at best, horror at worst. They thought of him as a dangerous animal, something less than them. Only Moa treated him as an equal.

They would not let him go. He was smart enough to know that. They would not let him go until they were sure that he would not tell anyone about this place. Rail and Moa might be free, but he wasn't.

He stared at the painting, as if *she* might provide the answer. The girl in the painting on the wall, with the white hair and the expensive dress. But she was, as ever, silent.

She was peeping around the corner of a street stall, waving out at him with a smile on her face. It was the same girl as the one he used to talk to in his room above Cretch's laboratory.

Kittiwake caught his look, and turned to the picture. "You like this? I bought it in . . ." she trailed off. "Oh, hello. It seems that we have a guest."

Rail squinted at it. "What?"

"Lelek. Can't you see her?"

"Lelek is here?" Moa cried.

"Where?" Rail asked, coming closer. "I've never seen her."

"I saw her once," Moa was saying. "A few years ago. At least, I think it was her."

Kittiwake pointed at the waving girl in the painting, half-hidden by the stall. "There she is."

Vago, not for the first time, was left utterly stranded. This time it was too much. "Lelek?" he asked.

"Lelek," said Kittiwake. When it became clear that it wasn't much of an explanation, Moa supplied the rest.

"She's said to be good luck," she said. "She appears in pictures all over Orokos. She's done it for a long time now. Nobody knows how she got there. Probability storm, maybe. It's really rare to see her." She peered closer. "Look at that dress. She must have been from a rich family. The probability storms get everyone, rich and poor. It's about the only equality we have in this damned city."

Vago just stared. He felt somehow betrayed that other people knew about the girl. He could have told them how he had seen her many times in his room over Cretch's laboratory, but he chose to keep silent. Vago said very little unless he had to. It was his way.

Kittiwake lost interest. "Walk with me, all of you," she said. "There's somewhere I have to be. You might like to see it, too."

"What's happening?" Moa asked.

"I'm going to show you how we're going to escape from Orokos," Kittiwake replied.

3.6

Kittiwake led them away from the shipyards, on a route around the north side of the cavern towards the western wall. There were more communities here than on the steep south side where Moa had languished. Kittiwake was hailed and greeted as she went.

When they reached the western wall, they went through it, and there was the ocean.

They had all seen it before, of course, but never like this. Their eyes had adjusted to the dimness of Kilatas, and then to the even darker tunnel which Kittiwake led them into. Then, suddenly, the tunnel opened and they were standing on a ledge, fifty feet above the waves that crashed and sprayed beneath them. They were on the side of the Orokos plateau. Above them, as high as they could see, the colossal flanks of the plateau rose up and up until they became a mass of cranes and outposts, guard-towers and metal walls. It made Moa feel as if the whole island were leaning forward, about to topple onto them and crush them like ants.

Before them was the endless water. It was mid-morning, and the sun in the east cast the long shadow of Orokos across the waves, but in the distance the ocean sparkled. The air was crisp with salt. Some way to their left, one of the immense waterfalls that spewed from the canal vents thundered down from an unguessable distance above them, misting the air. The sky was untroubled by clouds. And far away was the horizon, the beautiful horizon and the promise of what lay beyond.

They stood there for some time, each thinking their private

thoughts. Only Rail seemed restless, scanning the water, craning out as if he could see around the curve of the island.

"We're perfectly safe," said Kittwake when she noticed him. "I have lookouts to warn us if any Dreadnoughts are nearby. We haven't kept hidden all this time without being very, very careful." She waved to their left with one hand. "See? The noise of the waterfall drowns any sound that might come from Kilatas. The holes in the wall that let in sunlight are so high up that no Protectorate ship can see in. If I believed in any gods, I'd say they put that cave there just for us." She raised her head and looked out to sea. "But I don't. I believe in chance. And chance is what is going to help us escape Orokos forever."

Vago had been watching the black shape of a jagbat wheeling in the distance, a mere speck to the others but easily visible to him with his superior vision. Now he tilted his head curiously, his interest piqued.

"How will you escape?" he asked.

"We're going to sail right out of here. We're going to sail to the land that's just over there."

She was pointing to the horizon. Vago looked.

"There is no land," he said.

"It's beneath the curve of the horizon," Moa supplied. "You can't see it."

"Then how do you know it is there?" the golem asked.

"We have clues," Kittiwake said. "There have always been rumours, for as long as anyone can remember. But there is also evidence." She was having to raise her voice over the roar of the waterfall. "I come from a long line of fisher-folk. The sea has been in my blood for as long as I can remember. But the

175

Protectorate doesn't let just *anyone* sail anymore. They have specially sanctioned fishing boats, and Dreadnoughts to make sure nobody else takes to the water. I remember sailing when I was a child, and it was the most . . . perfect feeling I can recall. Then they forbade us, because we were ghetto-folk, and I never sailed again on the open water. That is torture for me, golem. Do you understand? The sea calls to me, and I can't answer."

Rail had sat down on the lip of the ledge, his feet dangling over the drop. He'd heard about this before from Moa. Moa was rapt, however. She never tired of the tragic romance of Kittiwake's past.

"I found a bird, like you did," Kittiwake went on, glancing at Vago before looking into the waves again. "I found its body in a net when I was young. There was no bird like it that anyone had seen. It caused quite a stir, I recall." A flurrying wind blew, ruffling her white ponytail. "That was when I began to believe that there was something beyond Orokos. That this place wasn't the limit of our world but a prison. And out there, hidden just out of sight, there was something else."

Her eyes had become unfocused, as she drifted on the tide of her dreams. Now she caught herself, and sharpened once again.

"Of course, the bird wasn't enough. But we kept watch. And over time, we found more signs. Things were washed up, caught by the scavengers that collect rubbish from around the base of the island. Things that people couldn't explain. Strange items. Always from the west. Usually the Protectorate got hold of them, but some we kept.

"And then, one night, we saw the lights in the sky."

Moa couldn't suppress a smile at this. The very thought of them made her heart swell.

"Out there." Kittiwake was pointing. Vago looked. "After night had fallen. Strange glows that lit and flashed and faded, like a thunderstorm of many colours. And we heard sounds, too, tiny pops and crackles, as if the sky was being torn. But the colours: yellow and white, bright orange and blazing pink. Not even a probability storm has those colours. We saw them, and we have seen them many times now. Something is over there."

This was too much for Rail. "Something that could be a sea storm, or the glow of some luminous monstrous jellyfish, or any of a hundred things that we can't even guess at," he snapped. "Something that doesn't give anyone even the *slightest* reason to believe that there is land there."

Kittiwake's expression was indulgent and faintly pitying. "Your friend is not convinced," she told Moa. "He swallowed the line we were all given long ago by the Protectorate, that there is nothing else but Orokos in all the world. It's a tricky hook to get out, but one day maybe he'll cough it up."

Rail rolled his eyes. "Well, when you've killed yourself and all the people you'll take with you, I'll just keep chewing on that hook."

"Rail!" Moa snapped, but he ignored her.

"What does he mean?" Vago asked, addressing Moa rather than Kittiwake. But it was Kittiwake who answered.

"Have a look," she said, pointing to their right. "The test is about to begin."

She produced a small pair of brass binoculars and gave them to Moa. Moa turned them towards the thin lines of white that were tracking across the blue of the ocean from around the side of the plateau.

It took Moa a moment to identify what they were. The tiny

crafts were little more than streamlined hunks of wood with crude miniature engines driving propellors. Each was about half the size of a man, speeding along without riders. They had begun in a straight line, all heading in the same direction, but several of them had started angling away as the chop of the waves changed their course. All of them, however, were heading out to sea.

"Drones," Kittiwake said. "It's never quite been determined exactly how far from Orokos that ships are allowed to go. It seems to fluctuate."

There were seven drones in all, and by now they had made quite a distance away from the island, and the pack had mostly split up.

"Here we go," said Kittiwake. "Any moment now."

And there they were, breaking the surface, bobbing up out of the ocean. Skimmers. Moa turned her binoculars onto them, a trickle of chill sweat running down her spine. These were the things that had killed her father.

At first, they seemed like smooth metal balls about two feet in diameter, with four red lenses that looked uncomfortably like eyes spaced around their upper hemisphere. As Moa watched, they rose a little way, until they were hovering a few inches above the water. They swivelled towards the drones that were speeding across the waves.

"How many do you see?" Kittiwake asked. "Three?"

"That's right. Three," Moa said. Kittiwake grunted in satisfaction. Moa was about to ask how Kittiwake knew, when they were almost too far away to see without binoculars. But then the Skimmers erupted into life.

They shot across the sea, raising fins of spume behind them. As they went, a multitude of blades unfolded from their round bodies and began to spin. By the time they reached the drones, each one was a whirling blur of sharp edges. They smashed into their targets like cannonballs, reducing them to splinters in moments. Then they sped off on a new course. Another drone was torn to shreds, throwing bits of wood into the air . . .

. . . and the Skimmers stopped, coming to a dead halt. Three of the drones were still heading out to sea, but the lethal machines were making no attempt to catch them. They sank back down to sea level, waited for a moment with their red eyes above the surface of the water, and then descended and were swallowed up.

"They made it," Moa breathed. She looked up at Kittiwake, who was grinning. "Three of them got through."

"Four of them didn't," Rail reminded her.

"But three of them *did*," Kittiwake said. "They'll run out of fuel before they get far, but they got past the killing zone." She twitched an eyebrow at Rail, a tiny expression of triumph. "It's taken us a long time, but we've established a pattern. Different numbers of Skimmers appear at different times, in different places. At first we thought it was random, but it isn't. And we also learned that there's an outer boundary as well. If you get far enough away from Orokos, the Skimmers will stop chasing you."

"So all you have to do is break through!" Moa finished.

Kittiwake made a noise of agreement. "Now we know when the best time is to sail, when there will be the fewest Skimmers in the water."

"The best time to sail?" Vago asked.

"It's quite simple. We've set explosives all along the wall that separates us from the sea. When the time comes we'll blow it open, and every man, woman, and child in Kilatas will sail out of Orokos and head west. The more boats we build, the more targets

179

the Skimmers have to take out. They won't be able to get us all. Even given that our boats are slower than those drones, our estimates are that about thirty-three percent will make it through."

"Thirty-three percent?" Rail cried. He got to his feet and faced Kittiwake in disbelief. "You're saying that only one in three will even get past the Skimmers? That the rest will die?"

"That's the risk we're all prepared to take," Kittiwake said. Her voice was hard. "One in three. Do or die. And we'd rather have a one in three chance of living than the certainty of rotting in this place for the rest of our days."

"But you don't even know if there's anything out there!" Rail argued. "You have a one in three chance of getting out into the open ocean, sure, then a one in a million chance of actually *finding* anything. Half your boats would sink in the first storm!"

"We only need to make it over the horizon," said Kittiwake. "There's land over there."

"And what if there's not?"

"Then at least we died trying. But there *is* land there. We've seen the signs."

"And what if you get there and they don't want you? Or that place is *worse* than this one is? Have you thought of that?"

Kittiwake gave him an indulgent smile. "Rail, this plan has been my life for a long, long time. There's nothing you can come up with that I haven't already thought of. It comes down to a matter of belief. It's a leap of faith. We can stay here with our dreams just out of reach, or we can risk everything to reach them."

"Nothing's worth risking that many lives for," Rail said.

"Some things are," Kittiwake replied.

Rail shook his head and looked at Moa for support, but there would be no help there. He could see by her expression that Kittiwake's passion held her entranced.

She'll get sucked into this, he thought suddenly. *She'll get sucked into this mad scheme if we stay here.*

"I'm glad you came back now, Moa," Kittiwake said. "You were almost too late. It wouldn't have been right to leave without you. Your father believed so much in what we are doing."

"You're leaving?" Moa asked. There was a tremble in her voice. "You're really leaving?"

"In seven days. That's when we have the best chance of making it. We sail in seven days."

And with those words, Rail felt his world teeter. He realised now what a mistake it had been to bring Moa here. This place wasn't a sanctuary — it was a trap. A trap for dreamers like her. A whole town full of people caught up in Kittiwake's delusion, and Moa was the perfect candidate. He knew what she was thinking. She believed in a world outside Orokos, just like she had always believed. And here was Kittiwake offering her this one chance to reach the places that she visited in her sleep, the wonderland that she imagined must exist out there. But it *didn't* exist. And Kittiwake would die finding that out, and she would drag Moa and everyone else in this insane town with her.

All at once Rail wanted nothing more than to leave Kilatas, to take Moa away from this place for good.

Before this place took Moa away from him.

3.7

"I want to go with her," Moa said the next day. It was so depressingly inevitable that Rail didn't bother to even respond at first.

"Did you hear me?" she persisted. "I said I —"

"I know what you said," he interrupted, and then lapsed into a sullen silence.

The two of them were sitting on the edge of the lake, watching small fishing boats glide around. Morning sunlight glowed beyond the great tears in the rock wall high above, leaving Kilatas in twilight.

They had spent the morning wandering. Rail was bored. Kittiwake expected them to work for food, but they had enough to last them a while. They had bought it from outside with the proceeds of their theft from the Mozgas, and it was certainly better than the slop that most of the people in here were getting. Besides, Rail didn't see the point of joining in if this place was going to be gone in a week's time.

Moa watched him uncertainly. She had expected him to argue, at least. This blankness disturbed her.

"Remember when we were going into that district full of Revenants?" she said. "Remember what you said to me then? You said sometimes you have to a take a risk."

Rail didn't reply. Then he asked, "What about the artifact?"

"What about it? We can take it with us."

"Take it *where*? To Kittiwake's little paradise? You really think I'm going with her?" He laughed softly. "Not a chance."

"You have to come," Moa said, suddenly distressed. "You can't stay."

"Moa, I am *not* becoming part of that woman's insane freck-ing scheme, and neither are you!" Rail snapped. "Don't you understand what we have? For once in our lives things have turned our way! With that artifact we can do anything we want. Nobody can catch us. We can make ourselves rich. We can have enough money to eat when we like and what we like, we can buy a place to live that's *ours*, we can sleep in proper beds every night. We've been given a chance to change our lives here and now — a chance to make *this* a better place for us. And you want to throw that chance away and go looking for somewhere else, somewhere that might not even exist? Why?"

"I don't want to be a thief," she said quietly. Her eyes were closed, and the black eyeshadow made them invisible. "That's just making this whole horrible world that little bit worse."

Rail threw up his hands. "I can't believe I'm hearing this. You talked about taking a risk. Well, we *took* a risk. We stole from Anya-Jacana and we got away with it. There's no way Finch could have gotten into Territory West 190, and even if by some miracle he did, he'd never get into Kilatas. We're safe. We did it. Now's the time we should be thinking about what we can do with what we have. Not talking about running away." He turned and glared at her furiously. "One in three, Moa. That means you have a two in three chance of committing suicide if you get on those boats. You want to go out the same way your father did?"

"Don't you *dare* bring my father into this!" Moa cried. She got to her feet and began stalking away across the boulders, up towards where the huts and shacks clustered in the distance and the shipyard beyond.

Rail caught her before she got very far. "Don't you walk

away!" he said, grabbing her arm and pulling her around. "We're having this out now. Because I don't want to stay another day in this place. I can see what it's doing to you."

"Listen to yourself!" she replied. Her voice was harder than he had heard it for a long time. "You think you know it all. You're thinking: *Poor little Moa, easily led, she's fallen under the influence of this terrible town and I have to save her.* Well, this time I don't *want* saving. And I'm not going to pass up the only chance I'll ever have of getting out of this city!"

Rail was about to respond, angry at her ingratitude, but she cut him off.

"Think!" she snapped at him. "Think about where you are! Think about Orokos! Why would someone build a place that constantly rearranges itself? A place that creates things like the Revenants and then keeps changing around so that we can never be safe from them? And then to trap us here so we can't ever get out! Why would anyone *do* that? *Who built the Chaos Engine and why?*"

Rail didn't have an answer to that.

She dropped her voice to a more reasonable level and went on. "You can't just think about what's happening now. You have to think about the past. You have to think about why we are how we are. The Faded built this city and then disappeared. Why? Is it a punishment? If it is, we've forgotten what we're being punished for, so there's no lesson being learned here. Don't you see? There's something wrong with this city, and while we're still here it won't ever be right. You talk about a better life, but no matter how rich you get you'll never be anything other than a ghetto boy — not with that tattoo on your arm. You'll never find a doctor who can fix you so you don't need a respirator, because they won't work on a ghetto boy. You could make all the money in the world and it wouldn't be any better."

"You want to run away," he said quietly.

"No," she said. "I want to start again."

"What about me, Moa? What about my chance to fix myself, to be able to breathe the air again without this thing on my face? That'll never happen if I leave Orokos."

"Then *stay!*" she cried. "But I'm not going to be condemned here. There's *more than this,* Rail! And I will find it if it kills me."

"That," replied Rail quietly, "is exactly what it's going to do."

They had nothing to say to each other after that. In silence, the two of them trudged back across the boulders to the paths that ran towards the shipyards, and Kittiwake found them there. She had been running, and she looked grim. Two guards were with her.

"I've been looking for you two everywhere," she said. "Have you seen the golem?"

"Not since yesterday," Rail replied.

Kittiwake stared coldly at them. "He's gone."

"Gone?"

"He overpowered his guards. That *thing*, that creature you brought with you . . . he's escaped."

3.8

Far, far above where the secret town of Kilatas hid within the black rock of the island, the city of Orokos went about its business, and Finch went about his.

He had never been the kind of boy who gave up easily, and he was certainly not giving up on finding Rail and Moa and their strange companion, even after all hope seemed to have faded. But he was forced to admit that things didn't look good for him at present. To all intents and purposes, his quarries seemed to have vanished.

He slouched at a streetside café, sipping tuzel and watching the passing traffic. Carts clattered over the cobblestones. Gyiktyuk riders daintily bobbed above the heads of the people passing to and fro. Spicy aromas rose from food stalls, and colorful knick-knacks were laid out on rugs to tempt passersby.

None of it interested him. He barely felt the faint warmth of the sun on his skin. The faces he saw were only marks to him, potential victims for pickpocketing or mugging. Even the beautiful ones, the girls with smooth faces flashing joyous smiles as they laughed and talked — even they didn't do a thing to stir him. Finch didn't have a soul that was capable of appreciating the finer emotions.

Twice now he had been bothered by Protectorate soldiers who recognised a ghetto boy and wanted to see his tattoo, but he sent them away by flashing the pass Bane had given him. It gave him a mean kind of satisfaction to rub his presence in their faces. Here he was, dirtying up their city just by being here, and they

186

couldn't do a thing about it. He could get used to being in the favour of the Secret Police.

He swirled the remains of the tuzel around in his mug and looked into it, obsessed with his own thoughts. Where had Rail and the others gone? How had they given him the slip? Their trail was easy to follow after he had pursued them out of the Revenant-infested district. They had stopped being careful, for they thought they had gotten rid of him. Though he was some way behind, he caught up fast. And then . . . nothing.

He had traced them to a bar owned by a man called Whimbrel, and there he had hit a dead end. Nobody had heard of them. Nobody knew where they'd gone. Nobody had seen a golem. Finch could tell that people were lying, but they got angry at his questions and threw him out. Everyone around here, it was the same. People kept their mouths shut. How very annoying.

He sold Moa's glimmer visor for a handsome amount of money and got himself a room in a tumbledown inn for a few days. During that time, he made contact with the local thieves. Once he mentioned Anya-Jacana, they were willing to listen to him, even if her power didn't impress anyone here. There were other masters and mistresses across Orokos. He made a deal with the local thief-master, an offer of a reward for information. The thief-master agreed to have his boys and girls keep an eye out for the golem. It made Finch uneasy — if they found the golem, they might find Moa and Rail, and that meant they might find the artifact. But there was no other way that he could see to track them down.

Still, time had passed, and there was no sign. It was like they had sunk into the ground.

He was seriously considering a little light torture on the owner of the bar where Rail and Moa had last been. Then a filthy little urchin popped up next to him and gave him a gap-toothed smile.

"What do you want?" Finch asked.

"You said you was lookin' for a golem?"

"That's right," he replied, his interest suddenly piqued.

"I seen a golem."

"When?"

"Just now."

"Where?"

"How much you offerin'?"

Finch studied him carefully. "You a thief?"

The boy shook his head. "I jus' heard about it."

Finch thought about that. He made an offer of about one-tenth what he had promised the thief-master. It was still a fortune to a young boy. The urchin's eyes lit up. He didn't even bother to haggle.

Finch got up from his chair. "Show me," he said.

And with that, he was back on the trail.

PART FOUR:

The Null Spire

4.1

They were after him. Somewhere in this maze of tenement slums, in the shadow of the colossal metal wall that surrounded the city, Vago's pursuers were drawing nearer. He wasn't sure that they had spotted him yet, but he had certainly spotted them. He recognised them, though they wore no official uniform or insignia. It was in the way they dressed and moved, their arrogant confidence. He couldn't have said how he knew what he knew, but it made him no less certain. The Secret Police were coming.

But why? What did they want with him?

The sun was sinking in the west, behind the wall, painting the cloudy sky in tones of velvet and gold. He slunk through slowly darkening streets and tried to remain unseen. For someone his size, looking the way he did, it was no easy task. But he had to find his maker. He had to find Tukor Kep.

The escape from Kilatas had been simple for him. What had been harder was making the decision. He had felt a small regret at abandoning his bird to the care of Kittiwake, but that seemed petty now. It was a child's thing, and in deciding to seek out his maker he felt he had become somehow older. He didn't need the bird anymore.

But the real obstacle was Moa. He hated to leave her behind. She needed protecting. But this was something he had to do, for his own sake. And besides, a bitter voice in his head told him, it was Rail she wanted and not him. She might have been kind to him, but it was really pity — pity for his horrible ugliness. He would always be behind the boy in her affections. And the boy

191

didn't like him, wanted to get rid of him. Sooner or later, Moa would have sent Vago away.

Very soon, the boats would sail. Perhaps Moa would be on one of them. Perhaps Rail would not. Vago meant to be back in Kilatas in time to join her. She couldn't send him away if they were on a boat together. There would be nowhere to send him *to*.

But in the meantime, there were answers that he couldn't live without. He couldn't leave Orokos behind without knowing who he was, where he had come from. This could be his last chance to find out.

And so he had broken free of Kilatas. They would never have let him go; he was a prisoner there. But he believed that, when he returned, Moa would take him back. Moa would forgive him. And if Rail refused to go with her, as Vago hoped he would, then she would be glad for a guardian on her voyage.

Did he believe in the land over the horizon? He didn't know. But he knew that Moa was the only good thing he had found in this world since he had first come awake in Cretch's attic.

Getting out of Kilatas would have been impossible for any normal person. The route up to the surface was guarded in many places. Secret paths wound through endless tunnels that an intruder could lose himself in forever. But Vago took the more direct route. He went up the outside.

Kittiwake herself had unwittingly shown him the way, when she had taken them to watch the baiting of the Skimmers. He had noted then how rough the stone of the island was, the flanks of the great plateau on which the city sat. The climb would have been suicide for anyone but him, with his endless reserves of energy and his long, strong fingers with their machine-assisted grip. That was why they didn't think to watch it.

192

He disabled his guards with ease. Something in him — fear of Moa's disapproval, probably — made him gentle, and he managed not to hurt them much in the process. After that, he went out to the ledges and began to climb. Bomber birds buzzed him, curious at this strange being with wings that crawled up the side of the island like an insect. A jagbat came to investigate, but he crushed himself into a fold in the rock until it went away.

He was moving at a speed many times that which a human climber could have managed, but it still took him hours to reach the top, where the great perimeter wall of Orokos began. He was forced to be careful up there, for there were soldiers; luckily the watchtowers were mostly empty and it was easy to clamber up the outside of them. The people had long ago learned that it was pointless to watch the sea for enemies. Nothing ever came to Orokos. If popular wisdom was to be believed, nothing ever would. All their enemies came from within.

And so he climbed up the city wall and back down the other side, making his way along the many rocky outcroppings and abandoned buildings that pocked its surface. That done, he had found himself in the urban sprawl once again. This wasn't a wealthy district but it was far from a ghetto: a relatively new housing project for factory workers, built on the ruins of the last.

On reflection, he should have made his escape at night. But time was short if he wanted to return in time to join Moa, and he couldn't afford to waste another day waiting for the sun to set. Perhaps if he had been more patient he might have avoided being seen, and maybe the Secret Police would not be after him now.

But no, it was hopeless. He was impossible to miss. The city was just too crowded for him to travel in secrecy, night or day, without the kind of street knowledge that Rail had.

Everywhere he went he would be met with fear and panic and revulsion.

And yet he was still determined. He would find the man who'd made him. The man whose face he remembered behind the glass window of a containment tank. Though he had no plan and no idea how to go about it, he would find the answer to his own being, somehow.

First, however, he had to get away.

He had stolen a tarpaulin from a cart and wrapped it around himself, but it didn't hide him from the eyes of the citizens. The buildings here were all inhabited, so there was no help there. Eventually he went to ground in a vast rubbish dump. It was a huge enclosure where heaps of discarded devices and household filth were picked over by scavengers for parts that could be sold to Coders. The scavengers ignored him, and from the highest heaps he had a good view of the surrounding area. He burrowed in among the junk and waited. It was just as well that he had no sense of smell.

With his telescope vision he tried to keep track of the movements of his pursuers. They were stopping people in the street, talking to them, asking them what they had seen or heard. Already rumours of the monstrous thing that prowled their streets had spread throughout the Territory.

He was hunted. Perhaps he would always be hunted. That was why he had to get away from Orokos. There was no place for him here.

Darkness gathered, but his vision cut through the gloom. The glimpses he caught of the Secret Police showed that they were getting closer. They would find him eventually.

When the last glow of the sun had left the sky and all but the

194

most desperate scavengers had gone home, he spotted his pursuers sneaking through the gate of the rubbish dump. The time had come, he decided, to make his move.

He emerged from the heap of junk that had concealed him and headed for the opposite end of the dump.

At ground level, the refuse piles rose around him like mountains. There were no arclights here. The only illumination was that which glowed from the cloud-scratched moon overhead. He prowled on all fours, wings half-open as if in anticipation of flight. It was deathly silent, except for the distant scrape and curse of a few late-night prospectors.

The Secret Police would be spreading out across the dump, searching. He had seen the telltale bulge of thumper guns under their coats. After his incident with the Revenant, Vago was no longer sure that he had anything to fear from aether cannons, for aether didn't appear to harm him. But thumper guns fired explosive pellets. He didn't want to try his luck against them.

Something moved to his right with a clatter. He whirled, crouched to run or to attack. But it was only a piece of junk that had shifted loose. Carefully, he made his way onward, moving ahead of the Secret Police towards the high concrete wall that surrounded the dump.

He reached it without seeing anyone. He listened for a moment. Nothing. *Let them search the whole dump*, he thought. He would be elsewhere.

He cleared the wall in a single leap, landing cat-like in the street on the other side.

Right in front of one of the Secret Police.

The man was as startled as Vago was — but Vago moved quicker. As he tried to pull his gun, the golem grabbed his wrist

195

in a bone-breaking grip and threw him aside. And then suddenly the street around him was swarming with figures in black trench-coats and jackboots, guns levelled. He bunched to spring —

"Don't," said one of them, who had the thick muzzle of a thumper gun zeroed on him. "You wouldn't make it."

He was surrounded, backed against the wall of a rubbish dump in the white glow of an arclight. Six of the Secret Police stood in a rough semicircle, their weapons trained on him. He crouched like a dog at bay.

They had *herded* him. They had let themselves be seen closing in on him from one direction, knowing he would go the other. And he had fallen into their trap. He saw now, in the deeper shadows of the street, the lurking shape of Finch, the thief-boy who had followed them all this way. Now it made sense. The boy must have called the Secret Police.

Vargo snarled, his lips pulling back over his metal fangs. He had a purpose, and not even the Secret Police were going to stop him.

"Don't!" the man warned again, seeing Vago's intention. But the golem didn't lunge forward as the Secret Police had expected. Instead he sprang sideways, leaping from a crouch to sail over the heads of his attackers. One of them fired his gun in surprise, blowing a hole in the concrete wall, peppering them all with tiny, stinging shards of stone, raising a cloud of dust. There was confusion for a few seconds. By the time it was over, Vago was gone, swallowed by the alleys.

4.2

"Granpapa!" Ephemera squealed. "Come quick!"

"Alright, alright, child," Cretch muttered as he shuffled in from the other room. "What are you shouting about now?"

"It's Vago!" she said. "Look! Vago's on the panopticon!"

She turned the periscope-like viewer of the panopticon towards her grandfather, who put black-goggled eyes to the screen. He fiddled with the focus knob until it suited his failing vision, and there he saw an artist's rendition of his former assistant, a sepia-coloured sketch of the golem. Beneath it, words appeared and faded. They were too small for him to read easily.

"He's wanted by the Protectorate!" Ephemera announced gleefully. "They say he's very dangerous and we shouldn't approach him. And you're supposed to take your goggles off when you look at that thing."

Cretch ignored her. The picture switched to something else, a news item about the Protectorate unearthing a band of terrorists in one of the nearby ghettoes. He sighed and sat down in his red armchair. He was tired and weary. He always was, these days.

"I knew he was bad!" Ephemera said. "I told you!"

"Yes, you told me," he said.

"I told you, I told you!" she began singing, dancing round the room. "I told you, I —"

She pulled up short and the song died in her throat. Standing in the doorway, as if the panopticon sketch had come to life, was Vago. Silence fell.

197

"How did you get in without being seen?" Cretch asked after a time.

"Climbed the tower. Through the window."

"I knew you'd come back in the end. There's no place for you in this city. You were always safer here."

Vago turned his face from Cretch to Ephemera, who cringed away from him. He looked around the room. It was warm in here, despite the chill of the night. The furniture was a little battered and dusty, but it was real furniture, not just bare wooden chairs and makeshift tables. Cretch and Ephemera looked plumper than before, their cheeks fuller, but Vago knew it was just a contrast to the people he had gotten used to, who were lean and hungry and spent their lives under the threat of starvation.

Suddenly he saw quite clearly how savage the divide was between the wealthy and the ghetto-folk. People like Cretch took decent water, food, and warmth — the simple necessities — for granted. For the folk of Kilatas, for the men and women and children in the ghettoes, for Rail and Moa, it was a struggle just to raise themselves up to this most basic standard of living. And the Protectorate made absolutely sure, by branding the ghetto-folk and keeping them penned in their special areas, that the poor stayed poor.

"It's safer here," he growled. "But it's no better."

Cretch levered himself up from his chair. Ephemera ran to him and hugged herself to his legs, wide-eyed with fright.

"Are you here to kill us?" Cretch asked. "I'm an old man. I'm not afraid. But I won't let you hurt her." He put a thin, veined hand over his granddaughter's head.

"I'm not here to hurt you," Vago said.

"Then you've come looking for your maker?"

"Yes."

"Well, then," Cretch said. "Come with me."

The chamber at the top of Cretch's tower was much as Vago remembered it. There was his little corner by the window, among the brass pipes and ticking cogs. There was the painting, leaning against the wall, which he used to talk to. The painting had a drape over it again, as it had when he first found it. Someone had covered it up.

"I'm sorry I beat you, you know," Cretch went on. "I'm sorry I did that. It's just . . . you reminded me of her. That's why I took you in. A probability storm stole her away, and a probability storm gave me you. Like a sick joke. It took away my beautiful granddaughter and gave me another child in its place, a child of metal and dry flesh. I beat you sometimes because you . . . made me think of what I lost. Of her."

"Your granddaughter? Ephemera?"

Cretch shook his head sadly. "Her name was Evanesca. But I've heard the rumours. Even an old man like me has heard the rumours." He looked at Vago with his expressionless black eyes. "Now she's known as Lelek."

Vago moved over to the painting and reached for the drape.

"Please don't," Cretch said. "I saw her in that painting, days after it happened. She just . . . *vanished.* The Storm Thief took her. And then I saw her in that painting. It was horrible. Like a nightmare. Like a ghost." He pinched the bridge of his nose between his goggles, as if to stifle the pain of the memory. "I had to hide it from Ephemera. She was too young to understand then. It was just after her parents had died. She doesn't even remember she had a sister. . . ." He swallowed; his throat was dry. "I threw out every picture in the tower, but I couldn't throw out that one. In case . . . in case there was a piece of my grand-daughter in there. So I put it up here. I hid it."

Vago understood now why he had seen the girl more often than anybody else had, and why she had followed him to Kilatas. This was her home. And during the lonely days and nights that he had talked to her, they had become friends, of a kind.

Vago pulled the drape clear. Cretch averted his eyes.

"You're her grandfather," he said. "Look at her."

And there she was, leaning against the railing of the canal, her white hair falling about her shoulders, waving out of the picture at them.

As if drawn against his will, Cretch slowly looked. His face tightened, then became soft again.

"She looks happy," the old man said. "Don't you think . . . she looks happy?"

"Sometimes she's happy," said Vago. "Sometimes she's sad. But she's still here."

Cretch was unable to take his eyes from the picture of his granddaughter. "You seem older, Vago. Not as young as you once were," he said absently.

"It's hard to feel like a child when you see what the world has become," Vago replied.

"That's why we shelter our children as best we can," Cretch replied. "The contentment of ignorance is all too brief." He was still staring at the picture. His face scrunched up suddenly, and tears leaked from the edges of his goggles. "Oh, my Evanesca . . ." he muttered. "Forgive me."

But the girl in the painting was still.

After a time, Vago flexed his wings awkwardly. "You said once that you had suspicions about my maker," he prompted.

200

"Ah, yes," Cretch said. "Well, it's quite simple. When I first found you I was fascinated by the machinery that is integrated into your flesh. Much of it was Fade-Science. But some of it was made after the Fade, and if you look closely you can see the maker's mark on the components."

"The maker's mark?"

"It's a tiny engraving to let you know who manufactured it. Like an artist signing a painting."

"Where did I come from, Cretch?"

"You came from the Null Spire," said Lysander Bane, stepping into view from behind a row of pipes with a thumper gun trained on the golem. "The Protectorate built you. *We* built you."

Vago tensed instinctively, dropping into a crouch. But there was nowhere to run here. It was too tight. The only way out was through the window, but he wouldn't make it. He might have tried anyway, but there was something about this man, something . . .

Vago *recognised* him. He felt like he knew Bane, but he couldn't remember why. The face he had seen peering into the tank in his earliest memories? No, not him. That was Tukor Kep. Then how did Vago know this man?

"It's time to stop running," Bane said. "There are more of us on the stairs. You can't get away from the Secret Police. Come back with us. Come home."

Vago glared at Cretch, who was backing away. "I'm sorry," Cretch mumbled. "I'm sorry."

"What do you want with me?" Vago snarled. "I'm just trying to find my maker. I'm trying to find Tukor Kep."

Bane looked surprised, and then he burst out laughing. "Oh, no, it seems you don't understand at all." He sobered and grinned. "You *are* Tukor Kep."

201

4.3

Kittiwake's summons wasn't so much a request as an order. Rail got the impression that she wasn't going to be in the greatest of moods. He was right.

The activity in the shipyard was at fever pitch. The people of Kilatas raced to finish the last ships for the great exodus. Every ship floating meant that the people of the town had more crafts to spread themselves across. That gave everyone a better chance of survival when they took on the Skimmers. The prospect of the approaching deadline had put new strength in tired bodies. They were finally going to do what they had come here to do.

Whether it would work or not was, as Kittiwake had said, a matter of belief.

Rail and Moa were shown into her shack amid a frenzy of clanging and hammering. It was dark outside, but torches burned everywhere. The great holes in the western wall had been covered over by blackout sheets so that no light could be seen from the sea. The shipwrights would work through the night. Rail despaired of getting any sleep with that din going on.

Kittiwake didn't even bother greeting them as they came in. She had her back to them, looking at the painting on the wall.

"Do you know what you've done?" she said quietly. Moa cringed at the suppressed anger in her voice. "Do you know how many lives you put in danger by bringing that golem here?"

The shack was eerie by candlelight. Shifting shadows lurked in the hollows of their faces and in the corners of the room. They had searched every inch of Kilatas, but Vago was nowhere to be found. Somehow he had gotten out.

"He's not an enemy!" Moa said. "He wouldn't do anything to —"

"How do you know that?" Kittiwake snapped, focusing her wrath. "What do you know about him? This *thing* you brought into my town? Do you know how careful we are about who we allow to know about this place? Freck, if it wasn't for the fact that he brought you back to us then we wouldn't have let him in at all. And I'll have words with Whimbrel next time I see him. The fool, letting something like *that* in here!"

"Don't take this out on her!" Rail said. "*You* let him escape. And you were happy enough when we brought you the bird, weren't you? I notice you haven't been shy about using that to inspire your little followers out there. We couldn't have brought you that without bringing you the golem, too. How were we to know what he'd do?"

That stung her. She had indeed made a speech the day before, telling Kilatas about how they had found another bird from a foreign land: a good omen for their departure.

Moa was on the verge of tears, but Rail wasn't intimidated. He met Kittiwake's gaze steadily. "You can throw around blame all you want," he said. "Doesn't change anything. What exactly did you bring us here for? So you can shout at us?"

Kittiwake cooled a little. She stalked to the other side of the room, loosened her white hair from the ponytail, and tied it up again, tighter than before.

"The painting," she said. "Look at the painting."

So they did, turning their gaze to the painting, the street scene in which they had seen the mysterious girl Lelek several days before. She was there again, but now she was standing in the foreground, frantically pointing at something. There, behind the rows of houses and just on the edge of the picture, was a thin black tower. The Null Spire.

"What does it . . . what does it mean?" Moa asked.

"What do you think?" Kittiwake said, disgust in her voice. "She's telling us where Vago's going. Or where he's already gone."

"He's not a spy!" Moa protested. "He's not!"

"You listen to me," Kittiwake said, her voice threatening. "In less than five days we are going to sail. I have been planning for this moment most of my life. Those people out there are my responsibility. I will *not* have this destroyed. Not now. If the Protectorate comes down on Kilatas as a result of what you've done, we're going to sail anyway, even if we have to go through a fleet of Dreadnoughts to do it. If we don't sail at exactly the right time, there will be more Skimmers than we planned for, and more boats will sink. Every death will be on your heads."

She turned away, looking out of the grimy window to the shipyards. "I brought you here to tell you this: I want you to find that golem. I want you to make certain he tells nobody about Kilatas. If he *has* told anyone, I want you to let me know. It might be the only chance we have." She closed her eyes regretfully. "You have to make up for your mistakes. That's the way things work in Kilatas. Maybe it's too late already, but you're going to try. You have until we sail." She looked over her shoulder at Moa. "Or you don't come with us at all."

"No!" Moa gasped. "No, you have to let us come with you!"

Rail said nothing, his head dipped in thought and his face hidden by his dreadlocks. The candlelight made an arc along the black edge of his respirator muzzle.

"I suspect that would suit you anyway, wouldn't it, Rail?" Kittiwake said.

Moa glared at him accusingly. He raised his head. "You know what I think. Both of you do. I wouldn't sail with you if you paid me." There was a silence, during which he felt the heat of Moa's sense of betrayal. He knew she still expected to persuade him, but he was adamant. He wasn't going.

"Vago's just angry!" Moa cried. "You treated him like a prisoner. Of course he wanted to escape! You'd have done the same." She wiped her eyes with the back of her hand. "You say you're all about freedom, but look at you! You excluded him the same way the Protectorate excluded us. It just keeps going. We always need someone to pick on, someone we can feel better than. But you're no better than anyone else!"

Kittiwake shrugged. "Maybe. Maybe not. Just find that golem. If he betrays us, Moa, I'll leave you here to rot with the rest of them." She gave a snort. "Now get out of my sight. The guards will show you back up to the surface."

Moa had begun to sob. Between Kittiwake's harsh words and Rail letting her down, she was crushed. Even she had started to believe that she might have brought a Protectorate spy into their midst. "But how are we even supposed to catch up with him now? How are we supposed to find him inside the Null Spire?"

She didn't ask how they were supposed to get *into* the Null Spire. That would be the easy part. They had the artifact for that.

"It's your problem," said Kittiwake. "I suggest you get on with solving it."

Moa turned to Rail, and in her eyes was a question. He felt something twist painfully deep within him. She was pleading. She was begging him to help her, because she couldn't do it alone.

Rail wanted to leave Kilatas behind, to forget about Vago.

205

He wanted Moa to be safe, and he wanted her to stay with him. Together they could use the artifact to make their fortunes.

But that wasn't what she wanted. She would risk anything to get to Vago, to win back the opportunity to sail with Kittiwake. Even though Rail thought it was suicide, even though the chances were slim to none, she would try, even if it meant breaking into the Null Spire itself.

There was a long silence. If Rail helped her, then she would end up sailing with Kittiwake. Even if she wasn't killed on the boats, she would still be gone forever. If he didn't help her, then she would go to the Null Spire in any event.

If only there were some way, he thought. Some way to make her change her mind and stay. But she had gone past that point now. There was no turning back for her. She believed that she could really escape this place, and if she didn't sail then that dream would be turned to dust and she would have no more reason to live.

In the end, there was no choice for him. He couldn't bear her tears, and he couldn't ever say no to her. This was what she wanted. She wanted it enough to stand up to him about it, when everything else she let him decide. She wanted it that much.

"We're wasting time," he said. "Let's go get him."

4.4

Vago, in the end, went with Bane willingly.

They took a gunboat up the West Artery towards the centre of Orokos, a long black craft with three turrets that each carried a pair of cannons. The Protectorate gunboats ensured that law and order was enforced in the canals and the docks.

Their progress was rapid, and as morning approached it was possible to see the Fulcrum and the Null Spire looming ahead, and nearby the great mountain from which all the water in Orokos flowed. Dawn mist clung to the flanks as the waterfalls spilled from their reservoir and were funnelled into the canals that went north, south, and west, dividing the city unevenly.

"You weren't hard to trace," Bane had told him. "A lot of people saw you coming out of that tower when you first escaped. You caused quite a panic, don't you remember? I went to see the old man soon afterward and found out what he had done." Bane's voice was flat and without emotion. "Your master had been very . . . foolish to hide you from us. He knows what happens to people who defy the Protectorate. We'll deal with him later."

"You were waiting for me," Vago said.

"We expected you'd come back eventually. After you got away from my men, we were certain of it. After all, you didn't cover your tracks well. It's hard, looking the way you do. We knew you were heading that way." He gave Vago an appraising look. "You made very good time, though. I'm surprised you managed to find your way back so quickly. Though this is quite a distinctive tower, and your eyesight is very good. And I suppose you don't need to rest or sleep."

207

Vago didn't reply. In fact, he had said barely a word the entire journey. He stood looking out over the railings of the boat, gazing at the rooftops and spires of Orokos, and thought about things. Bane had promised him answers, but not until they got to the Null Spire. In the meantime, he had a lot to think about.

You are Tukor Kep.

He was. He knew it, without knowing why. He knew Bane, too. But how? From where came this picture that blazed so vividly in his mind, of a face looking back at him from the other side of a window? The memories would not come yet, but something had been jogged free by Bane's words. Recollection was slipping towards him like a landslide, gathering momentum as it neared.

He was Tukor Kep, then. And, strangely, it felt right. But who *was* Tukor Kep? He would know soon, when Bane explained it all. But until then, he waited, and tried to make sense of his feelings.

Earlier that night, he had been listening to Finch and Bane argue on the jetty as they were boarding the gunboat. Apparently Bane had promised Finch some kind of reward for locating Vago. Now Finch wanted his money, and he wanted the Persuader removed, and he wanted to be gone.

"Not yet," Bane said. "I may need you again."

"That wasn't the deal!" Finch cried.

"Then I'm changing the deal," said Bane. He held up the device that activated the explosive band just below Finch's shoulder. "Or perhaps you think you'll argue better with only one arm?"

Finch flushed with rage, his wispy blond hair transparent against the red of his face. "What else do you want with me? I got you the golem!"

"We'll just wait to see what the golem has to say before I let you loose," Bane said calmly. "I get the impression that there's more than meets the eye in this situation. I'd like to know where he's been all this time. I'd like to know about his companions. And I'd like to know why you were *really* after them."

Finch was quick enough not to react to that, but it didn't matter.

"It's my job to seek out lies, boy," Bane said. "And I'm very good at my job. If you won't tell me the truth about why you're chasing those ghetto kids, then maybe *they* will. Stay here and find them. Bring them to me, alive. Same deal applies. If you don't get in contact soon, I'll make sure you remember me; and the last thing you hear will be three little beeps before your Persuader explodes."

Finch was virtually spitting with anger. His rotten fangs were bared in a snarl.

"I'd hate for us to be enemies, Finch," Bane said. "You've impressed me twice now. See if you can make it three times. We've taken boys like you into the Secret Police before, you know. It's a better life than the ghetto."

With that, he left Finch to seethe. The gunboat set off and carried them onward into the rising dawn.

4.5

"Here it is," said Bane, as they entered the great chamber, halfway up the Null Spire. "This is where you were born. Or rather, where you were *re*born."

Vago ducked through the doorway, his wings folded tight to his body, and stepped slowly inside. It was chilly and empty, its walls and floor metal. Circular gantries ringed the room high above his head. There were tall devices of strange design, like narrow, leafless trees of gold. Generators and banks of levers mixed with bizarre Fade-Science machines, all fused together in uneasy alliance. At the centre stood a cylindrical brass tank with a single, curved window of green glass in it. Soft white light from overhead flattened the shadows.

Vago crept closer to the tank. He recognised all of this. He had spent time here, a lot of time, studying this place. This room had been the source of great fear. He walked to the glass of the tank and looked in. A golem stared back at him in faint reflection.

Of course. The face he remembered looking in at him had been his own, reflected from inside the tank. It *was* Tukor Kep. But he had been looking at himself.

Then he hadn't always been this way. He had been human once, and he'd had a face and a name. Now he was a monster.

He turned his head slowly and looked across the room at Bane, who stood with a dozen members of the Secret Police, all holding thumper guns. Bane returned his gaze impassively.

"Tell me how I came to be this way," Vago said, his voice an old man's whine.

Bane detached himself from the group and walked slowly

into the chamber, running his hands over the devices. Now they were silent, but Vago remembered them humming with power, the tree-like golden structures flickering with energy that darted through their branches.

"There was a project. A project to create a soldier, designed specifically to kill Revenants. Our scientists thought they could do it, with some of the Fade-Science that we'd worked out how to use. With an army of soldiers like you, we could tip the balance of this war. We could drive the Revenants into extinction. But it needed a human brain, a human body. It needed to be a fusion of man and machine." Bane walked over to Vago and stood next to him as he gazed into the tank. "The experiment was far too risky to try on one of our own, so I decided to choose a subject. We had several ghetto-folk taking up space in our cells, awaiting . . . processing. I asked them if they would be interested in a second chance."

Bane let the sentence hang in the aching silence of the chamber. Vago didn't move.

"I volunteered," he said. Of course he had volunteered. No wonder he had remembered the face in the glass as being his creator. He had created himself. That face was the last sight of his humanity before he went under, and the procedure of turning him into this fusion of flesh and metal began.

"*I want to live.*" Bane put a hand on Vago's shoulder. "That was what you said. You'd do anything, even this. You'd rather give your life to the Protectorate than die. This was your act of redemption."

"Redemption?" Vago croaked. He stepped back from the tank, his wings drooping. "Redemption for what?"

Bane took his hand away. "You were a murderer. You killed

211

and robbed upwards of twenty citizens before we caught you. You don't remember?"

Vago felt numb. He knew he should be horrified, but how could he be horrified at something he couldn't recall? He couldn't make any connection between himself and these crimes that Bane spoke of. He wasn't even sure whether to believe it all; but then he remembered the flashes of rage that had led to him attacking Cretch, and the way he had enjoyed the slaughter of the Revenants in Territory West 190.

"We trained you," Bane went on. "You had all the instincts, but not the discipline. We made you into a soldier. Then, when the time was right, we made you into a *super*-soldier."

"Look at me," Vago said, staring at his reflection. "Look what you did to me."

"Yes, look," said Bane. "You're faster, stronger, better than you ever were before. Kep, you're —"

"My name is Vago now," the giant snapped. His voice rang up towards the ceiling of the chamber. "It's Vago . . ." he repeated, quieter.

"Vago, then. It's a good name. You see, all the modifications we made seemed to take. You're fast enough and strong enough to take on a dozen Revenants at a time. You have a targeting system and enhanced reflexes. You've got a metal exoskeleton that allows you to not only absorb aether but to draw energy from it. You don't need to eat, you don't need to sleep — the only thing you need to survive are Revenants, and even then only rarely. You're powered by aether! As far as the Revenants are concerned, you're practically invincible. It worked! The project worked!"

Vago thought back to the escape from Finch and his mob,

through Territory West 190. He remembered how the Revenant that nearly killed Moa had faded away on contact with him. That really was how she had survived — he had absorbed it. He really *had* saved her life.

"What about these?" Vago said, flexing his wings.

Bane gave him an apologetic tilt of the head. "I insisted on wings. I wanted our soldiers to be able to fly, to catch the ghosts. But the physics are all wrong. Wingspan versus body weight versus gravity versus whatever else makes something like a jagbat take to the air. I don't pretend to understand it, but the scientists warned me. I wouldn't listen, though. Probably you can glide a fair distance with practise, but you'll never take off."

Vago digested this. After a time, he looked at his hand, flexed it, watched the jointed metal rods slide together along the backs of his fingers.

"Why don't I remember?" he asked quietly, his voice tortured by his throat. He raised his head and stared at Bane. "What happened?"

"You were like a newborn at first," Bane replied. "The process was hard on you. There was surgery, and electricity, and processes I don't even know the name of. You . . . retreated into yourself, I suppose. Became like a child again. We began conditioning you, coaxing you out bit by bit. But the probability storm took you away from us. After that . . . well, we learned the rest from the toy-maker Cretch, at least until you went wild and disappeared. The remainder of your story I would be very interested to hear."

Vago looked over at the group of Secret Police, watching his every move.

"What now?" he asked.

213

"Now we have you back. We resume conditioning."

"Conditioning?"

"We have machines that teach you how to think."

"How you want me to think," Vago corrected.

"Very good," Bane replied, mock-impressed. "You're picking up this game quickly."

Vago considered making a run for it, lunging at Bane, doing *something* . . . but his heart had been crushed, and he couldn't make himself try. It would mean his almost certain death, and for what? There was nothing for him outside in the city. He had no memory of his life as a murderer from the ghettoes. He knew who he was now: a creation of the Protectorate. How could he go back to Moa, knowing that?

He sagged. "Why do you treat us this way?"

Bane laughed in surprise. "What do you mean?"

"The ghettoes, the disappearances, everything. What you do to the ghetto-folk. Why?"

Bane's laughter faded. "Because you ruin our world," he said.

Vago met his eye, and saw that he was perfectly serious.

"We all have dreams," Bane said. "Mine is of a world of order, where everything has its place and everything works, where people can walk the streets in safety. A society of citizens who are happy because they are secure and because their lives are overseen by us." His face soured, and Vago could hear the disgust and hatred in his voice as he went on. "All I want is a society of good, healthy people with enough food to go round and enough jobs to satisfy everyone. But there are always you filthy ghetto-folk getting in my way. The poor and the weak and those with criminal genes who breed more criminals. The sick and the useless, taking up our food and our space. Don't you realise how small Orokos is, compared to its population? Already our hydroponics farms are stretched to the limit. Our fish stocks deplete daily; even the sea is not inexhaustible. And with the Revenants appearing all over the city we can never be certain of any kind of steady supply. You people are leeches, draining our society dry, and we can't allow that any longer."

Vago regarded him silently.

"But we can't just kill you. The citizens won't allow geno-cide. So we do it quietly. We take you away a few at a time, and then we shut down one ghetto and move all the inhabitants to another. One day Orokos will wake up and you just won't be there anymore. There'll be no poor, no sick, no criminals. Everyone will be happy and content. Then once we've defeated the Revenants, there'll be a new age. An age of peace and order and perfection, like there was in the days before the Fade."

There was one last thing Vago wanted to know. "What would have happened to me if I hadn't volunteered for this? What happens to all those who are taken away?"

Bane's face was stern, rigid with conviction. There wasn't a flicker of doubt there in the righteousness of his cause. "That's the most elegant part. As I said, we don't have enough food to go round, and wasting it on ghetto-folk is foolish. The nutrient gruel that we feed them to stop them from starving and riot-ing . . . it's made from the people we take away."

Vago lowered his head, and his features fell into shadow. The horror of it was too much. All of it was too much.

Bane motioned to the Secret Police near the door, and they came closer, guns aimed at the golem.

"Come, Vago," he said. "In a short while you'll understand that this is all for the best. That's what the machine does. It helps you understand."

Broken, defeated by the sheer cruelty of the world, Vago was led away from the chamber to finish his conditioning.

4.6

Moa shifted nervously, glancing around the gloomy interior of the Coder's workshop. Next to her, Rail was waiting, his eyes on the owner, who was counting out platinum chits onto a metal counter. Dim morning light shone through slatted windows behind them. It was cold, but Moa felt colder. She was utterly miserable.

Four days left. Four days before Kittiwake sailed, and the chance to reach her heart's desire was gone.

They had been ejected from Kilatas in disgrace. They were led up through the winding ways by stern-faced guards, passing the gates beneath the disapproving gazes of the sentries. Moa had spent most of the time sobbing, but nobody had any sympathy for her. Even Rail had been distant. That she could understand. He was going to help her break into the Null Spire. He was going to risk his life and his own dream of riches to get back Vago, who he had never liked anyway, so that Moa could return to Kilatas and subsequently leave him. There was absolutely no reason for him to be doing what he was doing, except because Moa wanted it.

That made her feel worse. Her own selfishness crushed her. How could she ask that kind of sacrifice from him? And yet, how could she not? She needed his help, and she needed Vago. Maybe the golem was in trouble. Unlike Rail, she had some real affection for Vago, and she would not leave him to his fate if she could help it.

"Trnsctn s vr," the Coder whirred.

Rail shook his head. "More."

The Coder remained still. It was impossible to tell what his reaction was. His whole body was encased in an interlocking exoskeleton like chitin on a beetle, and his features were hidden by a full face helmet of smooth black. Two bulbous, blank eyes glowed pale blue from within. There was a circular grille on his thin chest where his voice came from, flat and mechanical.

"Vry wll," he said, and continued counting out chits.

Nobody knew how much of a Coder was machine and how much was human. Coders liked to give the impression that they were integrated flesh and metal, like Vago was, but the truth was that only the Protectorate had that kind of science. Coders surrounded themselves in a shell of technology, but inside they were human, and ashamed of it.

Coders wanted to be machines, like the machine-god they worshipped. They believed their god lived inside the Fulcrum, inside the Chaos Engine. The probability storms, the Revenants — these were the evidence that their god existed, and that it was angry with them and needed appeasing. Coders were mechanics, whose purpose was to understand the fingerprints of the deity in circuitry and the interlocking of a gear or a cog. They could always be relied on to buy technology like a glimmer visor. Rail was selling his now, to make extra money for their passage up-Artery towards the centre of Orokos.

Unbeknownst to them, Rail and Moa were following the same route that Bane and Vago had gone the night before.

"Stsfd?" the Coder asked. Coder language was tricky to follow as they didn't use vowels, but Rail had enough experience so the half-spoken words were clear enough.

He scooped up the chits into a bag. "That'll do fine."

The transaction completed, Rail and Moa left the workshop and ambled out into the dull grey morning. Here on the canalside terraces, buildings rose to three or four stories, and each one was a different shopfront. Weathered staircases and walkways creaked under the weight of booted feet as people slid by one another on the narrow throughways. The air was full of the smell of gutted fish and dirt.

The workshop was on the third floor, so they made their way down to ground level where the jetties were and headed for the boats. Barges and haulers were slowly departing up-Artery, heading for the Fulcrum or the smaller canal networks that ran all through the city. None were going the other way; only a short distance west was the edge of the city and the colossal wall, where huge intakes sucked in the water and spewed it out on the other side in a vast cascade.

They walked through cobblestone alleys down towards the canal. Houses of dark stone and metal rose up around them. Neither of them said anything. Rail, in fact, had been virtually silent ever since he had agreed to try to rescue Vago. It felt like he was punishing her. After some time, Moa couldn't bear it any longer.

"It'll all work out, Rail," she said weakly. "You'll see. We'll get Vago back."

"And then what?" he replied. "Then you'll get on a boat and get yourself killed. One in three, remember? Or have you forgotten the odds of getting off Orokos alive?" He glared ahead into the middle distance. "That's even assuming Kittiwake knows what she's talking about."

She was about to reply, but he cut her off. "And another thing — what if she's right about Vago? What if he *is* an enemy? What do we know about him? Nothing! If he's at the Null Spire — and again, we've only got the word of some girl in a

219

painting for that — then he's probably already blabbing about Kilatas and our artifact."

Moa fell silent again. She didn't have an argument. He was right. And she knew now that she would never, never manage to persuade him to come with her. Even the prospect of losing her forever wasn't enough to make him subscribe to Kittiwake's plan. If only she could make him see what she saw, the spectacular lands that might be just out of reach over the horizon. If he could see that, then he'd know they were worth risking anything for. But there were no words that would make him understand.

Now that she felt herself and Rail splitting apart, she realised how tightly they had been entwined. Always together, always valuing the other more than anything else. But now this, now Vago and Kittiwake and the fact that they just didn't want the same things anymore.

She wished they had never found the Fade-Science artifact that was stashed in the inner pocket of her pants. She wished she had never gained the power to open doors. Some doors should stay shut, because once opened they could never be closed again.

As Rail haggled with a boatman for their passage upriver, she found herself thinking of the Null Spire, of what they would face when they got there. Maybe they could get in with the artifact she had. Maybe it was suicide. But she had to try. She knew that Rail didn't understand that, but she had to try.

"It'll be a little while till we set off," he murmured to Moa. She shrugged. It would still take the whole day and night to get to the centre of Orokos on a barge. Another day gone. Time was slipping from her.

Rail glanced about as he waited for the boatman to count the money he handed over. He hadn't forgotten about Finch, but he was fairly sure that Anya-Jacana's thief-boy would have given up and moved on by now. Finch couldn't be everywhere.

But right at that moment, a boy was watching them from behind a pile of crates, a boy who had heard a rumour. A rumour that someone was paying good money for information about a dreadlocked, dark-skinned boy with a respirator and a pale girl wearing green pants. He watched them get onto the barge, noted its name, and ran away.

Finch couldn't be everywhere, it was true. But it was amazing what the promise of a little money could do.

4.7

Darkness claimed Orokos once again, and the barge moved slowly onward, its engines labouring against the current. It was a large passenger craft with a dozen cabins, heavy and ugly, hung with chains and cables that clanked softly as it rocked in the sway of the West Artery. Tonight the moon was clouded and a fine rain fell, making the night unfriendly and impenetrable. Houses and buildings on the canal bank were invisible. The barge ploughed through the water, towards the heart of the city. The crew steered, half-awake, watching for the lights of other crafts on the massive canal.

None of them noticed the slender figure that attached itself to a trailing cable, nor did they hear when he scampered up it like a rat and slipped over the gunwale. Finch scanned the deck for crewmen and then slid into the shadow of the cabins, the rain erasing the drips he left in his wake. Stealthily, he tried the door next to him, and it opened without a sound. Within, metal stairs led down into the noisy core of the barge. He took them.

The boy who sold him this information had better have been telling the truth, Finch thought. If not, the boy would find himself with his throat cut before long.

The whole day had been a race to overtake the barge. He had hired a swift craft to take him upstream, and only as night drew in had he passed the boat he was looking for. He got out several stops upstream and waited, and when he saw its lights approaching in the rain he swam out to meet it. He had expended a lot of money and effort to get here, and he had used up most of the chits gained from selling Moa's abandoned glimmer visor already. But if it worked, it would be worth it. He wanted that artifact. And he wanted to kill Rail and Moa, just for the trouble they'd put him through.

But he couldn't kill them. Not yet. Bane wanted them alive, and while Finch was wearing the Persuader he was still Bane's man.

He found himself now in a short corridor of riveted iron. Hanging lanterns cast a green-tinted light, swinging with the movement of the barge. Several oval doors were on either side, each with its own porthole. All were dark. It was late, and the passengers had settled in for the night.

Finch peered in through the portholes. The faint moonlight coming through the small, square windows on the opposite wall was enough to outline the sleeping forms within, cradled in net hammocks. He passed along the corridor, looking through each porthole, until finally he set eyes on Moa.

She was curled up in her hammock, wrapped tight in a blanket like a caterpillar in a cocoon. But the hammock above her was empty. Rail wasn't there.

Finch glanced either way up the corridor, concern crossing his features. Where *was* Rail? Out on the deck?

No matter, he thought, sliding his dagger from its leather sheath. If Rail came back, Finch would deal with him. Time to get this done.

He turned the handle, pushed open the door, and stepped into the cabin, closing the door behind him. The rattle and drone of the barge's engine covered what slight noises he made. Moa didn't wake.

Finch crept towards her, his sodden clothes sticking to him.

The rain pattered against the window outside. She murmured and stirred, some dream-sense warning her of danger . . . but it wasn't enough to make her open her eyes. Not until she felt the cold edge of Finch's blade against her throat.

"Hello, pretty," Finch crooned, grinning his terrifying grin. "You have something I want."

Moa froze. Instinctively she looked about for Rail, but he wasn't there. There was only Finch.

"I hear you have a trinket," he murmured, leaning over her so close that drips from his hood fell onto her cheek. "Something very precious. Why don't you tell me exactly what it does, Moa? I'm *very* curious."

"It doesn't do anyth —" she began, but stopped as he pressed the dagger harder against her neck, hard enough to hurt.

He made a soft tutting sound. "Let's not lie to each other, hmm?"

She wanted to swallow, for her mouth had gone dry, but she didn't dare. Where was Rail? Why had he abandoned her like this? Frightened out of her wits, she had little choice but to answer.

"It opens doors," she murmured. "It makes things . . . so you can pass through them."

"That's what I thought," Finch replied. "Otherwise you'd never have gotten away from me the first time." He shifted the blade so that the point of it was under Moa's chin. She whimpered softly, tears gathering at the corners of her eyes.

"Give it to me."

She reached inside her blanket. She had slept fully clothed, for the cabin was cold. After a moment, she drew out the Fade-

Science device. Finch snatched it from her. He examined it from every angle.

"How does it work?"

"You put it on . . . you put it on your hand," Moa managed. A shiver of pure fear shook her body, but Finch didn't notice. He looked at her, eyes narrow in suspicion.

"Don't move," he said. "And don't make a sound. Or I'll cut you *really* bad."

He retreated a little and lowered the dagger, freeing up both his hands so he could put the artifact on. Moa entertained wild plans of making a dash for the door, but she knew she wouldn't get that far. She wished desperately that Rail were here; but then, part of her hoped that he would stay away. She wouldn't want him to get hurt.

Take it, she thought. *Take it and go.*

"It doesn't fit," Finch muttered. He looked up again at her and said again, angrily, "It doesn't *fit!*"

He tossed it at her and she caught it automatically. "Put it on," he hissed. "I want to see."

Moa did as she was told. She moved so that she was sitting at the edge of her hammock and slipped the artifact onto her hand. It went on easily, the amber disc nestling in her palm, a perfect fit. And then the colours came — the strange, swirling veils of colour, like the drifting hems of a probability storm. They danced slowly around her forearm, lighting the cabin with a soft radiance. Finch stared, amazed. Suddenly, he tore open his wet shirt and shucked it off one arm. His body was scrawny, white, and scarred. Around his upper arm was the dull grey band of the Persuader.

"You told me it makes things so you can pass through them," he said. "What about this?"

Moa looked bewildered. She had no idea what it was, or why he simply couldn't get it off himself. "I don't know, I . . ."

"Try!" he hissed. He still held the dagger in one hand.

She was about to warn him that she had no idea what harm it might do if she touched him with it, but she stopped herself. She didn't care if he got hurt.

She reached towards him. "No tricks, now," he warned. He had the dagger ready in his free hand.

"No tricks," she murmured, clasping her hand to the Persuader.

The colours flowed from her arm, gliding around the metal band. The Persuader and the surrounding arm faded until it was ghostly. Finch gave a yelp at the sight and pulled his arm back; as he did so, it slid through the transparent ring of metal, which fell to the floor with a thump.

He gave a breathless laugh. He was massaging his arm, which had become solid again. The Persuader was on the floor next to where Moa sat in her hammock.

"Throw it to me," he said. She picked it up and tossed it across the cabin. He caught it and slipped it into his pocket, then got his shirt back on. "Now then." He grinned. "I suppose I should thank you for helping me out of that little bind, but all you've done is remove the only reason why I shouldn't kill you." He smiled nastily as he took a step towards her, his blade sheening in the dim light from outside. "Without that Persuader, Bane's got no hold on me anymore. I can take that Fade-Science trinket and disappear. I wonder if it would still work if I just cut your hand off?"

But Moa had no intention of letting him near her. She slapped her palm down on the floor of the cabin, and the colours flowed. Finch had time for an instant of surprise before the ground beneath his feet became transparent, and then with a cry he fell through the floor and into the cargo hold of the barge. Moa, suspended in her hammock, pulled her hand away and the floor became solid once again.

For a short time, she just gazed at the empty room. She was unable to believe it had actually worked. But here she was, alone, in the cabin. Finch was gone.

Then she was moving. She tugged the artifact off and stuffed it back in the pocket of her pants. All she wanted now was to be away from this place, off this barge. Finch was down, but he wasn't out. She got out of the hammock, wrenched open the door . . .

. . . and came face-to-face with Rail.

The sight of him brought all the terror of the last few minutes boiling to the surface. "What were you *doing*?" she shrieked. "Where the freck were you when I needed you?"

Rail grabbed her arms, shushing her. There was something in his glare that withered her anger. He was frightened, too.

"The Secret Police are here," he said.

"What? What are they —"

"We have to go!" he hissed.

She didn't argue any further. The two of them hurried down the corridor, and Rail sped up the metal stairs to the door which led onto the deck.

"I was up top," he muttered as they went. "Thinking. Didn't care about the rain. I saw their boat pull up. They're searching for something. I think they're searching for us."

He grasped the handle of the door and looked back at her, his dreadlocks dripping and his respirator wet. "Are you ready?"

"Rail," she said. "Finch is here. He nearly got me."

Rail's eyes tightened. "We have to go," he said again, and he opened the door a crack.

Outside, he could see trenchcoated shadows moving along the sides of the barge. They moved quietly and with purpose, and they had thumper guns in their hands.

"We make a break for the water," he said. "If we can get to the side of the barge, we might be able to —"

"You go," Moa interrupted him.

"This isn't a time for —" he began to protest, but she cut him off again.

"I can't swim," she said.

"What?"

"I can't swim."

"You grew up next to a lake, your father was a fisherman, and you can't *swim*?"

"I was stung by something . . . when I was very young. They could never get me back in the water after that. . . ." She trailed away, realising how pathetic it sounded now. "Freck, Rail, we live in the middle of a city. I never thought it was important."

Rail's heart sank. "We're caught," he said.

"No! You can run. You can swim."

He turned away from the door, shook his head. "I'm not going. Not without you."

There was a long silence as they looked at each other.

"I'm sorry," she murmured, fresh tears spilling from her eyes. "I'm sorry for all of this."

He walked down to the bottom of the stairs where she stood.

"Come on, Moa. We got into this together." He embraced her gently. "I'd rather be here with you than anywhere else."

She slipped her arms round him in response, feeling the hard metal of the respirator pack beneath his jacket. She was still holding him when the door at the top of the stairs opened and the Secret Police came for them.

4.8

The cells of the Null Spire were like the corridors that had led to them: grey, featureless, and sterile. As they were marched to their confinement, Rail and Moa glimpsed rooms full of filing cabinets, dreary chambers packed with typing secretaries, and desks, desks, desks. It was a sombre place where echoes seemed hollow, and the atmosphere was that of soulless and clinical efficiency.

The Secret Police had taken Rail and Moa without a word as to why. Finch came with them, too. Though he wasn't under arrest, the Secret Police watched him closely nevertheless. He glared at Moa, still sore after being humiliated by her.

The first thing the Secret Police had done was to take the Fade-Science artifact from Moa. They'd even known which pocket she kept it in. That was what they'd been after. They'd known all about it.

Rail and Moa had been betrayed. And Rail had a good idea who had betrayed them.

At first he thought it might have been Finch, but after what Moa had told him, he ruled the thief-boy out. Finch wanted the artifact for himself, and he had wanted to kill Moa and Rail as well. That left only one other possibility: Vago.

Rail didn't say anything to Moa about his suspicions. She was smart; she would reach the same conclusion eventually. In the meantime, they languished in their cell and wondered what would happen to them.

At least they had been put together. That was one small mercy. Though everything else had fallen to pieces, they shared the same cell. Moa was hunkered on the thin, hard bench that served as a bed. Rail sat against the wall, his head tipped back and resting against the cool grey metal. Their cell was one of a curving corridor of many cells, but all the doors were solid and without windows, and they had no way of knowing if they were the only prisoners or if there were others like them.

Why hadn't they been separated? Surely that was the most sensible thing to do. Pull them apart, break their spirits, let them stew in their own thoughts. Unless, of course, it simply didn't matter. They had nothing the Secret Police needed to know, and any interrogation would be short. They had no reason to hold out. Whether they were together or not made no difference.

That made Rail depressed, and he sank into a mire of hopelessness.

He could tell Moa was feeling worse than he was. He wanted to say something to her, but he couldn't bring himself to speak much. He felt flattened and unable to pick himself up. Suddenly, all that had happened since finding the artifact — the flight from the Mozgas, Anya-Jacana's wrath, the journey through the Revenant district, Moa's brush with death, Kilatas, their pursuit of Vago — all of it seemed ridiculous. They had been living a fantasy, struggling towards some imaginary goal where things would be *different*, where they could break out of the straitjackets they'd been born into. But now Rail wondered if they had ever really had a chance. Like the city itself, life offered a certain amount of leeway, but it was apt to pull you back with a sharp yank if you tried to go too far. The illusion of freedom was important, but in reality they were not free at all.

Rail tried to console himself with the thought that at least they had tried, but it was cold comfort now. The artifact was gone. They could never return to their ghetto with Anya-Jacana after them. They couldn't go back to Kilatas. In a stroke, they had been reduced to nothing.

It was like Moa said: Why bother to struggle, when all your best efforts could be obliterated by a sweep of chance? Better to let the current take you than to swim against it. You would only exhaust yourself and the current would take you anyway.

She was marking time. He could tell. Three days left. In her heart, she still held out for the possibility that the Secret Police would release them in time to return to Kilatas. They might throw themselves on Kittiwake's mercy and join her in her futile attempt at escaping Orokos. Rail felt fatalistic enough that he might have even been tempted to join her. But they would not be released. The Secret Police didn't release ghetto-folk.

It was over.

4.9 The Secret Police came for them the next day. They had been given basic food and water, suffered the embarrassment of having to use the cell toilet in each other's presence, and passed a strange night. There was only one bed, and Rail had initially let Moa take it while he tried to sleep on the floor. After some time she had invited him to share the bed with her. They lay together in each other's arms, and Moa, exhausted, had fallen instantly asleep. Rail, however, had been kept awake by the warmth of her body, the feel of her bony frame, and the faint pressure of her breath against his throat. How casual she could be sometimes, not knowing what she was doing to him by letting him hold her this way.

For a time, he resented her for it. He had lost all hope, and he had accepted that. But now she had reminded him of something he had all but forgotten these past days: that he had one thing worth clinging to and fighting for, and she lay in his arms that night.

They were taken from the cell at midday by four burly, shaven-head guards. They were escorted down corridors and up stairs, passing nothing but doors, all closed and marked with some incoherant coding system. There wasn't a sound except for the squeak of the guards' boots and the tiny hum of Rail's respirator pack. They passed nobody else in the corridor. The Null Spire might have been deserted for all they knew.

Eventually they came to the office of Lysander Bane, Chief of the Protectorate Secret Police. It wasn't in any way special, merely another door. It opened into a grey room with one curved wall at the back, where a window looked out on to the Fulcrum. They had never seen it this close or from this high up before: an immense frozen whirlwind of glass shards, dwarfing the Null Spire. In front of the window was a grey desk, and grey metal cabinets stood along one side of the room. It was a fine day outside, but the window had a tint that dampened the sunlight and made the office seem drab. The only concessions to ornamentation were three paintings that were placed about the room. Two depicted scenes of troops marching, and one was a portrait of the Patrician in his black surgeon's smock coat and his faceless mask. On the wall was a bronze plaque, on which was engraved the legend WE WILL MAKE THIS WORLD RIGHT AGAIN — BENEJES FRINE. It was a quote from someone neither Rail nor Moa had ever heard of.

Sitting at the desk was Bane, reading a report. They didn't know his real name, but they had seen him on the panopticon, and they knew him as Grimjack. He didn't introduce himself.

Standing in the corner of the room like a hunched gargoyle was Vago.

Moa let out a little cry at the sight of him, but the joy on her face drained away as Vago stared back blankly at her. She pieced together the situation. He was standing on Bane's side of the desk, the light from the window falling on the metal half of his ruined face. She hadn't allowed herself to believe before, but as she saw him she knew what Rail had known: He was the betrayer. He was on Bane's side now.

She turned away from him, her face hardening. "She was right," she muttered to Rail, her voice full of rage and hurt. "Kittiwake was right."

"That would be Kittiwake of Kilatas?" said Bane, whose hearing was sharper than Moa had imagined. He didn't look up from his desk. "Leader of the previously secret — and very illegal —

underground community that is planning to try and sail away from Orokos two days from now?"

"No!" Moa cried, reaching out to lunge across the desk. He knew. He knew everything. Rail grabbed her arm and she reluctantly backed down. The two guards, who had remained in the room by the door, relaxed again.

Moa was trembling with suppressed emotion, glaring hatefully at the golem. Vago met her gaze for a moment, then wavered and looked out the window.

"Well. First Anya-Jacana, and now Vago. It seems you do have poor taste in allies," Bane said, putting aside a form he was reading with a brusque snap of paper. "Between him and your friend Finch, we already know all we need to know about your little adventures."

"The Secret Police must be scraping the barrel if you need kids like Finch to do your work for you," Rail said. He was determined not to be cowed. They were going to kill him and Moa anyway. He might as well be defiant.

"Finch is turning into quite the surprise, actually," Bane said. "I'm considering him for a trial apprenticeship in the Secret Police. He seems to have fallen into line nicely, all things considered. Doesn't even seem to mind the Persuader I had to put on him. Of course, you never can tell with you ghetto-folk, so I think I'll leave it attached to him for a while longer. Just to ensure his loyalty." He got up from his desk. He was much taller than Rail and Moa were. "I am hoping that you will be as co-operative."

Moa said nothing about her encounter with Finch, when she had helped him get the Persuader off his arm. Bane didn't seem to know about that, and Finch hadn't told him. She didn't know what it meant, or if it meant anything at all, but she wasn't going to help Bane out by telling him. Finch was the lesser of two evils at the moment. He was just a murderer. These were the Secret Police.

"What have we done wrong?" Rail asked. "Why are we here?"

Bane walked around to the other side of his desk. "Well, you're thieves. That's what you've done wrong. But we all know that's not really why you're here. After all, I'd be inclined to overlook something like that. You're ghetto-folk; it's in your blood to be criminals." He came closer, his brows creasing into a frown. "You're here because of the artifact you found. We very nearly didn't get it at all, you know. If Vago hadn't told us, we might never have even known you had it. All the time Finch was after you because of that artifact, and we didn't know. He's a tricky one; I admire that."

"So how did you find us?" Rail asked.

Bane felt indulgent enough to tell him. "Finch's Persuader has a device that allowed us to track him. Once Vago told me about the artifact I realised why Finch was after you. I sent along some of my people, both to help him capture you and to ensure he behaved. They arrived just in time, it seems."

Suddenly Rail understood why they were here, why they hadn't been disposed of already. The Secret Police already knew as much as they did about the artifact, so there was only one possibility left. He laughed suddenly.

"You can't make it work, can you?" he said.

Bane backhanded him across the face. It came without warning and was delivered without passion. Rail staggered backwards, then came back up again with his hand against his cheek. Bane gazed at him with dull eyes, flexing his hand. He had probably

236

hurt himself more than Rail, for most of the impact had been absorbed by the metal muzzle of the respirator. But the message was received. Rail didn't feel like goading him anymore. Flippancy would not be tolerated.

Moa was blinking back angry tears, but she held herself in check.

"How does it work?" Bane asked her.

"I don't know," she said through gritted teeth. "I put it on, and it works. I don't do anything."

Bane stared at her hard. "Would you like us to torture your friend until you tell us the truth?"

"I *am* telling you the truth," she snapped.

He looked at her a moment longer, then turned away. "I believe you are." He walked over to the window and stood there, his hands linked behind his back. "We've learned a lot about Fade-Science over the years. Some devices are designed to be used by only one person — they recognise the wearer and can't be used by anyone else. Perhaps you accidentally triggered something. Perhaps it was only that you were the first person who must have worn it in many, many lifetimes, and it reset itself. Who knows? It was just chance." He turned back with a salesman's smile. "Well then, I have a deal for you."

"A deal?"

"A deal. I'm not a man who believes in using force when I can achieve compliance. It's much less trouble if you work with me than against me."

Moa brushed her hair away from her face. "What's the deal?"

"Simply this," he said. "You help me with a little problem, and your friends in Kilatas can sail away quite happily. I won't try to stop them."

237

Vago, in the corner, shifted uneasily at this. Moa didn't respond, sensing that Bane was going to go on.

"You see, Kittiwake's calculations are all well and good but she hasn't accounted for one thing: She has been testing with unmanned crafts. But the Skimmers can tell when there are living beings on board a ship. If the people of Kilatas try to sail, the Skimmers will come in the hundreds. Not a single person will be left alive, mark me."

"How do you know?" said Moa, her voice quiet with the edge of hysterical anger. "How do you know that?"

"Don't you think we've tried it ourselves?" Bane said. His face and chest were shadowed by the light behind him. The Fulcrum glittered over his shoulder. "Don't you think, in all this time, that we might have tried it? And with better resources and better techniques than Kittiwake's shabby operation? We loaded people like you onto barges and sent them out to see what would happen. We did exactly what Kittiwake wants to do. And they *all* died."

Rail and Moa were stunned at the raw cruelty of this. Bane spoke as disinterestedly as if he had been talking about buying vegetables.

"Did you know that we tried to build flying machines once?" he said. "Oh, we have the technology. It's just that if anything nonliving takes to the sky above this city, it gets torn to pieces by airborne Skimmers. They come out of the water and swarm at it. Even gliders and balloons."

Rail felt a slowly squeezing dread in his belly. Bane was telling them too much. Would he really let them go with this kind of knowledge?

238

Bane walked up to Moa. He regarded her coolly. "You can help."

"Why should I help?" said Moa. "You just told me that the people of Kilatas will die no matter what I do."

"No," he said. "There is a way, perhaps, to save them. *If* you cooperate with me. There is a way that we can both get what we want. Kittiwake can sail away unharmed, and we can do the greatest service to our city that has ever been done in all of remembered history, in all the days since the Fade."

Moa was terrified. "What do I have to do?"

He stepped aside and swept a hand to indicate the colossal, alien construction beyond the window. "Use the artifact. Get us into the Fulcrum," he said. "We're going to rid this city of the probability storms and the Revenants and maybe even the Skimmers." He looked back at them, and something like fever danced in his gaze. "We're going to destroy the Chaos Engine."

There was a shocked silence from Rail to Moa. Was what he was proposing even *possible*? Did he really intend to try to get inside the greatest fortress in Orokos, where nobody had penetrated before? Did the Chaos Engine, the legendary source of the probability storms, even exist?

And yet, if it could be done, then they might shut down the storms . . . the scourge of their existence since the days of their ancestors . . . the phenomenon that had put Rail in a respirator, which had cost thousands, *millions* of lives through the havoc it wreaked and the Revenants it unleashed. They might make Orokos whole. They might kill the Storm Thief.

"Do you see that plaque?" Bane asked, pointing to the quote on the wall. " '*We will make this world right again.*' That's a sentence from one of the few surviving fragments of pre-Fade language we have managed to translate. Benejes Frine was an important man, the greatest scientist of the Faded, if our studies are correct. I believe he wrote that after the Chaos Engine wrecked this city. He lived in a perfect world and he saw it torn apart by Revenants. Now I'm carrying on his work. I'll make this world right again."

It was while considering this that Rail spotted someone else in the room, another witness to Bane's declaration. She had been listening all along, hiding behind the statue of the Patrician in one of the paintings. Lelek, the girl who lived in pictures. No wonder she had known where Vago was being taken when he disappeared. She had been keeping an eye on him. Rail wondered briefly what the connection was between the girl and the golem, but he knew he would get no answers from either of them.

He knew Lelek couldn't help them now. And Rail wasn't even sure he wanted to be helped. As much as he hated the Secret Police, he had to admit that Bane's plan was tempting. When they had the artifact, Rail had been thinking small-time. He would have used it to rob a vault or a rich family's house. Bane had bigger ideas.

You always wanted to change the world, Rail, he said to himself. *Now's your chance.*

"One condition," Moa said. "Rail comes with me."

"Agreed," said Bane.

Moa studied him a moment longer. Enemies they might be, but they all wanted the same thing. If she could get to the heart of the Fulcrum, maybe there would be a way to deactivate the Skimmers. Not only would Kittiwake and the people of Kilatas be saved, but the doors of their prison would have been blown off. They could escape. *Anyone* could escape.

"Deal," she said.

Bane nodded at the guards, and Rail and Moa were led away, back to their cells. When Vago and Bane were alone, the golem spoke at last.

"Even if this works, Bane, you don't really intend to let those ghetto scum from Kilatas be the first people to reach the sea, do you?" he growled. "Think of the publicity. A fleet of junk ships beats the Protectorate Navy to the prize."

Bane sat back at his desk and began looking through his papers again. "Of course I don't. Perhaps they are sailing to nowhere, perhaps not. But I'm not going to let some ragged group of outcasts become the inspiration for a generation of rebels. Our forces in the western Territories are assembling already. By tomorrow evening, Kilatas will be just an unpleasant memory." He turned in his chair and considered the golem, fingers steepled under his chin. "You will come with us into the Fulcrum tomorrow. I need to field-test your capabilities. It will be as good a time as any."

"I still have several days of conditioning left to undergo," the golem reminded him. "I would not want to be a liability to the Protectorate."

Bane smiled to himself. "I trust you won't be," he said. In fact, the golem had responded unusually well to the conditioning. Between the revelations about his ugly past and the truth of the present, his spirit had been broken even before the machine got to work on him. And besides, conditioning him properly was something of a waste of time. Once they had fully tested his capabilities, they would have to dissect him to get out all the prototype parts they had put into his body.

But there was another reason for him to be there: The

Fulcrum was home to the Chaos Engine, and the Chaos Engine was home to the Revenants. Vago was their ultimate weapon against the energy ghosts.

"I will do my best to live up to your trust," Vago said. He left Bane soon after, and Bane sat at his desk and dreamed of perfection. After a time, he began to plan.

Tomorrow they would go to the Fulcrum. Tomorrow they would change the world. There were preparations to be made.

PART FIVE:

The Fulcrum

5.1

Moa stood at the foot of the Fulcrum, her heart pounding. Before her and above her, the forbidden citadel of the Faded blocked out the sky. It was a bladed cyclone of metal and glass, glinting maddeningly in the midday sun. Hiding within were the secrets of a lost age, if rumours were to be believed. Since the Fade, nobody had managed to penetrate it. It had no doors, no windows, and its surface, though glass-like, was made of something utterly indestructible by any technology that the people of Orokos knew.

Moa waited at the head of three hundred Protectorate soldiers and Secret Police, in the great paved plaza that surrounded the foot of the Fulcrum. More guards prowled around the edges of the plaza, fending off curious spectators. Bane let them watch. They would see, for the first time in history, the defences of the Fulcrum breached. Or so he believed. Moa wasn't so sure.

There had been brief tests yesterday to ensure that the artifact worked in Moa's hands. It had performed superbly.

So they needed her. That was the reason she and Rail were still here. And Bane certainly didn't waste any time. He had obtained the approval of the Patrician and had assembled the forces he needed in less than a day. Moa wasn't sure what had provoked such haste. Maybe it was simply that planning made no difference when they hadn't the least idea what awaited them inside. And maybe it was just that Bane couldn't wait. She saw, behind his rigid composure, a burning passion for order. She knew that the chance to strike at the Chaos Engine was what he had waited for all his life. That was why he was leading them personally into the Fulcrum.

Moa didn't dare think of what would come next if she laid her hand on the flank of the Fulcrum and nothing happened. What if the artifact couldn't penetrate the skin of this place? Bane had invested too much in this; it was too public. The humiliation would be terrible for him if it didn't work. The last thing she would hear would be the sound of an aether cannon as it blew her soul apart.

She felt Rail's hand reach into hers, and she clutched his fingers tightly. The pressure helped to calm the fluttering inside her. Her ribs were a cage of panicked birds.

On their right stood Finch. He was no longer wearing his black, close-fitting clothes and cowl. Now he had on a long trenchcoat and jackboots, and his head was bare, his wispy white-blond hair straggling across a naked skull. He was dressed as one of the Secret Police. He bared his rotten fangs in a smile as Moa caught his eye, and she looked away hurriedly. Both he and Vago were Bane's men now.

Vago himself stood next to Bane. He was as silent as ever, but now Moa saw the horror of him. Whereas before she hadn't thought him ugly, he had become suddenly terrifying. Perhaps he had always been that way, only she hadn't seen it. He didn't appear to notice her, but she felt a pang of loss as she looked at him. He had been a companion to her once, even a friend, and friends were in short supply in this world. He had saved her life in Territory West 190. He had adored her. But since meeting Bane, he had become something different, and when he looked at her it was with disdain. She didn't know what Bane had done to him, but it had shrivelled him, and now he was like a hard blackened nut instead of the wide-eyed child she had met many days ago.

Rail had been right. She was too softhearted. She was too willing to believe the best of people, when it made more sense to assume everyone was a potential enemy until they proved otherwise. But when she said this to Rail, he surprised her by his response.

"No," he said softly. "Don't ever think that. That's what *I* think, and I wish I didn't. You have faith in people, Moa; you're willing to give. I can't do that, but being with you when you do it makes my life a little more worth living."

Her thoughts were brought back to the present as Bane walked over to her. He looked sternly down and said, "It's time."

Rail gave her hand a final squeeze and released it. She and Bane went ahead of the mass of troops, across the short distance to the base of the Fulcrum. It leaned out over them, for it was narrower at its base than at the top, and she couldn't help a feeling of vertigo. Bane said nothing as they walked up to the sloping side of the building. There was no obvious way in, no doorway or any part that might be better than any other. It was a complete unknown.

She looked at their reflection in the massive leaf-blade of reflective material. They were tiny in the mirror it made. She reached out and touched it. It was freezing, though the day was clear and warm.

Bane handed her the artifact. She put it on, and it swirled into life.

"I don't . . ." she began. *I don't know if this will work*, she meant to say, but she realised it was pointless. Words would not change anything. Bane pretended not to have heard her.

She put her hand again to the mirror, this time with the artifact resting in her palm.

247

Nothing happened.

Moa swallowed. Bane looked sidelong at her.

Still nothing happened.

And then the colours shifted, flowing from her arm and across the wall. Moa let out a sigh of relief, but her relief didn't last long. The colours were not forming a doorway. Instead, they kept on spreading, becoming thicker and brighter as they crept over the mirrored blade that she touched, and beyond. Waves of gauzy purples and reds flooded from her palm across the Fulcrum. Alarmed, she was about to draw her hand away when Bane grabbed her wrist and held it there. She met his gaze with fear in her eyes.

"It's not supposed to do this!" she said.

"Let's see what happens," Bane replied. He wasn't afraid. He could think of no price that he wouldn't pay to get inside this place.

The colours faded, draining from Moa's arm, sucked out of her. The artifact had no more to give. The veils that drifted across the surface of the Fulcrum had become absorbed into the mirrors, as if the building was drinking the energy greedily. All went quiet.

Finally, Bane released her, and she stepped back. She looked at the amber disc in her hand. There was no light there; it had lost the strange quality that had made it seem deep. She knew, without any way of being certain, that the artifact was only an ornament now. Its power had been leached. It was dead.

If the artifact was dead, then Bane had no more use for her. She closed her hand around the disc. She couldn't let him know.

She and Bane stepped back. The Fulcrum was just as it had

been. It was as if it had never been touched. And yet they were both waiting for something.

All at once, the Fulcrum turned red. As if it was a mirror that had turned towards a crimson sunset, every one of its reflective facets went the colour of rich, dark blood. No longer a tornado of ice, it was a frozen rose, jagged and deformed and threatening. The gasp from the assembled spectators was audible across the plaza, and some people shrieked and began to cry.

Then it began to unfold.

The shrieking of the spectators became panic. The troops looked at one another nervously and shuffled in the ranks. Their commanders ordered them to move back to a safe distance. Bane took Moa by the arm and marched her to where Rail and Finch and Vago were. Together they watched.

The Fulcrum was unwrapping, its uppermost parts peeling back like the petals of a flower. It was utterly silent; there was no grinding of gears or squeal of tortured metal as it bent. Bane was impressed. Incredible that a building could move like this. More evidence of how ignorant they were compared to the civilisations that had lived before the Fade ever took place.

They stood mesmerised as it uncurled and shifted, like a nest of snakes slowly writhing. The mirrors on its flanks were angling this way and that, making it seem as if the whole surface was in motion. And then it abruptly stopped, its top crowned with dozens of slanted tendrils of glass that had locked into place. It seemed bigger than before, like a pinecone that had opened up.

There was a breathless hush, deeper even than the silence that had attended its movement.

"We're in," said Bane quietly, and pointed.

249

He was right. At the base of the Fulcrum, the panels that had armoured it lay flat, offering a hundred entrances. All the way up the structure, the bladed mirrors had peeled back, opening the interior to the air.

"*We're in!*" Bane cried again, fierce excitement in his voice. He set off towards the Fulcrum, his troops in tow, Rail and Moa with him at gunpoint.

5.2

The temperature dropped the instant they set foot inside the Fulcrum, as if they had stepped through a curtain of cold air. Bane insisted on being the first in, and after him went Rail, Moa, Vago, and Finch with a small retinue of Secret Police. The soldiers followed warily behind, their eyes hidden by glimmer visors, their aether cannons held ready.

The openings fed into high tunnels with arched roofs that dipped in the middle. They were ribbed along the way and carved of some smooth substance that could have been either marbly stone or metal. There wasn't a join or seam to be seen — the construction was uncannily perfect. Wafts of cool air that tasted flat and lifeless drifted from the interior. Rail had the unpleasant sensation of walking down the throat of some great beast towards its stomach.

He was thinking only of escape, but escape at this point seemed impossible. Moa, next to him, was awed by the gravity of what was happening to them. They were *inside the Fulcrum*, something that nobody had done since the Fade. But Rail felt nothing of the grandeur of the moment. He knew for sure that there was no way the Secret Police would let them live after what they had seen. They were ghetto-folk — less than human, and very expendable.

Rail was searching for opportunity. Nobody knew what they would face inside this place. Uncertainty was his advantage. Once, he had wanted to be the greatest thief in Orokos. Now he just wanted to survive, and to get Moa out of here.

Bane — they knew that was his name now, for they had heard the other Secret Police refer to him — had taken the artifact from Moa once she had opened up the Fulcrum. Rail wondered why they were being brought inside along with the troops, but he reasoned that there might be more barriers within, and that Moa might be needed again.

The tunnel they were following went inward for some way before it ended. They stepped slowly into the room beyond, and there they gaped in wonder. Even Rail couldn't help but be impressed.

It was like a dream made solid. A colossal hall of black and purple, fashioned in several levels that were connected by curving ramps. Everything was made of some glistening material that was hard as stone but had been shaped like wax. Each part of the complex arrangement of balconies, free-standing platforms, bridges, and wedding-cake structures was rounded and smoothed. Soft light of an indeterminate colour, somewhere between green and blue, washed over the scene from globes that hung in the air like miniature suns. Trenches filled with a glowing liquid of the same hue traced back and forth across the floor, describing restful patterns.

The troops began filtering this way and that, spreading out to secure positions. They were treating this like the invasion of an enemy base. Bane, however, walked boldly out towards the middle of the chamber. His retinue followed him. Their footfalls made no sound, even though the surface they walked on was hard. The only noise was the whisper of clothes, the tap of weaponry, and the occasional hushed order from one of the soldiers.

Bane stopped and stood like a rock around which the troops broke. It was as if he was an explorer, having triumphantly set

252

foot in his new world, and he was now surveying the land he had claimed.

"Nobody's home," said Rail flippantly. Bane turned on him and fixed him with a steady glare. Finch grinned at his insubordination.

"Then we've nothing to fear," Bane replied. He produced a small black device, like a round stone of polished darkness. It pulsed softly as he held it up.

Finch eyed it appraisingly, calculating its value. "What's that?"

"This is why we know that the rumours about the Chaos Engine are true," Bane muttered, looking into the stone. There were tiny lights inside it, all rushing in one direction. "This is a piece of Fade-Science we found long ago. We've established that its purpose is to detect probability energy. Like a compass, it always points towards the Fulcrum. That means that somewhere in this place is the most powerful source of probability energy in Orokos. And that will be the Chaos Engine. This thing will lead us to it."

"And what then?" Moa asked.

"You'll see," Bane replied. He looked around the hall again, then consulted the device in his hand. "It's this way."

"Chief!" snapped one of the Secret Police at his side. "Movement!"

The soldiers had gone still, their cannons raised, a hundred weapons trained on the large black sphere that was floating down from the roof of the chamber. It descended unhurriedly towards the centre of the room, near where Bane and the others stood.

Moa clutched Rail's thin arm. He felt her nails dig in through his jacket.

"Hold fire!" Bane said.

253

The sphere dropped to a hover ten feet above the ground. Rail could see himself reflected in its surface. It was deadly silent.

"There's more," muttered one of Bane's men, and he looked to see several spheres, identical to the first, gliding downwards from the shadows overhead at varying speeds. They came to a halt at different heights, in an apparently random fashion.

"If you were the Faded," Rail murmured to Moa, "and you were building these things to provide a reception to visitors, would you make them look like that if they were friendly?"

Moa shook her head. She had a dreadful feeling about this.

"Me, neither," he said, and dropped his voice further so that nobody could hear. "Get ready to run. Something's going to happen."

As one, the spheres changed. Now their surfaces were not merely featureless black, but each displayed an emblem in deep red. They were stylised and flickered like a bad panopticon projection, but it was clear enough what the emblems were. Skulls.

Rail felt his heart plummet to his stomach. The great chamber, that he had thought resembled a dream, had turned into a nightmare.

The skull-spheres emitted a deafening scream, and a wind blasted through the chamber, blowing Rail's dreadlocks into a frenzy and almost pulling Moa off her feet. With the wind came an immense sensation of absolute terror that swamped them all, an animal panic that made Rail gag inside his respirator with the raw and suffocating strength of it. He had a moment to think *this is not real this is not real there's nothing to be afraid of* but then his thoughts scattered under the maddening fear that the skull-spheres transmitted. Like everyone else in the room, he lost his mind.

He barely knew where he was, only that it was the most awful place he had ever been and that he had to get out. But he couldn't make his legs move; his muscles had turned to water. The red skulls were everywhere, floating in the air, shrieking. He scrambled to get away, pawing over other bodies. When he looked down at them, their faces were horrible, distorted, eyes glaring and black. They were monsters — he was surrounded by monsters. Nothing else mattered but escape.

And yet there was nowhere to go. The monsters were everywhere.

He flailed in one direction, then another, then tripped over something and went crashing to the ground. It was one of the monsters, curled tightly into a ball. Instinctively he was afraid of it, but he seemed to recognise it, too. Something inside him prevented him from running. Nearby, someone was firing an aether cannon. He looked and saw some of the monsters had guns and were shooting into the air and at one another. He cringed under the force of the skull-spheres' din, and fell to his knees next to the whimpering shape.

not real

The sight of the curled-up monster somehow gave him the will to clamp down his fear, enough to grab snatches of sanity from the chaos. He reached down to the thing in front of him, wanting to uncurl it and discover what it was. His hands touched flesh. The cool skin of an arm. Moa. It was Moa.

the fear is not real it's not real it's not

He grabbed her and she shrieked, struggling against his grip. But she was too weak and too afraid to fight hard. He picked her up and the two of them found their feet. She was Rail's anchor, to stop him from sliding into hysteria again.

"Moa!" he cried. "Moa, it's me!"

But his voice sounded like a horrible clattering noise to her, and she screamed and tried to cover her ears. So he pulled her, dragging her in some direction, any direction. All around him he could hear men shouting and the squeal of aether cannons. There was a dead soldier on the ground before him.

just a man, not a monster after all

Some instinct made him reach down and tear the glimmer visor from the soldier's face. It was only later that he realised why he had done it. The soldiers were firing into the air, at invisible enemies. That meant only one thing.

Revenants.

He put the visor to his eyes and saw.

The Protectorate soldiers were in chaos. They were driven mad by the fear that the skull-spheres emitted, and they fought one another and anything else that moved. Some were fleeing down the tunnel towards the outside, some were shooting in all directions, others were huddled in fright. And between them went the sparkling shapes of the Revenants, swooping on manta-ray wings to possess the bodies of their victims. Already two dozen newly made Taken were attacking people. But most of the Revenants were not interested in the little force that had invaded the Fulcrum — they were headed through the tunnel, towards the open air.

Rail had a momentary vision of what the crowds waiting outside would see. They had opened up the Fulcrum, but the Fulcrum was full of Revenants. Like a wasp's nest that had been disturbed, the Revenants would swarm. Soon, the screams would begin. The Null Spire would be the first target, since Revenants always attacked Protectorate constructions before any other. After that they would flood the district. The nerve centre of Orokos would be compromised. The consequences would be disastrous.

They should never have opened the Fulcrum. They didn't know what they were meddling with.

But Rail couldn't think about that now. He had to get himself and Moa to safety. Somehow he had staggered a fair way across the chamber, and whether it was his imagination or not, the fear seemed to have lessened in him. The glimmer visor filtered out the worst of the hallucinations, and the presence of Moa give him courage. He had to be strong, to look after her. She needed him.

He remembered how he had almost decided that they should split up, that he would leave her to go with Kittiwake while he made his own way in the city. How ridiculous that seemed now. They couldn't do without each other. He would let nothing separate them again.

The cry of the skull-spheres was quieting now, and Rail saw why. Some of the soldiers had been smart enough to fire at the source of their distress, bringing thumper guns to bear. Several of the spheres had been blown out of the air. The skull-spheres were some mechanism of the Faded to incapacitate their enemies through fear. Each time one fell Rail sensed the pressure of panic easing a little, and he could think more clearly.

The soldiers were organising against the Revenants now, but Rail was intent only on escape. Moa, frightened out of her mind, was sobbing, but she had stopped resisting him, and they ran together towards a tunnel. Blobs of aether sizzled over their heads and Revenants glided and swooped, but the two ghetto children were not noticed by anyone or anything until they had almost reached the tunnel mouth.

Rail paused there and looked back. As he did, his visored gaze met that of Vago, who had been obliterating Revenants fearlessly. The golem was defending Bane, and several Revenants had already made the mistake of trying to attack him. They had been absorbed on contact. The ridge of his spine sparked with aether energy.

At the sight of Rail, Vago snarled, glowering in hatred. He threw his weapon aside and came pounding across the room on all fours, his metal-frame wings spread above him. Bane called him back, but Vago didn't hear or didn't listen.

Rail swore under his breath and pulled Moa into a run, and the golem came after them.

5.3

In the depths of Kilatas, beneath hundreds of feet of dank rock, men and women and children prepared for their departure. Tomorrow they would set out for the promised land. Tomorrow all they had lived for would come to fruition. Tomorrow they would run the gauntlet of the Skimmers.

None of them dared to entertain the thought that they would fail. They hurried to make watertight the last of the boats. The shipyards rang with industry. Each extra craft heightened their chances of survival by giving the Skimmers another target to distract themselves with. There was a constant supply of rough food coming in through the secret ways that led down from the city. People were spending the last of their meagre savings on supplies, and those who had remained above to guard Kilatas's doors were returning to the town.

Kittiwake walked with Ortolan towards her shack. To their right were the shipyards, a mass of scaffolding covered with clambering metalworkers and shipwrights. To their left were the cluttered docks where dozens of ships — rusty tubs, junks, tugs, anything with an engine — jostled at their moorings. They had checked and checked again the explosives wired into the western wall, ready to collapse it and let in the sunlight, to provide a route to the open sea. Except for the scramble to make the last vessels seaworthy, everything was in place. And yet Kittiwake couldn't shake the feeling that something was very, very wrong.

Just nerves, she told herself. But she didn't quite believe it.

Ortolan was a self-taught scholar and a natural genius. It was he who had worked out the complex algorithms that predicted in

259

what numbers the Skimmers would come. It was also he who had calculated the probabilities of survival based on the speed and number of the ships, the speed and number of Skimmers, and the distance across the killing zone (which also fluctuated from day to day, and had to be predicted and taken into account).

There was no appreciable difference in seasons in Orokos, no years or months. Anything longer than a few dozen days was referred to in a vague way, as "ages ago," or likened to another event, such as "back when we had the flood." So Kittiwake really had no idea how long it had been since she'd started assembling the people who would build Kilatas, how long it had taken Ortolan to make his calculations, how long they had spent making ships. But it had all come to this.

Ortolan was a small, mole-like man with slit-eyed goggles, a squat, hunched appearance, and a fringe of greying hair around a bald pate. He shuffled around in a battered brown coat, muttering to himself. Next to him, Kittiwake walked straight-backed, surveying all, her hair a tight ponytail and her face stern. She should have been ecstatic to see all this, to know that it was all finally going to happen . . . but something was sour, and she couldn't tell what.

She and Ortolan entered her dim shack, still talking over the impending departure, and she closed the door behind them. She stood there a moment, as if listening; then she looked around the room purposefully. Ortolan was rambling about a new idea he had for assigning townsfolk to boats. He noticed her expression.

"What's wrong?" he asked.

"There's something different," she replied. "The room doesn't feel right. Like something's been moved."

"You've been jumpy for days now," Ortolan said.

"I know." She cast around the room again. "There."

It was the painting. Lelek was back. She had been absent for the last few days, ever since she had directed Rail and Moa to the Null Spire.

The picture in the frame was completely different. Before, it had depicted a street scene — but now that could barely be seen in the background. Almost all of the picture was taken up by Lelek. She was so close it seemed that she was about to climb out of the picture, her face frozen in a scream, her eyes alarmed. One hand was spread as if pressed against a window, like she was trying to push through the painting and into the real world beyond. The other was drawn back in a fist, hammering at some invisible barrier.

Kittiwake felt a chill. She stood before the painting and studied it. The girl was so lifelike, it was hard to believe that she was only ink and water. There was a pleading in her eyes. Her scream was part fear, part desperation. Kittiwake looked closer. No, Lelek wasn't afraid for herself. She was begging, wanting the person on the other side of the painting to listen to her, unable to make herself understood.

"What does it mean?" Ortolan asked.

And suddenly Kittiwake knew. Vago's escape, Rail and Moa going to the Null Spire, and now this. It was a *warning*.

"Oh, freck. They've found out about us," she breathed. "The Protectorate. They know about Kilatas." She turned to Ortolan, her voice hardening. "They'll be coming."

"What? Eh?" Ortolan blustered. "How do you know? How can you tell?"

Kittiwake ignored him, stalking around the room. "We have to go. We have to sail. Right now."

261

"We can't sail now! The Skimmers will tear us apart!"

"If we don't leave now, we won't leave at all! If the Protectorate know about us then they already have troops on the way. They'll have Dreadnoughts assembling on the water by tonight. We won't get two hundred yards out into the ocean, and if we try to abandon this place and flee we'll just run right into the soldiers."

"But the Skimmers . . . !"

Kittiwake looked out of the window, arms folded, tapping her foot in agitation. "We can mobilise in a few hours. Most of the supplies are loaded. We can leave the unfinished ships behind. We just need to get everyone on board." Her gaze was flickering over the people working on the shipyards outside. "If we left today, what would be the casualties?"

"Ninety percent," Ortolan replied immediately. "We'd be facing seven Skimmers."

"Ninety percent," said Kittiwake, feeling slightly sick. "Versus one hundred percent if the Protectorate get here in time."

"If the Protectorate are coming at all," Ortolan added. He scratched the top of his head and sounded apologetic. "There's an awful lot of people who'll pay if you're wrong."

"And I might be one of them," said Kittiwake. "I know what's at stake here. I'm *not* wrong."

Ortolan peered at her doubtfully through his goggles. "Are you sure?"

"I'm sure I'd rather die than have the Protectorate take away our one chance at freedom," she said, and in the dull light from the grimy window she looked suddenly like a statue. Then she snapped a glance at Ortolan, and the illusion was broken.

"We sail. Now."

5.4

Rail and Moa fled down a smooth tunnel of pale blue, lined with metallic ridges and dotted with recessed lights that cast a soothing glow. Behind them, they could hear Vago getting closer.

"I'm on your back, scum!" came the wrecked voice from down the corridor. "There's nowhere to hide!"

"There!" Rail hissed. Moa, who was already out of breath, saw what he was pointing at: some kind of grille, like silver webbing, set low on one side of the tunnel. Beyond was a duct or a crawlway or . . . they didn't know what it might be. But it was too small for Vago to follow them into. Probably.

Rail skidded to his knees and grabbed the grille to see if he could pull it off. To his surprise, it melted away at his touch, leaving a round hole and darkness beyond. A featureless pipe, apparently, made of the same alien substance as the walls of the tunnel. They couldn't afford to be picky.

Rail ushered Moa in, and she went without hesitation. Whatever was at the end of that pipe couldn't be as bad as what was coming after them. But once inside she found it was barely big enough to admit her shoulders. There would be no space at all to turn around. The claustrophobia was overwhelming, the blackness total. They could easily get stuck in here, with no way to go but back. She was afraid of not being able to breathe.

But she had spent most of her adolescence as a thief, and she had gotten through narrower spaces than this before. She wriggled inward. The unyielding sides of the pipe pressed close to her.

Rail glanced nervously back up the tunnel just as Vago appeared, springing round the corner and racing towards Rail with his steel fangs bared. Rail crammed himself into the pipe after Moa, for he was almost the same size and thin as a rake. He bumped his respirator pack against the top of the pipe with a hollow clang. For an instant he thought that he would be stuck there, legs dangling out for the golem to savage. But he scrambled along, following the dirty soles of Moa's boots, and got completely inside.

Vago's face appeared in the circle of light at the end of the pipe. He reached in, his long arm stretching enough so that his middle finger scraped along the side of Rail's foot. But he couldn't get a grip, and by the time he tried again, Rail was too far away.

"I'll find you!" he howled after them. "I'll find you, you detestable ghetto spawn!"

And then, with a final curse, he was gone, and there was only the sound of their frantic breathing as they shuffled up the pipe.

Once they were far enough along, Rail awkwardly passed Moa the glimmer visor he had taken from the fallen soldier. It offered adequate nightvision, and since she was in the lead she needed it more than he did. She managed to put it on with a bit of jostling. The dim yellow-green scene that greeted her eyes was unremarkable — the pipe was as featureless as they had imagined — but at least she could see, and that eased the oppression of their situation a little.

"What happened to him?" she said, her voice echoing.

"Vago?" Rail replied. "He was a spy. He was like that all along. This is what he really thought of us."

"No," she murmured. "No, he's changed."

"He hasn't changed," Rail said firmly. "He was just a very good actor. He fooled us all." He sighed. "Now let's just get out of here. There were hundreds of exits, remember? The whole Fulcrum opened up. We need to find one."

Moa thought for a moment. "But what about the Skimmers?"

"What *about* them?"

"If we don't shut them off, the people of Kilatas will die."

"How do we shut them off? You think there'll just be a switch?"

"Why not?" Moa countered.

"Well, do *you* know where it is? 'Cause I sure as freck don't." Rail pushed her feet and she began wriggling again. "There's hundreds of Protectorate army soldiers back there," he said. "You think we can do it if they can't? If we get out of here now, we'll have time to get to Kilatas and warn them. Maybe by then Bane will have managed to shut off the Engine or something."

Moa chewed her lip. What he said made sense, but she couldn't help feeling that he was just trying to make her agree to escape with him. "Didn't you want to change your world, Rail? Don't you want to try?"

"I tried," he said. "And we ended up here. If we don't get away, the Protectorate will be the least of our worries. It's probably heaving with Revenants outside right now, and it's going to get worse."

"Then we go for the Engine. If we shut it off, the Revenants go away!"

"We are *not* heroes!" he cried, his voice becoming fuzzy as his respirator muzzle glitched. He grabbed the ankle of her boot, and she stopped. "Listen. There's nothing we can do. We have to look out for ourselves."

"It's because everyone only looks out for themselves that this world is the way it is," Moa replied quietly, and after that they went on in silence.

The pipe made several gentle turns and then began slanting upwards, passing through junctions with other pipes whose purpose was similarly unknown. Once they heard the distant hum of a massive fan and wondered if the pipes were to conduct air through the Fulcrum, or if they had some other purpose. The systems and mechanisms of the Faded were beyond their understanding.

They lost track of time. They were not sure how long it was before they saw light at the end of the pipe. Their progress had been excruciatingly slow. With weary relief, they crawled onward, until the pipe ended and they were at last able to move again.

It was a huge shaft, lit in soft green and crisscrossed by dozens of slender silver-coloured tubes. The surface of the tubes was partially transparent, and inside they could see clusters of wiring that were blue and organic and rubbery, like veins. Between the pipes, they could see down to the bottom, where still water lay below meshed metal flooring. Many small platforms, linked by metal ladders, led up from the base of the shaft towards the top, forming an uneven and broken spiral. They had come out onto one of these from the pipe.

"Up or down?" Moa asked.

Rail listened. The distant sounds of aether cannon fire could still be heard among the shouts of soldiers. There was a loud clanking noise from below as something was knocked over or thrown violently. There were people close by.

"Up," he said, against his better instincts. "Too dangerous to go down there at the moment. We'll see if we can find a way across to the other side of this shaft."

They climbed a short ladder to another platform. There was a panel of curious instruments set in the wall, covered in things that might have been buttons or faders. They could see now that there was a door of some kind on the other side of the shaft, higher up. If they kept climbing and walking along the platforms they would eventually reach it. Rail had just set his hands and feet to the next ladder when Moa sucked in her breath and clasped a hand to his shoulder. He looked back at her, and she motioned downwards with her eyes.

At the bottom of the shaft was Vago. He was prowling silently, his head turning left and right, wings half-cocked. Little bolts of aether fizzed between the metal blades that ridged his spine. He had absorbed enough Revenants in that first chamber to keep him going for a long time to come.

Rail froze where he was. Moa did the same. They watched him through the crosshatch of silver tubes, and willed him not to look up.

He crept into the centre of the room and slowed to a halt. Moa swallowed. There was suspicion in his movements. He could sense that he was being watched.

There's nothing for you here, she thought at him. *Just go. Just go.*

It was as if she had spoken aloud. He tipped his head back and his gaze found her.

"*There* you are," he growled.

Rail didn't need another prompt. He climbed the ladder as fast as he could, Moa close behind. At the bottom of the shaft, they saw Vago bunch and spring. He jumped a clear twenty feet and landed with uncanny balance on one of the silver tubes, his wings spread. As they ran along the platform to the next ladder, he jumped again, this time catching one of the tubes with his hands and pulling himself onto it. He was ascending the shaft far quicker than they were, and closing in fast.

Rail scampered up the next ladder. Now they had gotten most of the way around the circular side of the shaft and were nearing the door. On this platform was some kind of control panel, like a lectern, facing out into the centre of the shaft. On impulse, Rail kicked it, and was surprised to find that it gave a little. Though it was secured to the platform, it hadn't been meant to take heavy knocks. Rail kicked it again, hard, and it tilted. Again, and it tilted more.

Moa had reached the top of the ladder now. She saw what he was doing, and put her own boot to the task. Both of them kicked it, and it teetered. Rail shoved it the rest of the way, and it fell from the platform into the shaft, plummeting towards Vago.

The golem had heard the noise and saw the control panel tip towards him. But he was still barely able to get out of the way. It came crashing through the silver tubes, smashing them as it went and then bouncing off at a new angle as they shattered. The ruptured tubes sprayed an oily blue fluid. Vago calculated probable rebound trajectories and jumped to avoid the panel, but the tube he jumped on had been damaged and broke under his weight. The panel fell past him, ploughing a furrow of destruction down the shaft, and he fell with it for a few weightless moments before his hand clamped around an unbroken tube. He hung there as the panel finally smashed through the mesh floor and into the water at the bottom.

A rain of fluid from the squirting ends of broken tubes splattered down the shaft. He pulled himself up, his leathery brown skin streaked with blue. Then, with a howl, he sprang again, darting up the shaft in swift pounces, his fury at his prey redoubled now.

Rail and Moa hadn't waited to see the results of their vandalism. They had reached the door. But the door wasn't opening.

"Try pressing it!" Moa cried, as they attempted to decipher the featureless black panel which they guessed was the mechanism to let them inside.

"I *have* pressed it," Rail snapped back. He ran his hands over the surface of the door in an attempt to find a seam, but there was nothing.

Moa was at the edge of the platform, looking down. Vago was still coming, unstoppable. There was nowhere else to run.

"Make it work, Rail!" she pleaded desperately.

"You're the one that's good with locks!" he said. "Give me a hand here!"

"It's Fade-Science!" she protested, but she came to his side anyway. "What do I know about Fade-Science? You think I can just wave my hand at it and it will open?"

She waved her hand before the black panel to demonstrate the ridiculousness of this, and the door gave a gentle chime and opened. Rail looked at her in amazement.

"What are the chances?" she said with a shrug.

He grabbed her wrist and pulled her through the doorway. Beyond was a small room, not big enough to fit more than six or seven people in standing up, with rounded walls. It was like being inside an egg.

"Close it!" Rail urged her. They couldn't see Vago now, but any second he would appear, leaping over the edge of the platform. Moa flailed about, searching for something similar to the black panel that had opened the door, but the inside of the room was entirely smooth.

"I don't know! I don't know what to do!"

"Well, figure it out before Vago gets up here!" Rail told her.

Another chime sounded in the room the moment Rail said "up." At the same moment, the golem sailed over the edge of the platform and landed on it with a thump, six feet away from them. But he was a fraction too late. The door had already begun to slide closed. Before it had sealed entirely, they heard the golem crash against it with a thwarted shriek.

Then silence, and the sensation of movement. They were travelling upwards.

Rail looked at the ceiling of the room as if he could see through it to what lay beyond. Moa slipped her cold, pale fingers through his.

The two of them waited to see where the Fulcrum was taking them. It was all they could do.

5.5

"Hold them back! Hold them *back*!" cried the commander to Bane's right.

A volley of aether cannon fire was turned onto the creatures that were once their own men. The Revenants had possessed the husks of the soldiers, and those who had escaped that fate were now forced to mow them down. The Taken fell silently, and from their bodies rose ghosts of energy that were obliterated by the soldiers' weapons before they could attack. But there were always more.

The Protectorate forces that had penetrated the Fulcrum had splintered into a disorganised mess. The panic induced by the skull-spheres had driven men in all different directions, through the many exits from the vast chamber where they had first been attacked. Bane had managed to keep his head better than most, due to the training that all Secret Police received to strengthen their minds against torture. He and his men had fled the chamber to the tunnels, which were more defensible. Once out of there and free of the skull-spheres' influence, they had organised and gathered what pieces of the Protectorate Army they had come across. Though the situation was still desperate, they at least had a fighting chance now.

There had been talk of escape at first, but Bane had quashed that. There would be no escape. He held up the Fade-Science device that he had brought with him, the black stone full of tiny lights. It would guide them to the Chaos Engine. They were not leaving until the Engine was destroyed.

He was angry at Vago for deserting him. Part of the reason he had brought the golem was because he was the most effective weapon they had against the Revenants. But he had run off on some crazed vendetta of his own. Vago himself had warned Bane — he hadn't been properly conditioned yet. He had been taught to hate the ghetto-folk but not to control that hate. The golem was entirely unstable.

Bane hadn't lost Finch, however. The thief-boy was still at his side. Bane was surprised that he hadn't tried to flee, even with the threat of the Persuader hanging over him. He may not have been much to look at, but his sheer ruthlessness and his devious nature evoked a kind of admiration in Bane. When they got through this, he would see that the boy was schooled in the ways of the Secret Police. It was unusual to take in ghetto-folk, but not unheard of. It seemed a waste to squander talent like Finch's.

Finch hadn't been given a glimmer visor, but he was resource-ful enough to have stolen one from somewhere. Since then, he had been sticking close to Bane. He had no weapon that was effective against Revenants, whereas Bane was a dead shot with an aether cannon.

They had made their way deeper and deeper into the Fulcrum, keeping to the narrower tunnels where they could put up an effective response to any Revenants that came their way. Casualties were steadily mounting, but Bane didn't care. If it got them to their target, then every sacrifice would be worth it.

Their route had taken them up stairs and ramps. The path was lit by recessed lights and hanging globes that floated along with them. At each level they encountered new resistance, but the soldiers were growing in confidence now, and the Revenants couldn't stop them.

"It's close," Bane murmured. "It has to be close."

"Revenants to the rear!" came the cry, and there was a great surge as a horde of possessed soldiers and energy ghosts swarmed around the corner. The back end of the Protectorate group retreated up the tunnel, firing. Someone bumped Finch and he tripped, crashing into Bane and knocking him over. The two of them scrambled together comically before Bane pulled himself free and got up. He glared at the thief-boy.

"Clumsy idiot!" he snarled.

Finch grinned at him. "Sorry, Chief," he said, clearly not meaning it.

A salvo of aether shrieked down the tunnel, obliterating a dozen Revenants. Bane took a glance to be sure that the battle was under control and then pushed through the compressed mass of soldiers towards the front, where the vanguard was clearing tunnels ahead of them.

One of the commanders noticed him coming. "Something up ahead," the commander said. Bane looked. There was a massive, narrow arch, and through it he could see a soft glow of shifting colours.

"Secure that arch," Bane said. He checked his device and felt a twinge of excitement when he saw that all the lights in its black depths were rushing towards that glow. The soldiers raced up the tunnel, taking position on either side, and Bane walked behind them until he could see what was beyond. He stared for a time, speechless; then he went slowly through, drawn in by amazement.

It was the Chaos Engine.

The sheer size of it took his breath away. He stood in the midst of the largest chamber he had ever seen, over which the great machine dominated all. The walls, of honeycombed greenish-black, were rounded and squeezed closer at the top, so that the chamber was shaped like a flower bulb. Sunlight came from overhead in a gauzy beam, cutting down through the layers of many-coloured mists. The mists swirled and rippled with the stirring of the air in the upper part of the chamber, clinging to the tip of the Chaos Engine like it was a pen nib leaking ink into water. They were akin to the colours produced by the probability storms, the same as that created by Moa's artifact. These were the colours of raw probability energy, the colours of change.

He stood on a walkway, one of three that entered the chamber from three identical archways. The walkway led across to a central spike that towered high above them, a needle of metal that bristled with complex technologies. There it joined the other walkways in a ring around the spike. There were control panels of some kind there, recessed in the metal. This was the brain of it, then. This was where the Faded had given it commands.

He went out towards the spike, ignoring the warning cries of the soldiers. Like a moth to a flame. He couldn't resist.

Most of the body of the Chaos Engine was below him, like a miniature city spread out across the whole chamber. It was a mass of tiny spires and unfamiliar shapes, cut through by glowing trenches. Blinking lights and banks of switches nestled close to racks of black spheres that crackled with aether. Gyroscopes rotated silently while darts of light like fireflies flashed between them. He was above it all, only the thin metal of the walkway between him and a dreadful drop.

It was the most complex, most beautiful piece of machinery he had ever seen. The crowning glory of a forgotten people, able to affect reality itself. No technology that the Protectorate had could hope to match this; it was so far beyond them that it was like magic. Bane's heart swelled at the sight, the thought that one day *his* people might be able to invent something so grand. Given time. Given peace, and order.

He turned back to the arch, where the soldiers waited.

"Bring the explosives!" he called.

5.6

The elevator door opened with a chime, and Rail and Moa stepped out into the sunlight.

The room was irregularly shaped, with five walls of different lengths. The far wall, which was the longest, was open to the sky. Once, it had been covered by the folding mirrors of the Fulcrum, but now they had unfurled. One side of the room was taken up by a bank of panels covered in what Rail and Moa assumed were controls, but they had no idea what or how they would operate. In the centre was a sculpture of some kind, an arrangement of rods and spheres all in silver that stood on a pedestal.

Moa ignored the sculpture as she walked past, her eyes fixed on the sky, where thin trails of cloud drifted in a clear blue and the sun burned dazzlingly bright. Rail went with her, and together they stood on the edge and looked out over the city. The door of the elevator slid quietly shut behind them.

They were near the top of the Fulcrum, and the view was unlike anything they had ever experienced. Only those dwellings that clung to the flanks of Orokos's lonely mountains were higher than they were. The whole western side of the city was spread out before them, paled by golden haze in the distance. They could see the glittering path of the West Artery running straight to the lip of the plateau. They saw how it branched off into a thousand tiny canals on its way, spreading through the Territories like silver blood vessels. From up here, they could trace the walls between the districts that made the city a jigsaw. The great constructions of the Faded reared out of the cluttered mass of newer buildings. From this perspective, it seemed that the city since the

Fade was a mould that had grown on the gleaming bones of their ancestors' industry.

But for all that, it was wonderful.

"Did you ever think we'd be seeing this?" Moa whispered, her eyes welling.

Rail put an arm around her shoulders, and she leaned into him unconsciously. He was unable to tear his gaze from the scene before him.

"Never," he replied, and suddenly he understood her, if only a little. He caught a glimpse of her dreams, the mystical place where joy and awe lived, the invisible land that she visited when she slept. It was this feeling she was after when she talked of the new world over the horizon.

"Greetings," said a voice from behind them, and they whirled in fright. The room had been empty, and there were no doors from it except the one they had come in from. Yet there was somebody standing there now. He was a short man in late middle age, with a close-cropped brown beard. His clothes were of a fashion so old that they looked ridiculous.

"Who the freck are you?" asked Rail.

"Benejes Frine is my name," came the reply. He flickered uneasily.

Moa glanced at the device that she had thought was a sculpture, and saw tiny sparks of aether running up and down its complicated length. As realistic as it was, she had seen projections before. "You're not really here," she said.

"No," he said. "I died approximately six hundred years ago."

Rail and Moa looked blank. As a measure of time, years meant nothing to them.

"A long time," Frine clarified. "A long, long time. What you

277

are seeing is a reconstruction of myself, left behind in case anyone such as you should make it past the Fulcrum's defences. In case anyone should come wanting to know what happened here."

Rail frowned. The name Benejes Frine was familiar to him somehow. Then he remembered: the plaque on the wall of Bane's office. *We will make this world right again.* Benejes Frine had written those words.

"Are you one of the Faded?" he asked.

"That's what you'd call me," he replied. "The systems in the Fulcrum have been keeping track of you, updating themselves in line with your progress. For example, though we speak the same language, your dialect has changed so much over six hundred years. You would not understand me if I spoke to you in the way I would have done at the time I died. But the system remains current, and adapts. It is a marvel of what you call Fade-Science."

Rail couldn't quite believe it. This innocuous man in his strange garments was one of the Faded? He wasn't sure what he had expected, but it hadn't been this. Not someone so . . . normal.

"I expect you are after answers," said Frine, raising an eyebrow.

"Actually, no," said Rail. "I just want to get out of here."

Frine laughed heartily. "Don't you want to know *why*? Why Orokos? Why the probability storms? Why the Revenants and the Skimmers?"

"The Skimmers!" Moa cried. "How do we stop the Skimmers?"

"You can't," replied Frine. "Unless you destroy the Chaos Engine. They are all part of the system."

Rail shrugged. "Bane's probably doing just that right now."

"Yes, he is. But he doesn't know what he's doing. It was put here to *protect* you."

"To protect us from what?"

"From us," said Frine. "And from yourselves." He raised his hand. "Let me show you."

The device in the centre of the room sparkled, and a globe of light expanded from it. On the skin of the globe were pictures, moving pictures that swelled outwards and engulfed Rail and Moa. Then they were inside the globe and the pictures were all around them.

It took them a moment to recognise the vista. It was Orokos, but an Orokos that was clean and marvellous and alien. The only buildings were those of the Faded, and the skyline was a magnificence of spirals and coils and towers, arches and bridges and monuments. They could smell and feel the faint sea breeze on their cheeks. It was as if they were actually there, and it took an effort of will to persuade themselves that this was all some sophisticated illusion.

"This is Orokos as it once was, before the Fade," Frine said. "It was a place of peace. We believed that a society needed law and order, and the stricter the law, the greater the order. We liked that."

"Sounds like the Protectorate to me," Rail commented.

Frine nodded. "Indeed. You're more right than you know. You see, peace has a price. Prosperity breeds population, and Orokos is not a big place. Not everyone could have a job. Not everyone could have a family and a home and all the other things that they wanted. And that meant there were people who didn't like the way things were. They were rebellious and violent, and they brought disorder to our city when order was the most

279

precious thing we had. They were a problem, and we needed a solution."

"What did you do?" Moa asked.

"First we made them scapegoats. People like scapegoats, you see. It gives a very comforting us-versus-them quality to life. It feels good to be surrounded by people who are on your side." Frine's tone was faintly sarcastic. "Then we . . . got rid of them. I don't know how. They were just . . . taken away. Nobody really noticed." His expression showed what he thought of that.

"This is sounding more and more familiar," Rail said.

"It should. It happened in my time, and now it's happening in yours," Frine replied. "For hundreds of years, there was peace and order. Our government ruled with an iron fist, crushing dissention, and we were content. We didn't want anything to corrupt our perfect world."

The scene had changed, to the interior of a dwelling, breathtakingly splendid and strange. A couple lounged there, their expressions dull, eyes flat and vacant.

"But in the end, that was the problem," Frine continued. "We were so content that we became bored. You see, we're meant to struggle. It's in our blood. We're not supposed to live our lives to a plan. But that's what happened. We piled law upon law, rule upon rule, until the state told us what we should and shouldn't be doing and none of us really had to think for ourselves at all. We couldn't even be decadent; anything bad for us was outlawed. We had put ourselves in a prison, and even our jailors didn't realise it."

He shook his head sadly. "We came to Orokos long ago to escape the disorder of the world, to build ourselves a society that would be perfect in itself. But we became stagnant. We surrounded ourselves with Skimmers, so that nobody could get in or out without state approval. We alienated ourselves entirely from the rest of humanity. We didn't want them to taint us."

"Wait, wait!" Moa said, holding a hand up. "What do you mean, *the rest of humanity?*"

"If the rest of humanity is even there anymore," Frine said. "It has been a thousand years since we last contacted any of them, or they us."

Moa's leg went weak. "You mean there's more? More outside Orokos? It's really *true?*"

"Oh, yes," said Frine with an indulgent smile. "So much more."

While Rail and Moa were trying to digest this, the scene shifted again, and now they stood at the bottom of a colossal bulb-shaped chamber. Bizarre flying automatons glided above them, building the framework of something massive. The air was cold and tasted of aether.

"This was our solution to it all," Frine said. "Some of us, some of the best scientists and military men, we came up with a plan. We began to build a machine. We told the people that it was a new weapon, and they loved the idea of that. But what we were really building was the Chaos Engine. We were building something that would unleash havoc on the city. It was our masterpiece. We would paint a canvas of disorder over Orokos, and see what came out of it."

"Why?" Moa asked. She was still abuzz with a hundred questions, so much so that she didn't know which to ask first.

Frine looked at her, his eyes weary. The projector fizzed and the whole scene flickered and warped for a moment before snapping back into place. "Because we saw what we had become," he said. "We were empty, hollow things, mindlessly following rules that we had laid down for ourselves. There was no creativity anymore, no new thought or art; just people living like clockwork. We had no freedom left. We had given it all away. And anything that threatened our precious contentment, we destroyed. We were monsters. We needed to start again."

Rail and Moa couldn't believe what they were hearing. "*You* made our world this way?" Rail asked.

Frine nodded solemnly. "Perhaps you think this is Hell. You're wrong. I lived there, and it was worse than this."

They had never heard of Hell, but they didn't ask. There was already too much to take in.

The picture around them had changed again, and now they saw the Fulcrum from the outside. A terrific probability storm was lashing the city, pounding it with rain and sweeping thick veils through the streets.

"That first probability storm did more than we had ever dreamed it could," he said. "It changed everything. It shut down the power to all of Orokos, and it was a hundred and twenty-seven years before another storm turned on the old aether generators again. All our knowledge, all our wisdom, was stored in systems that had been inactive for generations. And by the time they had come back on again, everyone had forgotten how to use them. A hundred and twenty-seven years is a very long time. There were riots, starvation, terrible wars. The scientists who still remembered the old ways were lost in the chaos. The Skimmers would not let anything in or out. We started a new Dark Age. But that was the way it had to be. We had to begin again, you see. You call that time the Fade."

"You set the Revenants on us," Rail said flatly.

"Yes," Frine replied. "But that was an accident. We never meant for the Revenants to come. The Chaos Engine did that." He made a helpless gesture. "Rearranging things wasn't enough. It created an enemy that would match you exactly. There were not many at first, but the harder you tried to wipe them out, the more came. They were intended to be that way. You needed something to stop you from getting complacent, you needed chaos to stop yourselves from becoming too ordered. To stop you from becoming like we were. You see, total chaos and total order are just as bad as each other. There must be a balance. Even if it costs lives."

"It's cost *millions* of lives!" Rail shouted, swiping a disgusted hand at the apparition. He took a breath, calmed himself a little. "You were right. You *were* monsters."

"But nothing is different!" Moa cried, seized with a terrible despair at what she had heard. "You broke the world and nothing is different! The Protectorate controls everything in Orokos that the Revenants don't; they still send people like us to the ghettoes, or make them disappear. It's just like it was before!"

"Yes," said Frine sadly. "Yes, it is. We failed. We hoped that things would turn out differently if we wiped the slate clean, but they have turned out the same. It seems that though we can change our environment over and over, we are still trapped by our nature."

The projection dimmed, and they were back in the room again. The sunlight shone as before, but everything seemed changed now. Frine was pacing the room, his hands behind his back.

"If the Chaos Engine is destroyed, the Revenants will disappear, the probability storms will stop. All the systems in the Fulcrum will break down. Even the Skimmers will fail. Bane thinks that the Protectorate will control all of Orokos then, and there will be law and order and peace. But he would be treading the same path that the Faded trod, and he would come to the same end. A soulless world where all our decisions are made for us. Fortunately, however, he is wrong."

"He's wrong?" Rail said, brushing his dreadlocks away from his muzzled face.

"Quite wrong," said Frine, with a strange smile. "Funny that he appears to think of me as one of his heroes. Life is full of little ironies like that. I said I'd make this world right again, but I meant to do it by creating chaos. He means to undo my work. But he'll find out, like I did, that if you fool with chaos then you're liable to find a few surprises in store."

Moa didn't like the sound of that. Frine's smile became a grin.

"The Chaos Engine not only *generates* probability energy. It *harnesses* it. Once Bane destroys the Chaos Engine, he will unleash the most powerful probability storm there has ever been. This city will be turned inside out. All of Orokos will be utterly changed. Perhaps it will become a palace of glass, and all the people will be mice. Perhaps it will be a terrible slag-heap haunted by six-legged things the size of buildings. It could be a paradise of flowers and harmony. The possibilities are limitless. Once the Chaos Engine is destroyed, the world will start anew. We can only hope that humankind won't screw it up a third time."

"No!" Moa gasped. "No, you can't do it to us *again*! You can't gamble with all our lives like that!"

"It's too late," said Frine blandly. "The soldiers' weapons are advanced enough to overcome the automated defenses of the Fulcrum. And the Revenants can't stop Bane, it seems, though they're doing their best. The Chaos Engine is trying to defend itself, but it won't win. He is already at the core. Soon it will be over."

"Then *we* have to stop him!" Moa said.

"Oh, I don't think you'll have time," said Frine. "And besides, you have your own problems." He motioned at the door to the elevator. It chimed softly.

"There's someone here to see you," he said. "Good-bye." And with that he was gone, fading from sight as the Fade-Science projector turned itself off.

The door slid open, and there, hunched and massive and terrifying, was Vago.

5.7

"There's hundreds of them!" yelled one of the soldiers as his aether cannon spat shrieking pulses of energy into the swarm of Revenants. They had appeared as if from nowhere. They came from the walls, up through the floor, out of the arches that led into the chamber of the Chaos Engine. The Protectorate forces had formed a tight defensive ring around the spire of the machine, packed onto the gantry that encircled it, protecting the men who were setting the explosive charges. Others were strung out along the walkway that ran from the spire to the arch from which they'd entered. Their guns swivelled as they fought to bring down the creatures that swam through the air in shoals overhead. Occasionally one of them dived down to snatch a soldier and turn him into an aether-filled Taken. More gunfire could be heard out in the tunnels, where hordes of the possessed were surging against the remainder of the soldiers, trying to batter through with suicidal fury.

"They're throwing everything they've got at us!" said one of the Secret Police over the din.

"Then that means we're doing something right!" Bane replied. "Once we destroy this thing, they'll fade like smoke in the wind!"

"And how will you destroy it?" asked Finch, by his side. "We're pinned here."

"Then we have to fight our way clear."

The Revenants swooped again, spiralling down towards the cluster of men that surrounded the control panel of the Chaos Engine. A volley of aether fire drove most of them back, but some got through. They swept up a dozen soldiers and pitched them screaming off the walkway towards the machine far below.

"Explosives are all set!" a commander informed Bane.

"Good work," he said. "Advise your men to be careful with their targets. I don't want any accidents. We're packed too closely here, and there's a lot of gunfire flying around. The slightest thing could set those explosives off."

The commander departed to fulfill his orders, slipping along between the soldiers. Bane surveyed the state of his troops. The Revenants had whittled them down, and things were not looking good. There wasn't enough room to manoeuvre here. Whenever a Revenant managed to possess one of the soldiers, the Taken caused carnage with its lethal touch before it could be taken out. If they stuck here, the Revenants would batter them into extinction, eventually. They needed to retreat back to the tunnels, through the arch.

"How is the rear guard doing at holding them off?" Bane asked a soldier to his right — but the soldier didn't know, and neither did his commander.

"We'll have to send someone to find out," the commander said.

"I'll go," said Finch.

Bane turned and stared hard at the thief-boy through his visor. He was deciding whether to trust him. On the one hand, Finch was still ghetto stock, and it was too early to be sure of him. But then, Bane had brought him here to test his mettle as a potential recruit for the Secret Police, and this was a good chance to do so. Besides, there was no sense wasting a good soldier when he could send this ghetto rat instead.

"I'm smaller and faster than anyone you've got," Finch said. "Let me do it."

"Alright," Bane said. "But if you're not back here . . ."

"I know, I know," Finch snarled. "Three little beeps and *bang*. I'm not stupid."

"We'll see," Bane replied. "Go on then. Report back to me when you've assessed the situation."

Finch gave a mocking salute and a rotten grin. Then he was gone, slipping through the soldiers who were crammed onto the gantry around the spire of the Chaos Engine.

The thief-boy halted at the end of the walkway that ran across the chamber to the arch. It was littered with bodies staring sightlessly. There wasn't a drop of blood to be seen. Death by aether was so much cleaner than the alternatives.

Several dozen soldiers were standing by the railings, coordinating fire on the Revenants that swooped overhead in the haze of coloured mist that clung to the tip of the Chaos Engine's spire. The Revenants took two or three hits to dissipate, but each time one was destroyed two more took its place.

Finch paused. He would have to time his run. He had no weapon, and didn't even know how to fire an aether cannon. He would be an easy target.

The Revenants attacked in no pattern, and they came from all directions — above, beneath, to the sides. They swooped in gangs, swimming through the air on their crackling wings, tentacles trailing behind them. They were the essence of disorder, born of the Chaos Engine.

"Freck it," Finch muttered. In the end, like everything else in Orokos, it all came down to chance. He ran.

He heard the soldiers behind him open up to give him covering fire. His scalp prickled as aether bolts seared through the air around him. He saw two Revenants angle towards him, attracted by movement, but the soldiers had spotted the threat and they blew the energy ghosts into wisps. Finch sprinted with his head down, jumping over the bodies of the fallen, ignoring everything but the need to get to the other end. Soldiers flashed by him on either side, lighting up inside of the chamber with fusillades of aether. The noise was deafening.

With a fraction of a second to spare, he saw the Revenant that was swooping at him. It had slipped through the mesh of gunfire, appearing as a bright charcoal sketch through his glimmer visor. He half-dived, half-tripped over the arm of a sprawled soldier, hit the ground in a roll, and came up on his feet again. The Revenant missed him by inches. It coiled back on itself, ready to fly at him again, but the nearby soldiers had seen it by now and they blew it apart.

Finch didn't pause. He was running again, running until there was no more walkway and he was beneath the arch.

It was scarcely any better through there. The soldiers had been all but overrun. They had formed a wall across the tunnel that was being steadily pushed back. In a short time, it was going to collapse entirely under the weight of the Taken.

He could see Bane, gazing expectantly across the chamber at him, waiting for a signal.

Well, Finch would give him a signal. Finch would let him know that nobody, not even one of the Secret Police, could use and manipulate him the way Bane had. After Moa had removed the Persuader from his arm, he could have simply disappeared, gone back to Anya-Jacana, gotten on with his life. But he was vengeful by nature. He had returned to the Secret Police to await his chance to even things up. And now it had come.

Bane had thought he could make him a pawn. That was a mistake. He might have been a ghetto boy, but he would not be pushed around.

He held up his hand, and in it was a brass device shaped like a yo-yo. It was the device that would activate the Persuader that Bane had put on him. Bane tore his glimmer visor from his eyes, his face twisting in fury as he saw what it was. Finch, among his other talents, was a very accomplished pickpocket. When he had fallen into Bane earlier, back in the tunnels, he had stolen it from the pocket of Bane's trenchcoat. But that wasn't all he had done.

Once we destroy this thing, Bane had said, *they'll fade like smoke in the wind!*

"Let's see if you're right," Finch murmured. He twisted the device in his hand.

Bane saw what he did, but he didn't understand until it was far too late. He thought that Finch had pilfered the device to gain his freedom. It hadn't occurred to him that the thief-boy had managed to get the Persuader off. It was supposed to be impossible.

He only realised what had happened when he heard a noise in the pocket of his coat. A short, sharp beep.

He put his hand in there, felt it clasp around something cold and ring-shaped.

A second beep.

He pulled out Finch's Persuader. His blood ran cold. And all he could do in that moment was wonder how a boy from the ghetto had outfoxed him so utterly, before the third beep sounded and the Persuader detonated.

The concussion of the blast caught the nearby pack of explosives, and they went up, too, setting off a chain reaction that activated all the rest in less than a second. The result was catastrophic. The gantry that encircled the central spire of the Chaos Engine was obliterated in a cloud of flame. The force of it sheared the spire in half, smashing it into a pulverised mess that was blasted spinning in all directions. The tip leaned sideways with an ominous howl of metal and then slumped against the wall of the chamber, punching through and then snapping off. The body of the spire fell after it, pluming misty veils of probability energy. A chunk of the roof came crashing down, letting in the bright sunlight, and the whole avalanche of debris demolished one of the walkways and collapsed onto the great machine. Falling rubble crushed delicate mechanisms, cracked protective cases, flattened thin towers full of instruments. There were explosions from deep within the guts of the Chaos Engine.

The Revenants were in a frenzy now, whirling like maddened moths, spinning aimlessly this way and that. The Taken set up an awful keening, throwing themselves to the floor and flailing about or scratching at one another. The soldiers watched in amazement. Another explosion sounded from within the machine, this one much more violent. A gout of flame vomited from the depths of the chamber and sent huge chunks of metal wheeling through the air. There was a grinding noise coming from the Chaos Engine now, the noise of something broken that was still trying to operate. The air was full of a choking smell.

Then the Revenants began to fade. They started to smear as they passed through the air, leaving more of themselves behind with each loop and spin, as if they were watercolours on a paintbrush that was drying out. Their trails became fainter and fainter until there was nothing left at all. The Taken sagged at the same time, like exhausted animals, slowing and becoming feeble until they lay down on the ground and were still.

The Protectorate soldiers who had survived the blast — those who hadn't been near the centre of the chamber — stood stunned, at both the loss of their men and the disappearance of their enemy.

Finch pulled his glimmer visor off and tossed it over the railing of the walkway and onto the shattered hulk of the Chaos Engine below.

"Told you I wasn't stupid," he murmured with a fang-toothed smile.

The next explosion almost knocked him off his feet. Something in the depths of the machine was fatally ruined, and it was beginning to tear itself apart. The soldiers looked about in alarm as the structure groaned. Jagged sparks of aether were lancing across the inside of the chamber, and strange colours were beginning to swirl.

"Fall back!" one of the commanders was calling. "Fall back! Get out of here! This operation is over!"

Finch didn't need telling twice. He turned tail and ran for his life, with the sound of the Chaos Engine ripping itself to shreds echoing down the tunnel after him.

5.8

Rail and Moa felt the first of the explosions all the way up in the room near the top of the Fulcrum.

"Oh, freck, we're too late," said Moa.

"You're so right," Vago growled, stepping out of the elevator. "Your time has run out."

Rail was looking around the room for an escape route, but there were only two exits from the chamber. One was past Vago and into the elevator. The other was over the edge of the terrible drop at their backs, where one wall had folded away and left them with a panorama of the city. Neither was really an option.

"You can't run," said the golem. He was hunched low, his wings kinked sharply to either side like a cloak, their thin metal framework catching the sunlight. His yellow eye skittered from Rail to Moa, and his fingers flexed with a scrape of jointed rods. The Fade-Science projector, the bizarre sculpture of rods and spheres, stood between them, but it was silent now. Benejes Frine had left them to their fate.

"Vago, listen!" Rail said, holding his hands up as if to ward him off. "Can't you hear it? Bane has destroyed the Chaos Engine."

Vago's approach was slow and relentless. "Then the Protectorate has triumphed. As it always will."

"It's not what you think. Destroying the Chaos Engine is going to unleash the probability storm to end all storms. It's going to remake Orokos! And it'll remake *us* if we're still here when it happens!" There was another explosion, dull and heavy, and the room shivered. "Can't you hear? The Fulcrum is destroying itself."

Vago paused then, and suddenly laughed. It was a horrible sound. They had never heard the golem laugh before, and it was like the wheezing of a sick dog. "Then let it," he said. "Let it remake us all. Do you think I *want* to remain like this? The Protectorate will rise again, and this time there will be no Revenants to stop us!"

Moa shook her head. Vago was a different person since he had gone to the Null Spire, since he had met Bane. He didn't cringe any longer, and when he spoke he was more eloquent than he had been before. Something had changed inside him, something that made him like the Protectorate, something that made him hate Moa's kind.

"Vago, this isn't you," she said.

"This *is* me," the golem snapped. "That fawning, idiot creature that you knew before, *that* wasn't me."

The golem had advanced enough to cause Moa and Rail to retreat to the edge of the drop. Rail was calculating the chances of making a break for the elevator, but the golem would be too fast for them. Besides, Rail had no idea how he had activated it the first time. Even if they got past Vago, they couldn't escape.

"Yes, it was, Vago. That *was* you, before they got hold of you and filled your head with all their beliefs. You weren't Protectorate when we found you. Were you? Can you look me in the eye and tell me you were, that you were a spy all this time?"

There was an edge of desperation in Moa's voice, but Rail was frankly amazed at how calm she was being. At that moment he was struck by a fierce blaze of love for her, for the way she was, the way that she still fought to find the good in someone even when it was a maniacal golem bent on killing them. Her faith in people was perhaps the only weapon they had left now. Rail was all out of ideas.

"Tell me!" she demanded. "Tell me that you intended to betray us all that time!"

Vago didn't reply, and that was answer enough.

"What did they do to you?" she asked, softer now. "Don't you remember your friends?"

"We were never friends!" Vago spat.

"Yes, we were," she said. "And you saved my life once. That was the Vago who kept a dead bird with him because he thought it was beautiful. That was the Vago who was with me when I woke up after a Revenant almost killed me. We *were* friends. And it didn't matter that you were a golem and I was from the ghetto. We —"

"I used to be a person!" Vago cried. "A murderer! That's who I am! I *deserve* to look like this. I might not remember a thing, but what difference does that make to those people? They're still dead. And I killed them."

Moa was shocked into silence by the cruelty of his tone. She began to tremble, tears welling in her eyes.

"I don't care," Moa whispered.

Vago looked up at her, sunlight falling across the flesh half of his face. "What?"

Moa sniffed and wiped her eyes with her fingers. "I don't care. That wasn't you."

"Yes, it was," Vago said firmly. "You can't forgive me for that, Moa."

"Don't tell me who I can and can't forgive," she replied, and she seemed so frail and broken that she might have been blown away in the slightest wind. "I've seen what you were when you were like a child. You started again when you were remade. You're not evil, Vago. You just think you should be."

"Enough!" Vago yelled, and he pounced suddenly. Rail was ready for it, but it did him no good — the golem was simply too fast. Vago leaped at Moa, sideswiping Rail as he did so. His forearm smashed across Rail's face like an iron bar. If not for his respirator muzzle, Rail would have lost some teeth. As it was, he fell backwards, spun, and tipped off the edge of the drop with a cry.

Vago cannoned into Moa, bearing her to the ground and landing on her with one hand wrapped around her pale throat. She cracked her head on the floor as she fell, and the impact almost knocked her cold. But instead of unconsciousness, an almost unbearable pain flooded through her skull. She began to weep in fear and agony, her eyeshadow running down onto her cheeks in black rivulets.

"Do you forgive me now, Moa?" Vago hissed, his face close to hers. His fingers began to tighten on her throat.

"Rail . . ." she sobbed. "What did you do?"

"I think I might have killed him," the golem said.

There was another explosion, this one much louder. A monolithic groaning and creaking came from all around them. Vago looked up, then back at Moa.

"And now I'm going to kill you," he finished.

Moa was trying to shake her head, but she couldn't move it within his grip. "I don't want to die," she whispered. "Don't do this. Please don't do this. I want to live."

I want to live. It was the naked simplicity of it that broke

Vago's heart and cracked open the incomplete Protectorate conditioning that had fogged his mind. Suddenly the girl he was looking down on wasn't some filthy ghetto rat but *Moa*, a girl with a name, and she *had* been his friend once. She had been the only person in the world who had shown him kindness, when everyone else had treated him with hatred and mistrust. She had believed in him until the very end. And for all that, he had rewarded her with suffering.

Perhaps he wanted to be punished. Perhaps that was why he had made himself into this monstrosity. Perhaps that was why Moa's relentless faith in him made him angry.

He didn't know. But he couldn't hurt her anymore.

He loosened his grip on her and stood up. She curled into a ball, holding the back of her head, crying. He walked to the edge of the drop, and looked down at where Rail hung by his fingertips. Rail glared at him, eyes swimming with hatred.

"I thought I didn't hear you fall," he said. He squatted and reached down, pulling Rail up by the arms before dumping him on the floor. Rail scrambled over to Moa, and she hugged him in desperate relief and terror.

The next explosion rocked the room enough to make Vago stagger. It was followed by another, and another. There was the sound of tearing metal from somewhere in the elevator shaft, and smoke began to seep through the door. Outside, clouds were boiling, black thunderheads that spread from the centre of the city, forming out of nothing. A storm was coming.

Vago looked at the elevator door, then out at the horizon.

I want to live, he heard Moa say again in his mind.

He strode over to where Rail and Moa were huddled, and

with irresistible strength he picked them both up and bundled them each under one arm. They thrashed and cursed, and Moa pleaded, but he paid no attention. With both of them securely held to his flanks, he took two steps of a run-up and then jumped out into the sky.

5.9

And then they were flying.

It took both Rail and Moa a short while to stop their screams, to realise that they were not falling as they should have been. Though the wind tore at them and blasted their hair and rippled their clothes, they were somehow still aloft.

After the screams came a strange quiet, a time of raw disbelief, when they looked at the scene around them and couldn't quite credit what they saw. Vago's huge, leathery wings were spread above them like a canopy, held stiffly outwards, unmoving. The golem dared not flap them, for fear of going into a plunge that he would not recover from. He fixed them horizontally, though the strain on the muscles and mechanisms in his back was terrible, and they *glided*.

The city was laid out beneath them in all of its shabby magnificence, a colossal mishmash of old and new, beauty and squalor, order and chaos. Far to the south they could see the Coil, rising from its surroundings like two snakes entwined. They could see mighty buildings, towers and alleys and bridges, cranes and derricks and canals. The West Artery went straight ahead of them to the edge of the world, tiny barges and gunboats plying the water; Vago was following it to its end. He wasn't sure he could have turned if he'd wanted to.

Behind them, the dark red Fulcrum was flaking to pieces, a bruised heart of scabs falling apart in the violence of the Chaos Engine's death throes. Flame billowed out from it in great jets that flared and died in the gathering darkness. Overhead, the sun was being swallowed as the black clouds above the Fulcrum churned and spread. A shadow was creeping across the city from the inside out. At its core could be seen the insidious colours of a probability storm.

Soldiers were fleeing from the Fulcrum as it fell around them, and somewhere in that mass, Vago caught sight of a familiar figure. He was too far away for the others to spot, but Vago saw him. Finch was running across the plaza at the base of the Fulcrum, heading for the alleys and streets that he thought would shelter him. But he, like everyone else in Orokos, would have to face the storm to come. Perhaps it would make this lonely island a paradise, perhaps it would ruin it entirely. Perhaps the entire plateau would sink into the sea.

Orokos, the Random City, would have one last throw of the dice, and this time would pay for all.

Rail and Moa clung to Vago's flanks of metal and flesh, and they didn't say a word. They didn't dare to ask him why he had decided not to kill them. If they questioned him, he might change his mind and drop them. So they were silent, stuck between the glorious sensation of flight and the fear of falling that squeezed their chests.

In truth, had they asked, Vago would not have been able to give them an answer. His feelings had always been an alien place, even to himself. He could sense the tatters of the Protectorate conditioning peeling away from him, leaving him raw and bruised. All he wanted was to begin again, to be the child he once was. But there was too much he had done, too much guilt on his shoulders. He couldn't save himself. But he could save Moa. And for Moa's sake, he could save Rail.

They glided west, along the Artery, while the dark canopy of clouds chased them close behind. Above the Fulcrum now was a rolling ball of probability energy, a dim sun of coloured veils in which bolts of aether flickered and crackled. A terrible force was gathering.

It was some time before Moa realised that they were losing height fast.

She had been watching the jagbats that wheeled above the city, concerned that they might attack. But they were fleeing for shelter, sensing the oncoming storm. The pain in Moa's head had receded to a persistent ache now, and she managed to ignore it in the face of all that was happening. She had just begun to believe that they were not going to plummet out of the sky when she noticed the spires and rooftops were getting closer. She could make out details on the barges below when she hadn't been able to before.

"Vago . . ." she murmured.

"I know," he said. "We're too heavy."

Moa felt a lurch in her chest. Vago didn't look at them; he was staring rigidly ahead.

"I'm not going to drop you," he said. After a moment, he added, "Either of you."

"Where are we going?" Moa asked.

"Out," he said, and that was all.

Ahead and below them, the West Artery came to an end at the enormous intakes that were set in Orokos's perimeter wall. They were sinking towards it as the thermals that they had been riding lessened. Vago wasn't aerodynamic and was carrying too much weight. The rooftops of the city seemed huge now, a patchwork of uneven surfaces that skimmed by to either side of the wide blue canal. It was only as they got closer to the ground that

301

Moa realised how fast they were going. The water was a blur; boats sped past beneath them.

And looming up ahead, dozens of feet high, was the great grey wall that protected the city. Immovable. And they were going to hit it.

"We're dropping too fast!" Rail cried. The rim of the wall, blistered with guard posts that nobody manned anymore, was rising up before them.

Moa screamed, and she clutched herself to Vago's body. Then the wall was beneath, so close that Moa could feel the stone and metal thundering by inches from her. She screamed again . . .

. . . and then suddenly there was air, and space, and below them were the black cliffs and the dizzying drop to the sea. They had cleared the perimeter wall of Orokos by a hair's breadth.

Moa was panting, tears running from her eyes, while on the other side of Vago, Rail was clinging grimly on. Moa clasped Rail's arm across the golem's chest.

"Look," said Vago.

On the sea, there were ships. Dozens of them, junks and steamers and crafts that could barely keep afloat at all. They were sailing from a great hole that had been ripped in the cliffs, next to one of the massive waterfalls that plunged from the lip of Orokos. Kilatas had set sail.

Moa felt her heart swell with a pride and joy so great that she burst into fresh tears. Here, the shadow of the oncoming storm hadn't yet choked the light, and the green-blue waves were limned in sun-glimmer. But the ships were sailing, far out from Orokos now, and the Skimmers were nowhere to be seen. The city had let them go at last.

"Hold on," muttered Vago uncertainly, and he tilted his

wings a fraction. They began to drop faster, down towards the sea, down towards the ships that Kittiwake was leading out to the horizon.

Kittiwake's timing, it seemed, was excellent. Though Vago hadn't really known where he was going when he jumped from the Fulcrum, he had decided on the way that he would try to get his cargo down to Kilatas somehow. There they might have a chance of escaping the probability storm. But Kittiwake had set off early — for what reason, he didn't know — and now he could angle himself towards them without attempting to turn, which would have been necessary if he'd intended to put Rail and Moa anywhere near the entrance to the hidden town. The simple fact was: He couldn't fly, and he could barely glide. But it just might be enough.

The sea was coming up towards them, filling their vision. The ships' engines could be heard, clattering and clanking. Those that had sails were displaying bright colours. But Vago was over-shooting them, and making no attempt to correct his course.

"Aren't you . . ." Moa began, stopped, then decided she had to know. "Aren't you going to land on the ships?"

Vago laughed, but this time it wasn't malicious. "I can't land, Moa," he said. "This is going to be a little rough."

"You're going to land in the *sea*?" she cried. "Vago! I can't swim!"

The sea was suddenly too close now, and they soared over the ships full of upturned faces gazing in wonder. The constant whisper of the water was loud, louder, and a wall of blue was rushing up to crush them.

"Nor can I," Vago said quietly. "Rail will take care of you. Good-bye, Moa."

With that, he tipped his wings to vertical, and the braking of the air against them was so sudden that it almost tore them from his back. He clutched Rail and Moa, using his arms to stop them from being flung away from him. For a few instants he could do nothing but hold on as the savage deceleration wrenched at his body. Then he lost control and flipped over, his wings tangling around him. He let go of Rail and Moa. The three of them spun apart like a meteorite breaking up, and they smashed into the ocean.

Moa had wanted to scream, but at the last moment she had sense enough to snatch a breath before she was flung from Vago. The impact of the water almost drove it from her lungs, but she held on somehow. A muffling hand had closed around her senses, wet and cold and dampening all sound to a dull roar. She was too stunned to move, not knowing which way was up, not knowing where she was, only that the air wasn't there anymore, that she *mustn't breathe*.

Then reality collapsed on her, and she panicked. She thrashed wildly, but her uncoordinated flailing seemed to make no difference. She twisted until she could see the light and she struggled for it, knowing that light meant life. But she was sinking, sinking no matter what she did. Below her was an abyss deeper than eternity, blue shading into fathomless black, and it was sucking her down, down to where her lungs wouldn't work. Down to where it would be all over.

Her head went light. Suddenly the idea of fighting seemed foolish. It was so much easier just to relax and go with it. After all, wasn't that what she'd done all her life? Wasn't that how things were?

No. Not anymore. And she would not die here, not with her dream so close to reality. She would not give up now.

I want to live.

And with that thought, she began to struggle anew, striking up for the surface. But though her efforts were useless, though she was doomed here, she held on to every precious second even though her lungs felt like they were aflame and her pulse was thudding in her head. And she would not stop struggling. There was nobody to make the decision for her now but herself. She would not let herself go.

She held on longer than she would have thought possible, but she couldn't hold the air in her burning chest forever. She exhaled, and emptied herself.

A shadow in her dimming vision, swimming closer. Rail. Rail, grabbing her, and she was too weak to panic now so she clung to him. She could barely see him anymore, and though she tried to hold on, a part of her knew that it was already too late. She found a last ounce of defiance, but it couldn't save her.

Then Rail's lips were pressing against hers, his respirator hanging loose, and suddenly there was air, thin and unsatisfying but it was *air*, expanding her lungs, blown in from his. Their mouths came apart and her vision cleared a little, so that she could see him again. She felt him kicking upwards and she clung to him like a baby to its mother. Suddenly she wasn't afraid anymore. She trusted him utterly. For a time, she had forgotten that — but she knew now that her life was safe in his hands.

They broke the surface of the water together. Moa sucked in great lungfuls of air, while Rail slipped his respirator back in his mouth and did the same. Her dark hair was plastered across her eyes . . . but she was still breathing, and she held herself to him while he trod water. After a moment she began to cry.

"Where's Vago?" she asked.

Rail looked around, but there was only the ocean. "He's gone, Moa. He's gone."

The ships caught up to them a short while later, and ropes were thrown down to haul them on board. They emerged, dripping, on the deck of a battered old hulk. There, with the broadest of grins, was Kittiwake.

"You two are the luckiest kids I've ever had the misfortune to meet," she declared.

"You make your own luck," said Rail, smiling with his eyes. "Nobody ever tell you that?"

Kittiwake cackled, and blankets were brought, and Rail and Moa were led to the prow of the ship. Behind them was Orokos, massive and dour, and above it black clouds thickened and spread like an omen of doom. Ahead of them was horizon, and whatever lay beyond it.

Rail put his arm around Moa, and she leaned into him.

"You know what, Moa?" he said. "I think I've changed my mind. Maybe I will come with you to look for this new land after all."

Moa, wearied by grief and exhaustion, batted him on the arm. "As if you ever had a choice," she said.

He smiled behind his respirator and pulled her to him again. "No, I don't think I ever did," he murmured.

EPILOGUE:

Limbo

0.0

The sun rose and the sun set, and the currents took him where they would.

He could have tried to swim, if he wanted. He didn't want to. Instead he was curled, a foetus, his wings wrapped around him like a cocoon. He didn't sink, nor did he float. A trick of his construction kept him at a certain level of buoyancy. Gas pockets in his hydraulics, perhaps, or an effect of the aether stored in his batteries.

Vago was moved by the massive, blind whims of the sea. In the dark where no sunlight could reach, he floated in its freezing womb. Eyes open or shut made no difference; it was only when some predator came to disturb his rest that he had any sense there was anything in the entire world but him. Few predators came. The aether charge in his body deterred them.

He floated, and here he was nothingness. He had no need to breathe, no need to sleep. He had glutted himself with Revenants in the assault on the Fulcrum, and there was no telling how long the power in his body would last. Time was meaningless down here where there was no night or day.

Sometimes he thought about Rail and Moa, wondering if they had survived the crash landing in the sea, wondering if there really was another land over the horizon. Perhaps they were happy now. Perhaps they never made it. He couldn't say. This was limbo: a place of oblivion, a place where nothing was determined or certain. He liked it here.

He thought about Orokos, of the city he had left behind. The probability storm would have changed it utterly now. The Storm Thief's final rampage must have been terrible. What it was like, or if it was even still there, he would never know, unless the great flow of the oceans of the world took him back there one day.

And sometimes he thought about himself, about his life and what he had done with it. Down here, guilt and blame had no meaning. Was he a murderer? Was he really that person who had done those things, now that he had sheathed himself in a new body, now that the memories of his crime had gone? Was there ever any way to make amends?

He had no answers.

Could the sea forgive him, in time? Could it wash away his sins?

He couldn't say.

He had surrendered himself to the ocean, and he waited to see where it would take him. Perhaps, one day, he would bump against the flanks of a continent, and he would clamber back to the light. Perhaps there *were* no other continents, and he would end up back at Orokos. Perhaps he would float until his energy ran out, and the void took him.

In the end, it was all down to chance; but he knew one thing, above all else.

Anything was possible.